The Zookeeper's Tales of Interstellar Oddities

A collection of short stories
By Pamela Jeffs and Aiki Flinthart

To all the authors out there – both published and aspiring – don't give up. And find yourself a great tribe of fellow writers who can help you learn, grow, and push through the hard times.

Cover artwork by Pamela Jeffs
Interior artwork by Pamela Jeffs
Edited by Aiki Flinthart
Copyright © 2020 Aiki Flinthart and Pamela Jeffs
Published by CAT Press

All stories are original to this collection

A Cataloging-in-Publications entry for this title is available from the National Library of Australia.

ISBN-13: 978-0-6487736-0-3 (Trade Paperback)
ISBN-13: 978-0-9945928-9-7 (e-book)
CAT Press
PO Box 3388, Darra
QLD 4076, Australia

Heartfelt thanks goes to all the members of the Springfield Writers Group for their support and encouragement on this mad project. And to our awesome families who support our passion. Pamela's mum who babysat Pamela's gorgeous girls so Pamela could scribble, and who helped proof the collection. Plus, we both have Darrens in our lives, and they are wonderful.

Contents

The Zookeeper's Tales of Interstellar Oddities

By Aiki Flinthart and Pamela Jeffs
2020

Artwork by Pamela Jeffs

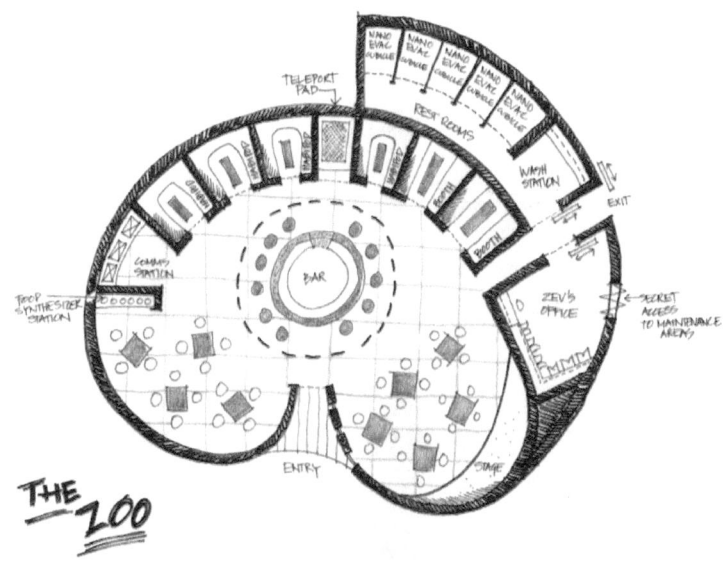

Artwork by Pamela Jeffs

1400 hours: A New Life

Ori Bligh

Current day

When the airlock opened, the stench hit first. Ori Bligh
gagged and hesitated in the entryway to Asteri Station. Sweat
and alien pheromones; rank, sick-sweet. A kind of damp,

inescapable awareness of…beings. Bodies. Too long unwashed because of the value of water on space stations.

All underlain by the staleness of air recycled through old scrubbers, the background heaviness of machine oil, and the lingering metallic smell of hot meteorites.

'Feck this shit,' she muttered. If only she could shut the door and leave the station; go back to the Inner Systems of the Hegemon Alliance.

A crewmember from the Hegemon transport ship that had brought her to this arse-end of the galaxy brushed past without apology and strode confidently into the depths of the station. His bootheels clanked on loose metal plates underfoot. After ten flips through the void to get here, he was probably glad to head straight for the nearest bar to drown any incipient flipvoid hallucinations.

Given a chance, Ori would risk full-on flip psychosis if she could turn the ship back now and go home.

But she wouldn't get that chance. Not for three years. Not until she'd paid her dues.

So, she studied her options for the here-and-now.

A narrow, curving corridor stretched away in two directions and neither looked appealing. Walls of bare metal scarred by old oxidisation and recent patches slapped over more meteorite holes than Ori was comfortable seeing.

A far cry from the gleaming white walls of her dormitory at the Grey Guards training facility, or the elegant sandstone and marble mansion she'd grown up in on Alpha-Five.

She sagged against the wall briefly, her situation sinking

in. She'd been an idiot. A naïve, gullible idiot. And this was the result. Instead of a plumb job in the Inner Systems—as a part of the Grey Guards' elite ranks her name and status entitled her to—she was stuck out on the edge of Hegemon-controlled space. A glorified take-thief.

Her parents expected her to be grateful. Everyone did.

And she was.

She scrubbed a hand over her short-cut white-blonde hair and grimaced. There was no-one else to blame for her stupidity. Her naivety. Only the Entwhistle-Blythe name she'd been born to had salvaged this much of her career. But out here that name was as likely to get her shivved as admired, so Bligh it was.

Here, she was on her own. And maybe that's what she needed to prove to her parents and the Grey Guards that her mistake was over and she could be trusted. She could do this. She could earn their respect again and get her life on track.

Swallowing, she threw back her shoulders and tugged down the fitted grey jacket, smoothing the lieutenant's bar on her sleeve.

Three years and she'd be back on her original career path. She just had to keep her nose clean.

She blinked to activate her ocular implant and pulled up the Hegemon Core computer's brief on Asteri Station once again for a final review.

The station had only three other Grey Guards and didn't see a lot of action. It had a reputation as a backwater populated by scum. Maybe two hundred permanent residents. Plus a lot of transients, drifting from world to world, job to job. Bounty hunters working for criminal syndicates.

Or traders hunting for new customers and products outside Hegemon space—shinies they could make a quick credit off in the rich Inner Systems, while trying to avoid legitimate taxes and controls imposed by the Hegemon Economic Alliance.

Ori had a thorough grounding in the Hegemon regulations that kept harmonious relations between the various Terran colonies and alien worlds.

How hard could it be to keep the peace in a place like this?

A door rattled open in the wall opposite. Bodies stumbled and tumbled out, tripping, shoving, fists flying. Voices raised. Three people attacking an elderly man. He lay about himself with a spanner, the heavy metal slapping into flesh. Two youngish Terrans and some insectoid dodged, trying to get close.

Ori dropped her bag. Time to earn her keep. She collared one Terran man and hurled him aside. His head clanged against the wall and he slumped bonelessly to the deck.

The second turned on her, fist upraised, swinging wildly. She sidestepped, caught the arm and flung him over her hip. He hit the plates hard, groaned and sagged into unconsciousness.

A fist blindsided Ori. Stars showered through her vision. She swore and backpedalled.

The insectoid swung another fist at her head. Dragonfly wings fluttered on its back. Her ocular implant picked up ultraviolet lights glimmering across its face. They were partially obscured by some sort of breathing mask. Tinkling sounds emerged from somewhere.

Her aural implant translated, the words humming in her mastoid bone.

'Get out of my way, Dirty.'

'Grey Guard Lieutenant Bligh to you,' she snapped. 'New security commander of Asteri Station. Stow it or I'll throw you in the brig as my first act of duty.'

The insectoid hesitated, lights flashing in quick, rippling patterns across its chest and face. Soundlessly, it spun on a white keratin foot and stalked away down the desolate corridor.

The elderly man lowered his spanner and straightened, wiping a smear of blood from his cheek.

'You okay?' Ori asked.

He nodded. She studied him, assessing his threat level. Not much. Older Terran. Wearing a maintenance crew coverall, frayed around the cuffs and stained around collar and sleeves. Faint smell of sewage. What looked like a permanent three-day growth of grey on his chin, and salted hair tied back in a long ponytail.

He, in turn, raked her with a shrewd scrutiny. 'You're tougher than you look, girl. New commander, huh? Thanks for the help.'

'Welcome. What did they want?' She toed one of the two unconscious Terrans. Still out. Sometimes she underestimated her gene-modded abilities and forgot she was stronger than most Terrans.

'The usual.' The elder snorted. 'Miracles I can't provide. Funding to fix all the problems on this voidfish-eaten rustbucket.'

Footsteps rang from her right as three newcomers approached. More Grey Guards. Three of them. Ori relaxed.

A gawky young Terran man with a prominent Adam's apple, and a small, brown-skinned Terran woman with big dark eyes. The third was an androgynous Glondian, Sergeant Yang, if memory of the report served. Gender-neutral terms of address were polite.

The Glondian was skeletally-thin and pale, one hand hovering by zis stunner. But Yang's vertical-slitted eyes were fixed on the old man, not Ori. Perhaps ze hadn't even seen her.

Yang's thin fingers twined into the elder's collar. 'What trouble are you making now, Zev Smith? Why can't you just stick to fixing the fecking toilets?'

'Feck you, Yang,' Zev said. He plucked the spanner from the toolbelt at his hip again and brandished it. 'I'll get to your fecking toilet when I get to it. I'm all that's holding this shithole place together, so if I say your shitter isn't important, it fecking-well isn't.'

'It is to me.' Yang stepped back, eyeing the spanner warily. 'I have to use the toilets in the Zoo and they're revolting.'

Zev bared yellowing teeth in a twisted grin. 'Tell me about it. No. Don't. I know, alright. When the Hegemon Alliance bothers to read my reports on what we need and I get more money, I'll fix your damned toilet. But no-one fecking listens to me, do they, so suck it up and shit wherever you can.'

Yang growled, one hand curling into a fist. Zev raised his chin, watery blue eyes glittering.

Ori strode forward. Time to intervene.

'Ten-shun, Sergeant!' she snapped in her best parade-ground voice.

Yang's head jerked around, eyes widening. A quick glance at her uniform and ze straightened, shoulders back. Flipping a sharp salute, Yang jerked zis chin.

'Yes, Ma'am. You're our new commander?'

The other two Grey Guards managed belated salutes, pulling themselves into some semblance of attention.

Ori nodded. 'Just came in on the transport. If two of you wouldn't mind cleaning up this mess for the maintenance master, perhaps, Yang, you would care to show me to my quarters and give me the tour?'

Zev Smith sniffed. 'Better take her to the Zoo and introduce her to Ab.' He grinned. 'Get the woman a drink and something cold to put on that bruise before it ruins her pretty face.'

Ori sent him a chill look. 'I don't drink on duty.'

Zev chuckled. 'By the time you've been here a couple of weeks you will, girl. Hell, maybe a couple of hours. We all do. The Zoo's the best place on Asteri. Only place that makes it worthwhile.'

In the distance, a muted alarm went off, a rasping buzz that sounded sick rather than frightening. Zev swore again.

'That's the rich water containment regulator. Better let me get back to it or it'll overload and this whole damned place'll blow.' He shook himself free of Yang's grip and stalked off, trailing obscenities.

Ori watched him. 'Is he serious about that?'

Yang snorted a laugh through slit nostrils. 'Who knows. The place is falling apart but it has been for the last twenty years I've been here.'

Zis lips parted, revealing serrated rows of fine, pointed teeth. 'Welcome aboard the Asteri, Lieutenant.'

A jerk of zis head indicated the other Grey Guards. 'This is Corporal Korvis, IT and comms specialist. Ensign Bahmra, psychologist and xenobiologist.' Before they could reply, ze added. 'You two take this pair of black-brains to the lock up until they cool off.'

They nodded and manacled the two sleeping men with anti-grav binders. With backwards looks at their new commander, the two young Terrans floated the prisoners away.

Yang picked up Ori's bag. 'Let's go. Shall we use the teleport pads?' Ze nodded toward a set of three scuffed circular pads inset into the wall opposite.

'No. Long time on the ship,' Ori said. 'Rather stretch my legs.'

She followed the Glondian through a maze of interlocking corridors, each as dilapidated as the arrival area. A brief glimpse of her musty, tiny quarters convinced her that a tour of the station was preferable to sitting in a bleak, grey metal tomb for the next few hours until lights-out rotation.

When her bag was stowed in the bio-locked room, she trailed her subordinate to the opposite side of the great, circular station. More for lack of any other plans than a real desire to go to this Zoo place or meet this Ab person Zev mentioned. The morning would be time enough to take up whatever minor duties existed here.

And, in spite of her words, the thought of a drink held a growing appeal. The more she saw of this place, the more bleak the next three years looked.

Yang led the way through a set of sliding doors. The smell of alcohol and old vomit overwhelmed the staler odours that dominated the rest of the station. Why did bars smell the same, the galaxy over?

Ori paused in the doorway and surveyed the space out of habit.

Thick, clear windows showed slices of the blackness outside, broken by the distant twinkling of far-away suns. Curved along the opposite wall were a set of four habipods designed to allow various lifeforms to relax in their own personal atmospheric mix. They were flanked by a couple of booths, the seats of cracked leather.

But the main floorspace was taken up by a scattering of battered metal tables and plain, cushionless chairs, surrounding a circular bar of dull silvery metal. Everything basic and spartan.

Overhead several faded glowtubes sputtered and buzzed unpleasantly. In one corner, a replica of some ancient Earth music-making device played a crooning melody that almost softened the atmosphere to something welcoming.

She made her way to one side of the bar and hitched a hip onto a torn cloth stool. A backroom door opened and a huge figure emerged and slipped behind the bar. Ori blinked.

An actual Aquanorian. She'd only ever seen holos and digitals before. They were notoriously reclusive. Sticking to their watery planet. Trying to rebuild after asteroid batterings had left it devastated almost five hundred years ago. Before Terrans had even left their own solar system.

She eyed this one dubiously. What was with the bright yellow and blue flowered shirt? Some sort of joke she didn't understand? Aquanorians were known for their subtle and obscure sense of humour.

The alien's highly mobile, scarred facial tentacles were ivory and teal. Didn't that mean it was fairly old? Rumour was they lived a very long time. And surely the even number meant it was male. She couldn't recall details of the species' physiognomy. Only that they were highly intelligent, long-lived…

…and responsible for the creation of the drug, black, that was the scourge of the known Hegemon population.

She pressed her lips thin. She'd seen what black did to people. Lost a good friend to its insidious addiction. But it was hardly fair to hold a single Aquanorian accountable for inflicting the drug on the entire galaxy.

She knew too well what happened when people started throwing blame around without listening to both sides of a story. Her throat tightened.

'Absinthe Krull,' Yang said, waving a languid hand, 'this is our new commander, Lieutenant Ori Bligh. Told you she was coming.'

'So you did.' Absinthe's voice emerged cultured but slightly burbling. Like her favourite academy teacher was speaking under water.

'Lieutenant, we call Ab the Zookeeper, for obvious reasons.' Yang indicated the Zoo. 'Asteri is a bit of a zoo as well, and he sort of looks after all of us. You need something, see if Ab can help.'

He gave a casual salute. 'I'll leave you to it. Meet you at 0800 tomorrow, for a briefing. It's 1400 local time, now.'

Ori returned the salute, glad of a respite from zis sarcastic intensity.

Absinthe inclined his bald head, his facial tentacles waving in an invisible current. 'And what can I get you to drink?'

She hesitated. Technically, she wasn't on duty until tomorrow. And it had been a very long trip after a very long few weeks, what with the trial. She glanced at the top shelf behind the bar and grimaced. The Blythe family gin brand had found its way even here. Seemed she still couldn't escape. Not that she wanted to.

'Blythe gin and redwater.'

He nodded. 'Good choice. Expensive, though.'

'I have the credits.' She tapped her wrist ident chip on the bar's reader. Eight credits deducted from the healthy account her parents had set up before she left. Blood money. Bribe money. Be a good girl money.

'I'm sure you do.' He poured the liquor.

Was that a hint of amusement in his tone?

'I hear you met Zev Smith,' he said. 'Our Effluvium and Detritus Eradication Manager.'

Ori almost sputtered her expensive drink onto the scratched metal bar surface. 'Nice title. Bit of a character. Word travels fast.'

Absinthe's tentacles jiggled in what she figured was probably laughter. 'Indeed. I hear everything. Comes with running this place for the last thirty years. People need help, they come to me. Besides, Zev's office is just behind the Zoo. As much as he likes to complain, he really does hold this place together with spit and shit.'

'Lovely image.'

'Suffice to say the station would be in serious trouble without his maintenance skills.'

There was a long silence and Ori frowned.

'Was that a warning?'

Absinthe's massive shoulders gave a close approximation of a human shrug. 'Just a suggestion. Leave well enough alone, no matter what complaints you might hear about him.'

His head came up, his dark, oddly-pearlescent eyes fixing on something behind her. 'And you might do the same for our Azilan friend, there. Hear you had a dust-up with him, too.'

Ori slewed around and observed the insectoid as it swaggered into a habipod. The atmosphere within thickened into mist and the faintest hint of ozone leaked out into the main room. The alien removed the breathing filter and its thin shoulders slumped. Lights on its chest flashed a soft purple.

'We can't pronounce his name,' Ab said, pouring Ori a fresh drink. 'So we call him Walter. Best to leave him to his own devices. Azilans are lethal hunters and they dislike Dirtys.'

Ori shot him a cold look for the insult.

He smiled gently. 'Sorry, Terrans. But Azilans have a long history of disliking Terrans. Three hundred and fifty year-long history. You know it don't you? Why they hate you?'

She shrugged. The story was shoved down every kid's throat at school. From the early days of Earth's colonisation efforts. Not long after the discovery of grey fuel and flipdrives made founding colonies outside of the original Sol system possible.

The story of two Earth explorers and their discovery of the first alien sentients.

A discovery that, as much as it was needed, Earth came to regret.

Beneath the Sea, Below the Sky, Beyond the Stars

Aiki Flinthart

350 years ago

The sea's grey linen surface rippled; a nebulous blanket, made soft and thin by age, thrown across the bedrock of the world by aeons-old hands. To my left and right, peaks of blue-grey granite framed the gaseous ocean's endless expanse and jutted into a clean turquoise sky. Rock bonded the heavens to the undulating sea in a way the razor-sharp, cloudless horizon didn't; part of both.

A bridge between worlds.

Between our world and theirs, hopefully. For Azil was

nothing more than clean sky, a few stony ridges…and the sea. Barely enough land for our scoutship to touch down on the high peaks.

I drew a slow, calming breath of thin atmosphere—cold and metallic with just a hint of the sea's acrid pungency. Enough oxygen to sustain humans. Barely.

My last breaths of clean air for a while, if all went to plan. Perhaps forever.

Hopefully not, but I was prepared, if I had to. The sacrifice would be worth it.

They were worth it.

'You sure about this, Kaido?' Ishmael's gruff question anchored me to the rock underfoot for a little while longer.

'Do we have a choice? We need her. We need the proof.' I stretched my neck and rolled shoulders aching from hours of being hunched over the ship's worktable. 'You heard the broadcast over the comms. The Hegemon has cut the exploration budget in favour of stabilising their hold over the colonies. Either we prove sentient life exists, or we're both going to end up back as water-miners in one of the belts.'

'Feck that,' Ish growled. 'I agreed to join Exploration to get *out* of the mines, same as you. Still don't know why Ex chose me, but I'm not going to complain. Exers live a bit longer than winers.'

I nodded but said nothing. My shoulders twitched, the scarred skin beneath my shirt pulling tight. I couldn't go back. Wouldn't. This had to work. For both of us. For all four of us.

I looked down at the edge of the sea where it caressed my

bare feet. Soft; the gas dry and faintly warm. Like a kitten pawing with claws retracted, waiting for the moment to dig in and hold.

Ish glanced towards the cool white sun where it edged closer to the horizon, his expression serious for once. 'You know this will change everything, don't you?'

'I know. That's why I need proof. Images aren't enough. They can be faked. I need some sort of hard evidence. Terra's religious factions, scientists... everyone. They need to know we're not alone.'

'How will they handle it?' He came alongside, keeping his booted feet well clear of the sea's wispy tendrils.

I chuckled. 'You're waiting until now to ask that? They'll handle it badly. As humans always handle the new and unknown. But we need to hear it. The only thing that might force humanity to work together to save ourselves is the existence of an alien species. That's why we're here, remember?'

I gripped his shoulder. 'Saving the whole damned human race by proving we're not as all-fired special as we like to think. Maybe we'll stop screwing up every planet like we own the universe.'

He snorted. 'Idealist. I'm scouting with a fecking idealist. I'm just here to earn enough money to get Emma out of the A-5 Asteroid Belt's water-mining shithole and into a living-pod on Mars.'

'I know,' I said. 'And she's worth it.'

A quick frown crossed his brow. 'How would you know?

You've only met my sister once.'

I shrugged and turned my face aside. 'That was enough. She's special. She's your sister, which makes her my family, too.'

That was all he needed to know, now. If he knew how close a family member I really was, he'd never let me take the next step. And if I was to save Emma, our son, and Ish then I had to go. I couldn't let my son grow up under the whip, as I had.

I scrubbed away the flush on my cheeks and studied the mountains intently. He let the silence lie, used to my occasional bouts of reticence.

Ish stared out across the undulating grey eternity. 'We've been here two weeks since you put that... creature... person... whatever... back. Why'd it turn up now?' His thick fingers scratched at the coarse red stubble on his chin and he glared at the gas as though daring something to emerge.

'Your guess is as good as mine. Maybe took a while to heal from her injuries?' I scraped dark hair out of my eyes. I should cut it before going in. Or dye it silver like hers. Present a more familiar image.

'I just don't like this,' he said. 'I still say we should get approval from the Hegemon, first.'

'We don't have time to wait weeks for a reply while they debate it in Council. We only have two weeks' worth of rations and half of that has to last us the return trip. I've got a few days, at best.'

'Well, we should have done tests on her.'

'She was dying, Ish.' I sucked another deep breath. 'Drowning in the oxygen after she fell off that airboat thing. She wouldn't have lasted more than a few minutes if we hadn't put her head back under the sea.'

'Autopsy, then.'

I sent him a level look. 'We're not repeating the mistakes of old Earth. We're here as guests and visitors, not conquerors with some god-complex. You got blood samples.'

'I know.' His fingers flexed. 'But they don't prove sentience. You're as much an exobiologist as I am. Don't tell me you didn't want to get the scalpel out.'

I pointed at a brilliant blue flash of movement overhead. Some sort of flying animal. 'Content yourself with the non-sentients.'

'You know it looked like she was pushed off that airboat thing, onto land, don't you?'

'All the more reason to find out who she is.' I pictured again the narrow, otherworldly shape of her face. The large eyes set wide beneath a broad forehead and silver hair that rippled even without wind to stir it. Flickering lights beneath her translucent white keratin.

And the two pairs of wings. A delicate, transparent tracery, like dragonfly wings. Fluttering restlessly. All four broken, grey ichor dripping until I'd patched them as best I could. Had it worked?

Ish raised a bushy brow. 'What if you end up on the wrong side of whatever politics are going on down there?'

I shrugged. 'Then I do. You know I have to go. It's why

we're here.'

'I know you're a damned fool, Kai. This world's not going anywhere. Wait for a backup team.'

'No way. This is our chance, Ish. We prove this and we're set for life. With a whole team we'd have to share credit and reward money.'

'Ya, I know.' His eyes narrowed. 'I just feel…' A scuff of his foot sent a piece of weathered granite into the sea. It vanished without a splash, without a sound. Gas swirled up and settled back again.

I gripped his thick wrist. 'Don't. Who the hell knows who's down there.'

His dark eyes flicked to me, then back to the smooth, opaque surface. 'You think they've been watching us this whole time? How?'

'If they evolved under there, they must have adaptations for low-light vision.' I shivered. Her eyes had had no whites. Just my image repeated in a hundred, oil-dark, compound lenses. Lips, with no hint of colour, covering a predator's sharp teeth.

'The guy who found her after we patched her up and I put her back, certainly had no problems seeing down there. He seemed pretty pleased to see her, too.' I chuckled. 'Assuming I was reading his emotions correctly. Pity I didn't have enough oxygen in my exosuit tank to follow him back to wherever he took her.'

'Do we know gender?'

I rubbed a hand over my face. 'No? Maybe we should use

the gender-neutral. They might not reproduce sexually at all. That's why I need to go find them again. To understand all of that stuff. But we don't have enough air tanks to last more than a day.'

Ishmael threw his arms wide and slapped them against his thighs, the sound ricocheting between the mountain ridges. 'What the hell am I supposed to tell the Hegemon Core computer if you don't come back?'

I smiled bleakly. 'Tell them we achieved our objective. You get all the credit for discovering the first sentient life form. You'll be famous. Won't have to give me the credit for first-contact, either.'

He hesitated, a slow, sly grin curling his mouth. 'Shouldn't give me ideas.'

I laughed and turned back towards our scout ship, beached on the rocks. The living-pod's curved pea-green shell nestled like a suckling pup against the silver belly of the ship. Giving us the space to work and sleep while we solved the problem of how to reach her again.

'C'mon. I need to finish the DNA splicing and give my body time to adjust before I go under. I think I've got the sequencing right this time.' Right, as long as I didn't give him a chance to read the program and see the truth.

'I still think you're mad,' Ish grumbled. His steps crunched the broken rocks as he stomped back to the ship.

I drew my boots on and followed him, glancing back twice. The sea's surface rippled. A silver head emerged. Dark eyes watched, blinked. Was it her? It must be. She'd reappeared three days ago—and every day since, just before dusk. Gesturing unmistakeably for me to follow her. Surely that meant something.

I raised a hand. She vanished.

Ish was probably right. I must be mad to attempt this. To body-mod to this extreme just so I could see her again. Marvel at her feather-light body and gossamer wings. Be certain she was real, not just a figment of my need.

I laughed softly. Surely people had done stupider things for science, or money, or love. I just couldn't think of any at the moment.

But this wasn't love. I knew what love felt like. Love was the ache of being incomplete; of not being with Emma. And the fear of loss that went with knowing she was at the mercy of the mine overseer.

No. This was…the fluttery anticipation of success, desperation, the thrill of potential discovery. Like a puppy, scrabbling at the fence to be free. The sensation had clogged my throat since the moment I found the alien—broken and gasping—on the sea's shore two weeks before.

Now, as then, I wanted to scream my exhilaration to the sky's emptiness. I was never going back to the water mines. Nor was Emma, or our son. Never. No matter what I had to do. But then, as now, hard-learned restraint clenched my teeth and fists until the urge subsided.

We entered the living pod, Ish stomping and muttering, me hiding a manic smile.

#

I swiped at the screen and tapped it so only the last entry showed. 'That should do it. Simulation shows my lungs will process the nitrogen dioxide from the sea's gas into breathable form. The xenon, ozone and other traces will be expelled by the new kidney adaptation.'

I stretched my neck. 'I should be able to breathe down there. I'll wear the exosuit and the nasal filters against spores and infections, but I won't have to carry tanks. Damned hard to talk to people when you're in a mask. We only have enough O2 for six hours, anyway.'

Ishmael raised wild, auburn brows. 'How long you planning on being gone?' He held up a transparent sheet of graphene and flexed it.

'Hopefully only a couple of days. A week if I must, assuming there's water. I'll take food.'

'That's a big assumption, mate.'

I pulled up the probe results and read them for the hundredth time. 'I don't think so. I'm sure these are lakes and rivers.' I poked a finger into the holo image of the landscape beneath the sea's surface. Valleys and basins. Had to be. 'Probe shows free water in the scans.'

I rotated the holo and pointed at a series of symmetrical arches and spires atop a plateau, about three kilometres from where we stood. 'And *that* has to be a city. *Has* to be.' I stared out the window at the sea that covered Azil. 'I have to see her…it…them. We need something uniquely theirs that shows sentience and couldn't be faked.'

Ish raised a cynical brow. 'About the only thing that fits that criteria is one of them. Any artefact can be declared a fake, you know that.'

'I'll find something.'

He snorted. 'Knowing our luck, the Core would refuse to class them as people. They still haven't recognised whales and dolphins as people, even though they were given sentient status two hundred years ago.'

A frisson of unease slivered through my stomach. No. She looked too humanoid for Core to pretend she was just a smart animal.

I reviewed the gene editing simulation again. 'I think I've got everything covered. What do you think?' A swipe at the screen hid the DNA splicing program and showed only the outcome.

Ish strolled over and read the feed. 'Looks good. Nice work. You're taking comms and a translator?'

'Course.' I tapped the still-tender spot beneath my ear. 'Mandibular implant. Not sure the translator will work, though. She didn't make any sounds I could hear.'

'Maybe they only carry in the gas?'

'Who knows. When I had her under the surface, she was unconscious the whole time. Maybe they write. Maybe they use interpretive dance.' I laughed. 'Guess I'll find out. How'd you go with the eyes and the wings?'

He scratched at his beard then pointed to a pair of contact lenses in fluid. 'Eyes are right to go. I can't mimic the compound lenses, but they'll cover your whole eyeball to protect against corrosive gas, if there is any. Enhanced vision through ultraviolet and infrared. Datalink feed to me. The wings...' He touched the microlattice and graphene work of art laid out on the bench. Two pairs of wings; like a dragonfly's; like hers. 'Yeah. They're ready, but...'

'But what?' I frowned. 'C'mon. We've been scout partners five years, Ish. What?'

'Take off your shirt. Let me see where they sit.'

Reluctantly, I complied.

He sucked a breath through bared teeth. 'Christ, Kai.' His fingers traced the old, thickened scars. 'I had no idea. The mine overseer?'

I shifted from under his touch. 'Better me than the person he *was* going to punish. Just fit the wings. Will the scars cause problems?'

'No. Doesn't look like the muscles are affected.' He pressed the contraption between my shoulderblades and muttered to himself while I stood, bare-chested, shivering, my fists clenched.

Finally, he handed my shirt back. His expression was grim. 'I can bond the mechanism to your trapezoidal muscles. And anchor them to your ribs and spine so they won't tear free.'

He picked up a small, elegant contraption of nanotech and tubes. 'This will sit between the wings. Flexing your traps will be enough to start the wings. The sea's gases are heavier than air, and Azil's gravity is less, so they shouldn't have to flap as fast as if you were on Earth.' He pointed at my jaw. 'Controls are linked to your comms. Tell it altitude, compass direction and distance and the software will control the wing function. But…'

'But?'

He sighed. 'Your muscles can't twitch fast enough to make them flap at the speed needed to lift you. So, the motor will do that. The battery will last a week.'

'What aren't you telling me?'

'It's going to hurt like Hell, mate.' He grimaced. 'A lot like Hell. Burning and sharp pains like you're being stabbed in the back with hot pokers.'

'Okay, okay,' I said, lifting a hand. 'I get the idea. Nothing I haven't felt before, then.'

His gaze slipped from mine and he cleared his throat. 'Just remember, if you get into trouble…' he pointed to the probe holo '… that city has nowhere to land a ship this size and no access except by flying, from what I can see. So your only way in and out will be these wings.' He paused then cocked his head. 'Still want to do it?'

We both knew the answer. This information would change his life and the lives of every member of humanity. Some more than others. That was the tricky thing about being partners for five years. Difficult to keep secrets when you're crossing the endless flipvoid of space in a tin can.

Not impossible, though.

I moved over to the window and gazed at the silent sea. 'Let's get started.'

#

A little over an hour later, I hefted the pack strapped to my chest and twitched my shoulders. Pain flared across my back and I ground my teeth against a gasp. The wings shifted, spread, then settled back flush with my spine, like a damselfly's. Like hers had. I stood at the edge of the sea and glanced back at Ishmael.

He tapped his hand. 'The wrist unit will send me biofeedback as well as controlling the data you get through the eye lenses.'

'Better go.' I coughed. 'Air here is a bit thin.' Each breath drove knives into my chest. My body couldn't pull oxygen from the air anymore.

After one last check of my equipment, Ish stepped back and nodded. I waded into the sea, feeling my way cautiously until the gases were up to my chin. I took a gulp of air by instinct and ducked beneath the surface.

Soft, pale sunlight lit the gas in an ethereal glow that deepened into darkness within a few feet. I could hold the breath no longer and let it go. The gases swirled, dancing and twirling in miniature cyclones.

The urge to breathe was irresistible. I sucked a breath and gagged on the acrid taste. Closing my mouth I tried through the nose-filters. Better. But each breath took willpower as my mind tried to tell me I was suffocating, breathing in toxins, dying.

Adrenalin pounded in my blood. My heart raced and I held a breath for the count of four, trying to calm myself.

The comm set in my jaw crackled static. *'Kai? Kaido? You there? You okay, mate? Talk to me or I'm coming after you.'*

'I'm here, Ish. Stop fretting like my grandmother. Breathing's fine.' My voice sounded deeper, like a sloweddown recording.

I tapped the datalink interface on my wrist and the contact lens display changed. Visual white noise faded and shapes jumped out at me. The black, cold shapes of jagged rocks underfoot. The surface sloped away steeply towards the east, as the probe's images showed.

I tapped again and faint green lines appeared. Surface contours from the probe data, showing me where I needed to go.

'Data link and visuals are good. I'm going to head towards the city. I'll drop the first transmitter at about one point five kilometres to boost the signal. Then the second just near the city.'

Now that I was out of sight, I ditched the supply pack, keeping only the two transmitters, a disruptor, and a stunner—which I holstered on my hips.

'Jeezus, Kai. I can't believe you're actually doing this. And you're still alive.' There was a long pause. *'There's a bit of interference with the comms and data feed, but I can compensate. Keep me posted? Don't do anything dumb.'*

I chuckled. 'Too late. Now shut up and let me concentrate. I'd rather not use these damned wings if I don't have to.' I almost told him where to find the note, then decided not to. Best wait until I was out of reach. I stepped carefully down the rocky slope, into darkness.

Into hope.

#

About half an hour later, the gloom lightened. Or, perhaps, I was used to it. The external temperature warmed, though my exosuit kept me comfortable no matter what. The sea's opacity faded and a vast world opened at my feet.

I checked the data analysis and sighed in relief. The atmosphere had a high percentage of xenon, but there was enough $NO2$ for my lungs to convert. I wasn't going to suffocate. Not yet.

With the soft grey gases drifting just above my head, I sat down on a boulder. Mostly because my legs gave way.

A broad valley swept down between the granite ranges, towards a distant, hazy basin that shimmered and sparkled like it was in direct sun. But what sunlight made it through the gas layer was sickly and pale.

Yet I could see clearly. Nearby, a patch of some sort of organic matter emitted a faint, yellow luminescence. And there were more. Everywhere I looked. Different colours, different strengths, different plants, if I could call them that. Up here on the mountainside, just a few patches. But further down in the valley the colours were deeper, richer, stronger.

I tapped the wrist unit and turned off infrared and

ultraviolet vision. The lights vanished, leaving only shadows and uneasy shades of charcoal and black. Hastily, I turned up the wavelength sensitivity again. Fae lights once again danced and swayed to winds I couldn't feel or hear.

The sounds! Now that I thought of listening, the plants seemed to hum like distant bees and clink like broken ceramic. A far away chime here. Then a ring so deep it resonated through my chest. A cascade of notes starting too high to hear and ending about middle C.

A small creature with pink-translucent glowing wings the miniature of my own fluttered past. But its wings tinkled like tiny brass bells as it flittered and danced through the air. I watched until it disappeared behind an outcrop.

My heart ached. A world that sang its own music. Together forming a chorus that sounded almost, but not quite, comprehensible. An underlying thrum and pulse that burrowed into my bones and into my cells until I trembled with its power.

I released a long-held breath on a sigh.

'Ish, you getting this? It's…beautiful. The sounds. The colours. It's…staggering.'

'You absolute, utter shithead, Kai. What the feck is this?'

'Ah, you got the note, then? Sorry. Couldn't see any other way to do it.'

'You used her DNA to mask yours! Your body will reject it. The gene mod is time-limited, you arsehole! A day or two at most. What happens if your DNA reverts while you're still down there?'

'It's okay. I'll be fine.'

'No! It's not. Did you really think I'd sit here and listen to you die? And what about food? And water? I used my exosuit to check on you and found your damned supply pack, too.'

'Too heavy. These wings hurt enough as it is. I told you I'd find water.'

'They might not be an oxygen-iron based life form, Kai. You won't be able to eat what they do.'

'I know. But I can last a couple of days without food. If I'm not back with anything useful in two days you can drop me supplies before you leave.'

'What the feck? Leave?'

'You have to. You'll run out of supplies for the run home if you don't leave soon.'

'You...you shit. You planned this. I always thought you had some sort of martyr complex. Now I know it.'

'Stop it, Ish. Go home to your family. Emma needs you.'

There was a long silence, full of anger and pain I could almost sense.

Dammit, Kai. He sighed into the mic. *You are my family. Go find your girl. I'm going to find a way to undo this feckery.*

I laughed and picked my way downhill, pausing occasionally to admire the view, or some bizarre specimen; and once to set the first booster. Twice I tested the wings, managing to fly a little further each time before the pain became unbearable.

When I was roughly halfway to the city, I stopped and rested on a ridge. Below was the valley in which the city nestled; a fairy-world of shimmering lights, ethereal arches, and delicate domed towers. Movement flickered between, above, and around the buildings, but too small for even the vision-enhancer to pick out the cause. People? Flying to and from their homes and businesses? Did they even have those? So many questions.

My heart pounded and my mouth was a desert. I hadn't yet found water. Something to be fixed soon. But I stayed where I was, just watching. Watching a world that wasn't human. I couldn't quite get my head around it.

How would they handle my appearance? Sweat prickled under my arms. We'd been so focussed on how humanity would respond to other sentients. Now that I was here, *their* reaction to *me* seemed a whole lot more… important.

A low-pitched buzz overhead caught my ear and I looked up.

There she was. Drifting down from above, soft, delicate; like an autumn leaf. At last she stood just a few feet away, poised to flee, wings jittering in quick bursts. Each wing was braced with what looked like a splint in some gleaming silvery metal. Repaired.

In one pincer-like, three-fingered hand, she held what might be a weapon—a long tube with a squeeze-closure handle. A close-fitting garment of some material that shimmered in the low infra-red range, disguised all but the sleek outline of her shape. Thin. Bipedal.

On impulse, I twitched my back muscles, setting the wings fluttering. Her eyes widened and the hand holding the tube fell. Shades of ultraviolet light flashed and danced across her face and exposed throat. Bewilderingly beautiful.

'Are you seeing this, Ish?' I whispered, trying not to move my lips.

The colours darkened on her skin and she peered at my mouth, hers moving as though in imitation. No sound emerged. More flashes of colour. Repetitions of the same pattern. The colours brighter each time. Faster, then slower.

'Shit,' I murmured. 'I think they communicate with ultraviolet light. Dammit. No way I can replicate that.'

'... violet light?... breaking up... getting audio not... ata or...mages... appening?'

Damn. Booster wasn't working properly. Or there was some other form of interference we hadn't accounted for. That meant the only record of this was locked in my wrist unit, pending upload to the ship's computer.

She took a hesitant step closer and reached out, touching my wings. She snatched her hand back, the lights flashing once more beneath her skin.

Was there *nothing* I could use to communicate? The only source of light I had was a small torch attached to my belt.

Useless.

A deeper buzz reached me and I looked around, seeking the source. She flinched, standing protectively before me as a larger specimen dropped to earth with a thud. His massive wings fluttered closed. Lights flashed rapidly beneath his skin and his eyes narrowed.

He, too, held a tube-weapon.

He pointed it at me.

She spun to me, gestured to my wings then to the sky. When I hesitated, she repeated the gesture. Was the hint of desperation just my imagination?

Reluctantly, I programmed a short flight into the wrist unit and launched myself skyward. White-hot pain lashed at my back. I shunted aside memories of older agony and gritted my teeth.

When I landed, the expression on her face was unmistakeably delight. By our standards, anyway. The exposed, shark-like teeth made me doubt the interpretation.

After another, rapid-fire, silent, beautiful conversation, she pointed skyward again. The larger—male?—pressed his lips together.

I took off again. This time it was worse. By the time I landed, trickles of hot liquid slid down my back and soaked into the exosuit. I didn't need the health-monitor to tell me it was blood, not sweat.

'...the feck are... doing? ... going on?'

I ignored Ishmael and concentrated on standing straight, not collapsing.

Another conversation. Closer to an argument if I was interpreting the arm gestures and dark-violet lights correctly.

'... back up here, Kai. Not worth...'

He was wrong. It was worth it. Maybe not for me, but I wasn't important.

'... what you can... bring anyth... doesn't mat... what.'

Again, wrong. It did matter what I brought back. Mattered more than he knew. To more people than he knew existed.

I waited. My tongue felt thick and sticky. My back muscles burned like someone had stuck hot wires into them.

The two argued, arms waving, lights flashing so fast and bright anyone looking this way couldn't help but see.

Uneasy, I checked the city. Nothing so far. But Ish had been right. Clearly, there were politics here I was about to walk into with no preparation and no way of communicating.

I took a step toward the pair. His weapon rose. She moved between us, her hand on his chest.

The lights on his face changed to a single pattern of spiralling geometry that was as beautiful as it was strangely ominous.

She froze, then shrank back, both hands held out as though to fend him off.

Without further ceremony, he spun her and wrenched at her newly-repaired wings, practically tearing them from her shoulders.

Her mouth gaped. The lights under her skin darkened to almost black... and went out. She slumped to the ground, her head buried in her arms.

My breath stopped. Time and pain ceased.

The weapon pointed at me and there was no mistaking the implacable blackness in his wide, dark eyes.

Our next actions would determine the future of both our civilisations. And the future of my family, and Ishmael's.

But what choice did I have? Without proof, our family was doomed, anyway.

I snatched out my disruptor and fired.

The ultrasonic pulse took him square in the torso. He jerked, staggered, and squeezed his weapon.

I threw myself to the side. A beam of energy skimmed icy fire across my arm, numbing it.

I shot again. This time at his head.

His carcass slumped to the stones, wings twitching. Grey blood oozed from his eyes and mouth.

Shit. Now what? The feeling in my arm returned, along with needle-sharp pain in the fingers.

I rose shakily to my feet and sucked a long, slow breath of the heavy air.

The world's music was a disharmonious din under my heart's thundering. Only my own harsh breath was real.

I drew another lungful and coughed knife-blades. A quick glance at the health-monitor confirmed my suspicion. The gene-mod was reverting. I had maybe an hour before I would suffocate in this toxic atmosphere.

There was no way I could go to the city, now. Even if his reaction wasn't normal, I'd be dead before I worked out how to say hello.

I glanced down at the broken-winged figure huddled at my feet. She represented salvation and condemnation in one.

Her existence would bring enough reward money from the Hegemon to get Emma and my four-year-old, never-seen son out of the water mines for good.

I'd promised Emma I would get her brother out—and promised him I'd get his sister out. But Emma would not want this. Not when taking this alien from her world could kill her.

And possibly plunge the Hegemon into a war with the first sentients we'd met.

Hesitating, I surveyed the city laid out below me; isolated and safe from the Hegemon. Beautiful in its strangeness. Blissfully unaware.

Then I gathered her into my arms and launched skyward, toward the ship. Pain lashed at my back and my mind.

'Ish!' I could only hope he heard me. 'Fill the hold and as many of our empty O2 tanks with the sea as you can. I'm coming back.'

As I flew, her blood and mine mingled and dripped dark onto the glittering, singing fields below. Marking the path to a future of both hope and uncertainty.

END

1430 hours: The Zoo

Zev Smith

'Fecking Azilans,' Zev sauntered up to the Zoo's bar and accepted a scotch from Ab.

'Only reason we didn't end up in a full-blown war after that,' Zev added, 'was because they weren't any more advanced than Terra. Just luck. We Terrans are idiots. Always have been. Especially Exploration and the Hegemon.' He gritted his teeth. 'Just don't know when to leave well enough alone.'

The new Grey Guard Lieutenant lifted her fine, arched brows. 'You always listen in on conversations?'

He chuckled. 'It's a public bar and that's not exactly a private fecking story. Learned that one at school.'

It'd been interesting watching the girl's face. She didn't

seem the sort to fit in here. Too Inner System. Too soft. But physically strong. And an expression of dark wariness in her pale eyes.

The next few days would show whether she would cause trouble for him.

He threw back the nip of straight scotch and cleared his throat. 'We Terrans should have left well enough alone when we found the Azilans. Plenty of other sentients around. Azilans have always caused problems. Not as much as the Derrians. Or the fecking Uher, though.'

Lieutenant Bligh swilled her drink in her glass. 'They're extinct, aren't they? The Uher, I mean. My cousin studied xeno-archaeology at university. I'm sure she said the Uher were ancient history.'

Zev curled a lip. 'Yeah. But when I was with Exploration we came across their ruins a few times. Always crawling with fecking treasure-hunters. Rumours that the Uher had an immortality formula and some special metallurgy processes everyone wanted to get their hands on.'

Bligh gave a biting laugh. 'Clearly their immortality formula was pretty crap, then. They're long gone.'

'Not so much.' Zev lifted one shoulder. 'Just had a prof from the Galaxy Collaborative University in here the other week. Had an interesting tale. Something he found on a planet called Helio. Want to hear?'

She eyed him from beneath long black lashes. 'Don't you have toilets to fix?'

'Don't you start, too.' He held up his empty glass. 'I get

breaks. Man's gotta eat.'

'You won't live long on that diet,' she said.

Ab refilled Zev's scotch unasked and leaned over the bar, his facial tentacles pulled tight into a bitter bundle. 'Living a long time isn't all it's cracked up to be. What did your professor friend find on Helio, Zev?'

The Weight of Time

Pamela Jeffs

Current year

The engines whine as *Arc Angel* prepares to fall out of flip. My stomach slews sideways as the void created by the ship's drive alters, spilling me out into a zone painted in ancient stars. My eyes sting at the sudden brightness. This is my fifteenth hop to reach this part of the galaxy and the experience gained in the doing never makes it any easier. I hate flipping. If only there was another option to get this far past civilisation.

A thud ricochets around the cabin, loud enough to wake the Creator himself. Metal screeches. Then a portion of wing, edges torn, floats past the viewscreen. Alarms blare, acidic.

Their pulse punctuates a flickering array of red and yellow lights on the ship's console.

'What the hell was that?' I snarl.

L.O.R.N, the ship's AI, responds, her metallic voice piping through the controls. 'Asteroid strike. Hull breach critical.'

'Habitable planets?'

'Class M, 300,000 kilometres away.'

'Is it the one we want?'

'Yes, Jonas.'

I lean forward. Helio—a cold world lit by the light of its supermassive black hole sun—hangs in the void like an eye glaring. Wreckages of ancient Uher satellites circumnavigate the planet; a planet light years past the borders of Hegemon-controlled space.

A whisper of excitement tingles down my spine. It's the dream of any academic—any space explorer—to prove a legend true. And this long dead planet is rumoured to harbour the vestiges of an advanced race. Never mind that said race, the Uher, was meant to have discovered the Immortality Formula before their sun went supernova and destroyed everything.

Yes. Helio could be my get-out-of–jail ticket from a series of expensive failures in recent expeditions, expeditions for which credits were borrowed from the Underground Banker.

Credits the Banker now wants back.

And I have no way to pay.

Professor Jonas Calbourne. That's me. Or it'll be Dead

Man if this Helio gig doesn't pan out.

I unclip my comms gauntlet from its cradle and transfer LORN to its interface. *Arc Angel* groans as I push up out of the control seat. I pat the main console.

'Sorry to leave you like this, girl,' I say.

'Engines powered down,' drones LORN 'Self-repair nanobots administered. *Arc Angel* will re-engage when complete and power into orbit around the planet to await our return.'

'That's if we make it back,' I mutter.

'Escape shuttle navigation set,' continues LORN, ignoring my comment. 'Ready to commence launch when you are, Jonas.'

#

The shuttle heads at sublight speed toward the planet. Being in such a small vessel gives me a real sense of my own scale in comparison to the universe. There is no denying that I am infinitesimal against the infinite. The depth of the indigo vastness calls me; the wonder of discovering something lost draws me to explore these cold reaches. It's my personal brand of addiction.

Helio looms large in the shuttle viewscreen. This close, the world gains more definition. Shadows lie behind the spines of red dirt mountain ranges and puddle wide in the deeper valleys. Patches of white against the russet denote the ragged shores of frozen oceans. A crescent-shaped plain ringed with mountains catches my attention.

'Set heading niner five point six, Lorn,' I say. 'Take us in.'

The escape shuttle engines change pitch as they increase speed in preparation to enter the atmosphere. I lean back into my seat and brace myself against the handles. A blip lights up on the sensor radar.

'A vessel has just emerged from flip, Jonas,' says LORN. 'Approaching at sublight speed. Its weapons array is engaged.'

'Who is it?' I ask.

'A gunner ship with forged Hegemon registration. The Banker's bounty hunters again, no doubt.'

Fecking hell. How did they find me this far out in space? I hit the viewscreen button on the console. The image feed transfers to the rear sensor display. The gunner, sleek as a comet, is closing in fast, the engines leaving a trailing red glow behind them.

The triple laser array on the front of the ship blossoms to life. Three green tracer beams detach from them, streaking through space before colliding with the aft of my shuttle.

#

Smoke. Alarms.

I raise my head off the shuttle's helm. Dizzy. Blood trickles down the side of my left temple and onto my flight suit. The viewscreen is awash with flame. We are entering Helio's atmosphere.

'Crit...critical malfunction,' hiccups LORN. 'Unable to

control descent. Impact imminent.'

I'm not giving up that easily. I grip the steering yoke and switch to manual control. I pull backward and to the left, angling the nose to 40 degrees—trying to ease the shuttle's hypersonic speed by twisting into the planet's orbital spin. The noise in the cockpit rises. A furious roaring of heat and light pummels the vessel's outer skin. I squint against the friction-bright viewscreen, cursing.

'Speed and distance, Lorn?'

Her voice pipes through my gauntlet instead of the ship's ruined comms. '29000 kilometres per hour. Ten seconds to impact.'

I press the retro thrustors to try ease off more speed.

This is going to be close.

#

The *trip-trip* sound of sparking wires wakes me. Still alive. It means the atmosphere inside the shuttle has been maintained. But for how much longer? I engage my flight suit's helmet, thankful when the clear, atmosphere-barrier settles into place. Then my ID implant, connected to my visual cortex, blinks awake before my eyes. My current medical status is displayed in bright green lettering.

Minor laceration to temple.

Severe bruising to ribs and right leg.

High blood pressure.

Emergency Hegemon Core computer communications

unavailable. Immediate return to Hegemon space required for medical unit deployment.

No chance of that any time soon. I try to roll over, but my right thigh is pinned under a metal strut. The bruise is already an angry purple. I push the beam. It slides free, the blunt edge pressing the sorest part of my leg on its way past.

Red backup lighting illuminates the cabin. The exit door at the rear of the shuttle beckons. I ease past the shattered control chair and brush aside the loose panels and their cascading falls of wiring.

The exit release lever doesn't work on the first go. I punch it and then slam it downwards again. The doors creak open just enough so I can slide through.

I blink in the new light. Dark orange bred from a cold sun and a hot sky.

The shuttle lies crumpled against the foot of a rust-coloured mountain. Caverns dot the height of the precipice, evidence that water once flowed on this planet.

LORN blinks awake on my gauntlet, her voice showing as a set of red audio lines. 'Congratulations on being alive.'

'Thanks for that,' I say. I survey the wrecked ship and wonder how the hell I'm going to get off this world. Then I recall the broken satellites orbiting the planet. Maybe there is some old Uher tech still here that might help me. 'What can you tell me about the place?'

'Compatible atmosphere. Iron and bauxite matrix in the surrounding rock. Nil water. Surface temperature, minus two degrees. I wouldn't take your flight suit off. Oh. That's interesting.'

'What?'

'The planet's core is warm. Liquid magma and evidence of H20.'

The holes in the cliffs are suddenly more interesting. 'Any of those caves lead down to a survivable temperature? A place maybe where the Uher could've survived?'

The gauntlet's viewscreen glows green as LORN maps the underground terrain in a series of illuminated lines. 'Yes. Several corridors.'

'Life signs?'

'Yes. But not in the cavern system.' LORN switches the display on the gauntlet. A red dot blinks. 'The bounty hunter has landed. One klick from here.'

Not interested in waiting to see who it is, I jog toward the closest cavern. My boots crunch and slip across the loose gravel as I head for the irregular-shaped maw of a nearby cave.

But the one hunting me is swift. Just as I gain entrance, a disruptor blast shatters the edge of the opening. I stop, hands up. The weight of the stunner hanging from my hip tempts me, but it's not a weapon made for killing, only incapacitating. It would be a mistake to draw it. I turn.

My heart skips.

I recognise the bounty hunter.

Rune Nevis.

She is dressed in her distinctive scarlet flight suit. Her helmet is tinted, black against the red. Rune, an Iscean female with a reputation for cold-hearted killing. And worse, a woman

I was stupid enough to have a one-night-stand with. Granted, at the time I didn't know that Isceans mate for life. Rune Nevis, no doubt, would have taken a great amount of pleasure in accepting the bounty to hunt me down.

'Rune,' I say.

I can't see her eyes, but her chin tilts. The translator function on my aural implant automatically activates when she speaks. 'Jonas.'

'The Banker sent you?'

'He did.'

I put my hands down and take a step toward her. Her sleek, silver disruptor remains trained on me, its hard lines a match for the hardness of her physique.

'Look,' I say. 'You have no reason to trust me. But I have a real chance here to make good on my debts. If you could just turn a blind eye—'

'It's too late for that, Jonas.' She lifts her weapon an inch, her finger tightening on the trigger. 'This kill is as much for me as for the Underground Banker.'

'Rune. Please.'

'There is no "please". I am not your claimed mate.'

I'm screwed.

Rune's finger squeezes the trigger.

I leap to the side. The blast flies over my head, hitting the cliff and shattering the stone. Fragments rain down around me, pins of stone nipping at the fabric of my flight suit.

Rune's growl scratches through the translator.

I surge to my feet and bolt for the caverns. Sprinting

through the darkness, I'm blind, bouncing off the close walls and uneven floor. LORN lights up a map of the cavern system on the gauntlet. The green illumination reveals the details of the underground corridor. I need to take the next left turn.

My pulse races. My ribs and bruised thigh ache. Behind me Rune's footsteps echo in the corridor. Her breath is loud, a virulent hiss in the darkness. Every moment hangs suspended, weighted, like it will be my last.

The deeper I go, the warmer it gets.

'External temperature is rising, Jonas,' says LORN, relaying the gauntlet sensor outputs. '20 degrees celsius. Atmosphere compatible. You can turn your helmet off.'

I press the helmet control switch. The visor melts away and a rush of warm air meets my skin. I inhale a deep breath, but almost choke on the unpleasant scent in the air.

'Lorn?'

'Sulphur vents in the side tunnels. The levels are not dangerous. Keep running.'

The corridor opens out. Concealed by the darkness, it is more a sensation of open space than anything I can see. The air on my face is moist. And there is noise. The cavern roars with the voice of rushing water.

Rune bursts from the passage behind me. The light around the sleek edges of her illuminated helmet is brighter than my own. I glimpse the broken white of a waterfall cascading at the far end of the cavern. A river sweeps by in front of me, its edges lapping at a red sandy shore.

I've nowhere to go and no time to react.

An ultrasonic blast from Rune's disruptor hits my comms gauntlet. Another shot and this time, the pulse strikes my leg. I crumple to the ground, grimacing against the pain. The affected flesh slackens and bruises, the molecules corrupted. My ocular implant relays my medical condition in facts, cold and hard.

Severe degeneration of muscular tissue.

Recommended amputation.

My vision wavers as Rune approaches. Her steps are smooth and clean, the lithe, compact movement of an apex predator. She kneels at my side and presses the disruptor to my forehead. Her helmet melts away to reveal her face.

She has aged in the years since I last saw her. Lines crease the fine blue scales edging her gold, reptilian eyes. Startling green hair frames her face, the light from my gauntlet catching glints of emerald in its depths. But she is still as beautiful as I remember.

And just as deadly.

Rune's lips part in a smile to reveal her teeth, the short perfect white crescents at the front framed by the longer fangs gifted by her reptilian genetics.

Her voice is loud, pitched to carry over the tumble of the falls. 'You end here, Jonas. In the darkness and the—'

The cave illuminates. Red rock and shore and jagged ceiling are revealed. The blue light rises like a wave from the lake, brilliant and cold. Brighter and brighter it grows, an underwater star, tendrils of phosphorescence colouring the water. The waterfall beyond cascades, a curtain of glowing silver.

Rune's attention is drawn away from me. The gun slips from my temple. Her expression, before full of confidence, turns first to wonder, then horror. She steps back, her gun now aimed over my shoulder. It trembles in her grasp. Her face twists, mouth turning down into a hard frown.

She fires.

Pulse after pulse.

I duck and turn. The light in the lake has coalesced into a single point of brightness. Except when it emerges, it is no star at all.

It is a creature, its body made of both shifting shadow and light—a body that cycles, black smoke and blue phosphorescence, never settling on a shape, just the suggestion of one. It steps clear of the river's brilliant waters, shoulders broad like mountains forged from fractured fire. Three meters high at least, it towers over us both.

Water trickles away in rivulets down its chest and neck. It stalks past me, carrying with it the scent of salt and sulphur.

Again, Rune fires. The shot connects, but the monster absorbs it—swallows it with a ripple of half formed flesh. Light glows around the hit site for a moment then fades.

The creature reaches Rune. Its back is to me, a coiling, seething expanse of fluid muscle. With one massive fist, it tears the gun from Rune's grip and throws it into the roiling river. Then it presses a hand to her chest. Energy explodes through the touch, phosphorescent blue.

The bounty hunter falls unconscious to the ground.

The creature turns to me. Its brows furrow over the broad bridge of an almost-there nose.

'Lorn?' I whisper, hoping for some insight, some salvation.

But the gauntlet's electronics are fried. LORN is back on *Arc Angel*, and the rock above us too thick for ship's comms to penetrate and reach my aural implant.

#

Rune lies unconscious on the dirt. The creature, silent, carries me away from the edge of the glowing river and higher up the underground beach. It's flesh, although ephemeral-looking, feels solid and warm under my back. The creature rests me gently against a smooth boulder.

'Are you Uher?' I ask.

The alien's chin lifts sharply; its blue, backlit gaze catches mine. It doesn't answer. Instead its eyes fall to my injured leg. It tears back the flight suit fabric and gently probes the wound, fingertips sinking into the spongy flesh left behind by Rune's disruptor. I wince at the sharp pain and jerk away from the pressure.

'It hurts,' I say.

The creature's brow furrows. Finally, it speaks, my translator decoding its gurgling voice.

'The damage. There is much.'

I look down. The flesh on my calf is black. Corrupted.

The alien gurgles again, 'I fix.' It makes a cutting motion

across my thigh. 'I fix. You live.'

I bite the inside of my cheek. I don't want to die here. I nod, a clipped movement. 'Okay, but can you at least tell me your name?'

'No name,' comes the reply.

'I've got to call you something,' I say. I consider the blue phosphorescence eddying through the creature's body. 'How about Phosper? That okay?'

The creature seems pleased. It presses its hand to its chest. 'I am he. Phosper. It is good.'

Phosper's touch is gentle as he ties a length of fabric, cut from my flight suit, around the upper part of my leg. I hiss as he pulls the knot tight over the bruise I earned from the crash topside.

I expect an amputation knife next but instead Phosper holds up a single finger. The light skipping through his ephemeral form travels to gather in the tip, the blue phosphorescence matching the colour of the gently glowing river adjacent. The tip is lowered to my skin, the touch a searing brand.

Blood sheets hot across my thigh as the flesh is severed. I bite back a scream as Phosper's touch scores through skin and sinew and bone. The damaged section of leg finally falls away. Phosper's hand closes over the open wound. Like before, when he touched Rune, the alien's hand burns blue for a moment. The pain of the raw wound eases, but the weight of an unfamiliar power fills my blood. Too strong, too potent for my body to process. My stomach turns. The last thing I remember is vomiting out fluid glowing with phosphorescence.

#

I wake. The river has gone dark but a blue fire burns brightly on the red beach. The waterfall continues to roar behind us, hidden now in the darkness. Rune, bound hand and foot sits across the fire staring at me, her glare baleful.

'This is your fault,' she snarls, her long venomous fangs glittering in the uncertain light.

'Sorry to disappoint you.' I rub a hand over my face then realise I am in no pain. Not anywhere—my ribs, my bruise, or more importantly my leg. I run my palm down my thigh. It ends at the stump above where my knee used to be. But the wound is closed, healed over as if it were months ago that the flesh was separated away.

I look around for the giant but he is nowhere to be seen. 'Where is Phosper?'

Rune's eyes narrow. 'If you mean that creature, it returned to the water.' She lifts her bound hands. 'Left us here to perish.'

I shake my head. 'Why would he heal me and build us a fire if he didn't mean to return?'

The blue firelight flickers in the depths of Rune's gold eyes. 'Why did it leave me bound?'

I smile. 'Perhaps because you fired at him.' I pat the stunner still holstered at my side. 'Perhaps he was worried you would undo his good work and try to kill me again.'

'It would be right.'

'Are you ever not a huntress?'

'Are you ever not a scoundrel?'

Movement at the edge of the river ends the conversation. Phosper stalks into the circle of firelight, an elongated white worm-like creature wriggling in his fist. He throws it on the fire where the animal squirms for a moment then falls still. Spitting and crackling, it starts to roast.

'Food,' says Phosper pointing. 'Finish cook, then eat.'

Rune's pert nose wrinkles at the fish-like smell. 'I prefer my food raw.'

Phosper shrugs. 'Then be hungry, snake woman.'

Rune hisses a profanity my translator cannot decipher.

Phosper ignores her. 'How you come here?' he asks, looking at me.

'In a shuttle.' I point up to the roof of the cave. 'My ship is orbiting your planet.'

'Why?'

'I am a Professor of Ancient Races for the Galaxy Collaborative University. I came here to look for evidence of the Uher.'

'No Uher here. Long ago die. Left me.'

'Did they leave anything else behind?'

Phosper's facial features move, playing like smoke in wind. His luminous eyes flare bright then fade back to embers. 'Only me.'

'And what are you?' asks Rune, her voice cold.

Phosper turns to look at her. 'I their experiment. Their

secret. Their formula.'

My heart skips a beat. 'Formula?'

Phosper points to the ceiling of the cave. 'Uher made me. But star fell. Uher died. I cannot. I escape a cage and flee from cold up top. Find river. Stay here.' He lowers his hand and pokes at the worm on the fire. 'Food, warm and water is good.'

My mind is reeling. I came to find evidence of the ancient race, to find their immortality formula. Could it honestly be this easy? A creature with answers served on a plate? A living breathing immortal?

Ideas start forming in my mind. And questions. Can I convince the alien to come back to the university with me? Who do I speak with about the genetic extraction of the formula from his DNA coding? It could kill him, but the price is worth the benefits, right? Maybe if I can repair my flight suit somehow and convince Phosper to take me topside. I could incapacitate him with my stunner and use Rune's ship to transfer him to *Arc Angel*. Of course, I would need to find a way to convince Rune to help me or otherwise dispose of her altogether…

Possibilities.

So many possibilities.

My thoughts spin, filling my mind with visions of freedom from the Banker, of funding and professional recognition. All my doubters, they'll see me in a new light. Professor Calbourne—Galactic Humanitarian.

And all to be gained at the cost of a single creature's blood.

Phosper's blood.

Phosper leans over and pulls the cooked worm out of the fire. With delicate fingers, he tears the warm meat apart and divides it into three equal portions. He hands a serving to me then smiles, the glowing edges of his teeth peeking out past his shifting lips.

And something about the act of his simple hospitality swings my perspective. Phosper is more than just an experiment. He is a living, breathing alien in his own right. I grit my teeth, unwilling to acknowledge the thoughts battering at the edge of my resolve—

I'm a better man than this, aren't I?

A man of principals.

Phosper saved me.

He healed me.

He's feeding me.

He deserves more.

The thoughts flood through me, relentless. My determination crumbles. Credits and accolades be damned. I'll need to find another way to repay the Banker.

But Rune is still a problem. I glance at her, but she is no longer there.

A chill crawls down my spine. Phosper has noticed the bounty hunter's absence also. He is on his feet, eyes glowing as he surveys the darkness beyond the fire. I hobble to my good knee, letting my shortened leg hang limp in the air. I am no use to Phosper physically, but perhaps I can warn him if I see her.

But she comes from an unexpected quarter. Rune falls

from above, dropping onto Phosper's shoulders. Her red flight suit catches the light and strikes a sharp and vibrant contrast against his translucent darkness.

They grapple and for a moment their bodies entwine, a kaleidoscopic column of red and black and phosphorous light. Then Rune's mouth opens and she plunges her wicked tipped teeth into Phosper's neck.

The immortal roars as Rune's venom pumps into his flesh. He swings, arms flailing but cannot gain purchase on the viper-fast bounty hunter. I watch in horror as his movements start to slow.

I fumble for my stunner, dragging it clear of the holster. The trigger is a cold line against my fingertip. I send a pulse into Rune's back.

It hits the mark cleanly. The bounty hunter's hands slip, her teeth slither free of Phosper's neck. It is enough of an opening for Phosper to get hold of her around the throat.

Her last look at me as Phosper squeezes the life from her is one I recognise. The same I saw on a day long ago when I told her I didn't love her.

Betrayal.

Rune falls to the ground, dead. Phosper stands swaying. The phosphorescence in him has travelled and focused on the wound in his neck—his body a dark swirling husk, a starburst of light at the throat. His chest heaves in great gulps of air. He stumbles and falls to one knee.

I crawl over to him and place a hand on his shoulder. 'What can I do?'

'What happens to me?' whispers Phosper.

I lean in and look closer at his wound. Phosphorescence is leaking out of the twin punctures left by Rune's teeth, two glowing rivulets. The light in his body grows dimmer. The immortality formula of the ancient Uher, it seems, is fallible— undone by the venom of an Iscean.

I help ease the centuries-old alien flat to the ground. His eyes, now dull blue, search my face.

'What happens?' he asks again.

Tears prick the back of my eyes. There is something unnerving about seeing fear in such a kind yet powerful creature. I choose honesty.

'You are dying, my friend,' I say. 'But I am here with you. You will not pass alone.'

Phosper's eyes droop, and then open again. 'At this end. A gift I give to you.' He places his palm on my shoulder. His transfer when it comes is gentle, a mere trickle of warmth through my blood, not the overwhelming sensation from earlier. Perhaps my prior exposure to his power has eased the way.

My arms grow stronger, my eyesight also. Years seem to fall away and I have never felt as healthy. Then I realise what he is doing—transferring the immortality formula to me. No, not an immortality formula, but one that grants strength and extreme longevity.

The gift as it enters me is tempered with Phosper's emotions. His sadness filters through the link, the sense of the loneliness he has felt at being the only one of his kind for as long as he can remember.

But it is his thankfulness at our coming to him that breaks me. Tears track down my cheeks and onto the now dead alien's chest as the last of his gift fills me.

#

Rune is not quite dead. Not yet. But she is close to crossing that horizon. Her emerald hair, fallen free of its braid, frames her face. Her eyes, open, gaze at the dark ceiling overhead. I kneel by her.

'You are finally rid of me,' she whispers.

'You deserve this end.'

'Do I?'

'Yes.'

'You're glad then?'

'Not really. I didn't want you dead.'

'So a part of you does care for me?'

Guilt wars with my anger at her. I hate that she murdered Phosper, hate that she took my leg, but I also know she was not always like this. Once she was beautiful, both inside and out.

A ghost of a smile touches her lips. 'Will you miss me?'

My anger slips away. In this moment, with the prospect of extended life stretching before me, I realise that centuries are a long time to ponder things lost and poor decisions made. A long time to live with regrets.

I press my lips together before answering. Recognising the

truth is easier than I expect. Even though I never loved her back, it was nice to know that I meant something to someone, somewhere in the galaxy.

'I will,' I say.

Rune's gaze softens. Her finger gently touches my cheek. 'And I am sorry,' she whispers. 'For everything I did. I just didn't want to be alone.'

Then her eyes close. Her breaths fade. Her hand drops.

I brush a stray lock of hair away from her cheek.

And now I am the one alone, left with the weight of time settling around me.

END

1500 hours: The Zookeeper

Absinthe Krull

'He's right about centuries being a long to time live with regrets.' Absinthe flicked his glass-polishing towel over his shoulder and sighed, shaking away unwanted memories. There was no point in wishing he'd made other decisions, all those years ago. Done was done. All he could do was help others make better choices.

He narrowed his eyes, studying the young Grey Guard lieutenant. She carried a heavy burden of some sort on those slender shoulders. When she thought no-one watched, her soft mouth tightened into misery. She was a long way from her Inner Systems lifestyle, too. Must be difficult for someone so young. Perhaps a distraction was in order.

He forced his facial tentacles to relax and let them drift. 'Discovering Helio is a pretty impressive tale, but nothing on finding an actual live Uher.'

She didn't look up from her empty glass. He slid the Blythe gin bottle closer but she shook her head.

Zev rocked back on his stool, the fabric seat creaking beneath him. 'Don't fecking try to tell me that someone has found one of those Uher bastards alive.'

Absinthe shrugged. 'A Yasti came in just the other day. Granted, he was blind drunk on redwater, but he claimed his great grandfather invented the dycerium space vessel hulls and that the original sample of metal was taken from the hands of a live Uher Overseer two hundred years ago.'

A cynical smile creased Zev's worn lips. 'Bullshit. That feller was yanking your tentacles. You sure he wasn't high on black and spinning hallucinations?'

Absinthe's tentacles fell still, all humour having fled. 'Not in my bar,' he said. 'You know I don't tolerate either black dealers or addicts.'

Zev sniffed and scratched the shoulder of his stained coveralls. 'Too true.'

The new young Lieutenant looked at Absinthe, studying him with open curiosity.

Her comms buzzed and she held up a hand. 'Bligh here. What?'

The tinny voice of her second-in-command, Sergeant Yang, swelled over the Zoo's muted hum of conversations. 'We could use some help at Dock 2, Lieutenant. If you don't mind starting early.'

'Be there in a minute.' She sighed and jerked her chin at

Ab. 'Don't stop. I'd like to hear before I go.'

'Thought this would be an easy posting, didn't you, girl?' Zev chuckled. 'I have to go, too, though. Hurry it up, Ab. Tell us what else your Yasti friend had to say about the Uher.'

A Corruption of Flesh and Mind

Pamela Jeffs

200 years ago

An ancient portal orb. One metre in diameter. Kain brushes his fingertips across its polished surface The iron-hard sphere of silver is shot through with threads of gold.

Stunning, he thinks.

'An Outer System border patrol found it floating just past Hegemon space,' says Mercor, his black, sclera-free eyes amplified like an Earth owl's behind his old style Terran glasses. His clawed fingers scratch his chest just above the Galaxy Collaborative University logo on his lab suit. 'They brought it in last night.'

'You've tested the material?' asks Kain.

'Yes,' says Mercor. 'It's a form of alloyed Telluric iron.'

Kain glances up. His vision blurs for a moment then sharpens. He ignores the glitch with practiced skill. 'You're sure?'

Mercor smiles, his long front rodent teeth looking too bright against his black lips. 'Positive. My third PHD was in metallurgy. Trust me. I know metals.'

'Now please tell me this metal is super rare and could only have been manufactured by a certain highly advanced, extinct, alien race,' says Kain.

Mercor's nose twitches with excitement as he points to a small, seven-pointed star stamped into the top of the orb. 'Consider yourself told. Look at the mark—it's Uher for sure.'

Heat rushes up Kain's neck as he recognises the ancient stamp of the Uher dynasty. Has he finally been given his ticket out of this damned university?

He squeezes Mercor's shoulder. 'Now tell me what I really need to hear. How old is it?'

Mercor swipes his finger across his handheld datapad. A hologram blinks awake above its jet-glass surface—a carbon dating graph outlined in luminous green. 'Reports catalogue it as five thousand years old. Close to when they died out.'

Kain stands back and pushes his fingers into his blond fringe. 'We need to work out if it can still be activated.'

Mercor stays silent.

Kain drops his hands. 'You've already run diagnostics on it, haven't you?'

'Well, you were late to work again and I couldn't wait to find out.'

Kain bites back his irritation. Mercor is the assistant researcher—he had no right to proceed without being overseen. 'Well then?' he says testily. 'What did you find?'

'Radiant energy signatures.'

'And?'

Mercor grins. 'Intact quantum cell resistors. The internal components are old, but the device is still operating and well under critical heat load limits. We should be able to activate it.'

'Yes!' Kain spins, fist-pumping the air. His vision blurs again. It takes longer to resolve this time, but does. He's been dealing with the ever-increasing effects of a black downer. He's just starting to skirt the fine line between feeling great and the onset of physical degradation—but this...this news makes him feel like he's just taken a new pellet of the drug.

He has a functioning Uher portal orb.

An image of himself swimming naked in credits alongside three beautiful Terran women and a bathtub full of black fills his mind. He shivers. Twenty years of research into experimental dimensional portals has culminated in this moment.

A moment when he can finally forget the day, three years ago, when he threw away his career by attacking the Head of University Research in a black-fuelled rage. He only wanted more funding. And was denied it. The Head has walked with a limp ever since and holds a grudge the size of a planet against

Kain.

Yes. Kain's had plenty of time to regret his actions and fantasize about changing his lot. Time to dream of wealth, money, power and drugs. He has big dreams. And all will come true if this portal works.

#

Kain's boots beat a steady tattoo on the floor as he heads for the particle x-ray labs. His research into Uher technology suggests that to activate the orb and facilitate the portal, raw electricity must be directly applied.

Energy. Yes, a shitload of energy is what they need. And Mercor reckons he can jerry-rig the equipment to syphon it from the x-ray cores.

Kain's fingertips begin to tingle. *Damn.* He should have taken another pellet of black before he left home this morning. The effects of last night's hit are wearing away faster than he anticipated. His heightened adrenaline at the orb's discovery has burnt it from his system.

It's a delicate chemical balance to maintain.

For the first four hours after taking the drug, he's lucid but functioning on a base plane. For the next ten he feels invincible, running on enhanced energy and a sense of wellbeing. But the hours he's in now—the hours of the downer—can go from bad to debilitating, fast.

That's why Kain always keeps a pellet on his person. A just-in-case pellet.

He reaches into his pocket and palms the small tablet. Taking it will ease the downer effects but he'll be incapacitated. He can't swallow it yet. Not until he has four hours alone to let the initial effects pass, and certainly not in front of Mercor. Last thing he needs is his only staff member to desert him. Kain reluctantly slides his hand out from his pocket. *I can wait. It's not like I'm an addict.*

I am in control.

#

University rules and sanctions be damned. Kain skirts protocols to proceed with the orb's activation. He's nervous, but not enough to stop.

Despite his twenty years of research into the orbs, knowledge on the actual function of the Uher tech is scant. Only hints, found in ancient Iscean texts. Suggestions that the orbs lead to manufactured monoverses—dimensional storage areas used by the Uher.

Once, Kain dreamt of discovering vast archives maintained within an orb. Or even better, actual Uher technology that could be brought back and utilized in the greater good of the universe.

How things changed.

Kain shakes his head. God, he was naive back then—back in his younger days. A time before the University Head kicked his career to the curb. Now life is simpler. All that matters is seeing if the portal works, and if it does, stealing the tech to sell to the highest bidder for as many credits as he can get.

And in celebration of that outcome, the portal should be activated.

The portal *needs* to be activated.

Kain heads down the battered corridor toward the x-ray labs. Mercor follows. The wheels of the trolley the Yasti pushes squeak across the crumbling vinyl floor. One of many things left unmaintained by a lack of funds to these lower sections of the university.

Kain pushes the double lab doors open. A man standing by the output console turns. Kain grinds his teeth. It's that feckwit from upstairs.

'Shaw,' says Kain. 'You almost done here?'

The man's blue eyes rake across the covered trolley. Mercor shifts, his uneasiness a palpable chill against Kain's shoulder blades.

'Oh, look,' says Shaw. 'The Portal Brigade. What's under the trolley sheet? Some fake credentials to convince the Board to keep funding you.'

Kain bristles. Shaw's work on advanced space flight flipdrive technologies is considered important to the university, especially with the flip psychosis pandemic afflicting the Hegemon's fleets of traders. The Hegemon Council itself funds his research. He has access to the better labs in the higher levels of the building and whole teams of staff working for him.

In the old days when they both worked in the lower labs, Shaw was okay, but now, his elevated status has turned him into a dick.

But status doesn't get you everything. The university suits upstairs don't like being too close to any old-school grey-fuelled technology. That means Shaw still needs to come down here to use the x-ray labs.

'Yeah, good one dickhead,' says Kain. 'How about you get the hell out of my x-ray lab and tootle off back upstairs to your team. They'll be getting lonely without your arsehole to sniff.'

Shaw's eyes narrow. He steals a glance at Mercor, his disdain for the Yasti rolling off him in waves. 'They may be arse-lickers, but at least they're human.' His lip curls up. 'Maybe it's time I put in a word with the janitor—tell them the basement's becoming overrun with rodents.'

'Feck off,' snarls Kain.

Shaw shrugs. He reaches over and unplugs his datapad from the input socket. Then he collects a piece of dull-looking metal from the x-ray chamber—a piece of dycerium, the newly discovered organo-manganese compound found on the planet Axx.

'I'm done here anyhow,' he says. 'I've got *actual* work to do.' He tips up the sample to show them. 'Turns out this stuff is highly explosive in powder form. If I can harness it as a fuel, that'll mean faster void travel. And possibly no more flip psychosis issues. See...that's the kind of work real scientist's do.'

Shaw stalks past Kain, shouldering him into the trolley. Kain scowls, but Shaw is already away, moving down the hall.

The lab falls into silence. Kain glances back at Mercor. The Yasti's whiskers twitch nervously.

'Ignore him,' says Kain. 'You're twice the person he is, and ten times smarter.'

'Yeah,' says Mercor. 'As if Dirtys like him are respected any more than I am throughout the galaxy.'

Kain frowns. 'I'm a Dirty too.'

'And a man without respect.'

Kain chuckles. 'Yeah, I guess I can be an arsehole at times, too.'

'You certainly can,' replies Mercor.

Kain slaps Mercor on the shoulder. 'Lighten up buddy. I'm looking out for both of us.'

The Yasti's eyes glitter like ebony glass. 'Is that why I'm stuck working here in the labs with you?'

'Don't lie to yourself. You love being here with me,' replies Kain.

#

The trolley sheet slides away from the orb with a quiet slither. A convex reflection of the ceiling appears on its shining surface. Mercor opens the larger of the two x-ray chambers and wheels the trolley in. Meanwhile, Kain lifts the hatches to the x-ray cores. Green-grey light spills out past the opening, illuminating the room with its sickly pallor.

Mercor hands a three-pronged power lead to Kain. 'I've attached a set of suction applicators to the surface. Plug these into the core output and we should be good to go.'

It's pure adrenaline this time causing Kain's fingers to tremble as he connects the cables. What they are doing could get them both sacked. Not that he cares. If he told the Board what he had, it would be given to Shaw before he ever got the chance to make any credits. Fortune favours the bold. And the bold don't give a feck about the Board.

Kain taps the activation panel. Electricity bristles, pouring down the cable and into the Uher's machine.

Air booms outward from the orb. Kain is hurled backward and slams against a wall. A tower of rippling light blasts upwards to scorch the ceiling. Lead panels lining the internal partitions of the chamber give way. Several bounce off the orb but leave no mark.

The room falls to silence, flickering lights, and the stink of burnt ozone. Mercor crouches, huddled on the floor, his paws covering his head. Kain straightens, rubbing his bruised hip. He moves closer, his steps tentative, yet tight with restrained excitement. He leans in, heart hammering as he examines the bright surface of the illuminated orb.

The portal is active.

He can see past the veil.

Mercor gets up. Kain chuckles.

'What is it?' asks the Yasti.

'I see a room,' says Kain. 'The portal leads to a room.'

#

The orb has been jerry-rigged to hang from the ceiling. Its gently glowing surface ripples in the breeze dropping from the ceiling vents.

Mercor holds up a backpack. 'A travel pack. Light. Water and food rations. I've also put a stunner in there.'

Kain looks into the bag. The stunner, silver and black, gleams back at him. The weapon is a stern reminder that he will be facing the unknown alone. There's no way of knowing if the portal can be activated from the other side, so he needs Mercor to stay here, just to be sure the doorway is maintained.

'You sure you still want to do this?' asks Mercor.

'Absolutely.' Kain grabs the bag and slings it across his shoulder. 'Just keep the portal open.' Then he checks his comms gauntlet. The signal is strong. He smiles at Mercor. 'See you in a bit.'

The yellow light embraces him—a tingling warmth trickling across his skin as he is drawn across the threshold.

The room beyond emerges, cowering in the quavering light of the portal. The air, cold and crisp, smells metallic with disuse. Kain looks back. The sharp edges of Mercor's form are visible through the portal. The Yasti smiles and gives the thumbs up signal.

Kain takes a deep breath. Time to discover what secrets lurk here—what secrets he can sell.

He flicks on his torch. Its acid white light cuts through the room. Polished surfaces brighten; walls, ceiling and floor all crystalline and glittering like old Earth quartz. But the room is otherwise empty except for a mirrored door in the far wall.

There is no mechanism to open the portal from this side. Good thing Mercor stayed behind to watch his back.

The exit door shudders on Kain's approach, and then melts away. Its surface cascades down in a matrix of sliding particles. The technology is unfamiliar and interesting. Kain pauses, torn between wanting to explore the mechanics and wanting to see more. But the vista beyond the door catches his eye.

And all thoughts of doorway technologies dissolve.

A crystalline landscape extends for miles past the threshold—a flat plain of indigo-blue metallic grass ringed by silver mountains. And more.

From the grass sprouts a forest of statues set on low pedestals, each one carved from stone, pale and translucent. They stretch away into the distance, an army so vast as to lap the foothills. A violet sun shines down over them all.

Over the carved likenesses of what Kain surmises to be effigies of the Uher race.

Kain leaves the small building housing the portal gateway, disappointed. He's found a fecking art gallery. Still some credits might be made selling the statues on the underground market. But that would mean getting the orb out of the university unseen—would mean having to silence Mercor somehow…

He doesn't want to hurt the Yasti. Mercor's been a dependable presence over the years. But Kain knows Mercor will balk at outright theft. He hasn't lost hope that undiscovered Uher tech will salvage his career, so his loyalties still lie with the university. Can Kain convince him, or blackmail him? Possibilities, devious and cunning, flood Kain's mind as he approaches the closest sculpture. He'll find a way—has to find a way.

The face of the carved Uher is ethereal. Wide features dominate, with long-lashed eyes and a smooth, hairless skull.

So this is what the Uher looked like? For some reason, Kain never thought to imagine their faces—to him they were featureless aliens with a knack for technology.

A breeze ruffles its way across the plain. The air, neither hot nor cold, touches the grass, setting the tips to dancing. Music rises from the movement, a soft tinkling of chimes that adds a layer of life to the crystalline landscape.

As Kain wanders from statue to statue, he sees artful differences in the works, differences that give identity to each subject. Yes. This lot will be worth a pile to the right investor.

He glances up at one Uher, a male, who is carved broader in the shoulders than the rest, a wicked steel blade hanging from his waist. A strange choice of weapon for a highly advanced alien. A soldier, perhaps?

Kain's comms crackles to life. Mercor's voice crunches through the speaker, blurred by the thin signal connection through the portal. 'Status update?'

Kain traces a finger down the smooth cheek of the Uher statue. The stone feels warm to his touch.

'The orb leads to a gallery of some kind, Mercor. It's full of sculptures.'

'As in artworks?'

'Yes. Carved statues. Pretty striking work.' Kain blinks and activates his ocular implant. Visual data streams back to the lab. Mercor gasps across the comms link.

'Is that a sword at the waist?' asks the Yasti.

'Yeah,' says Kain. 'Pretty weird, huh. I would have expected more advanced weaponry.'

'Do any of the others have swords like that?'

'Hang about. I'll find out.'

He looks around. The next statue is a female with a scar running down the side of her nose. Heavy, carved jewellery hangs draped around her muscular neck. A high-tech looking blaster is holstered at her hip. A more suitable choice. He looks further down the aisle. So many different figures—all armed and bejewelled and scarred. But no others carry swords. Kain shrugs. Maybe this sword guy was someone special.

'No. This looks to be the only one.'

'O…hang…signal…breaki…'

Kain's comms link collapses into static. 'You still there, Mercor?'

Nothing.

A rock settles in the pit of Kain's stomach. He is alone.

Kain knows he should head back, but isn't ready to yet. He looks at the carved warrior. The alien's essence, captured in the stone, seems almost life-like. Kain smiles. This Uher's face and those of his brethren will be the first the modern world sees of a race long turned to dust. The thought excites Kain. These aliens have been forgotten for thousands of years. Their legacy held only in the few fragments of their technology left in the galaxy.

Market it right and people would pay to see them.

Maybe I should open my own gallery. Charge a bomb to enter and offer private rooms to black suppliers on the side. Could he convince Mercor to join him in such a venture?

Possibilities. So many possibilities.

Kain places his hand on the bare, muscled chest of the soldier statue. 'You are going to make me a lot of money,' he says. 'You and your buddies.' Kain's fingers slide down the stone.

Click.

An all-but-invisible button depresses at his touch. Warmth erupts, blossoming off the stone and suffusing his palm. Kain blinks, stepping back. The chest of the statue brightens, glowing red. The warm light spreads, saturating it. Arms, legs and torso ripple, the stone transforming to pale flesh. Then the alien's great chest moves as it draws in a long, deep breath.

The Uher's eyes open, two silver orbs framed by white lashes and lids. Its hand rises to rest on the hilt of its sword. The neck swivels and the being's glistening, terrible gaze falls on Kain.

'Filos ee' ehthros?' it asks.

The translator beeps in Kain's ear. 'Unable to recognize language.'

He stumbles back a step further. The scientist in him reels at the prospect of a living Uher. The human in him is terrified for his life. Kain reaches into his pocket, fingers trembling as they brush across the black pellet resting there—his security.

He takes another step back and the eyebrows of the statue furrow over its slim nose. With a rasp, the Uher pulls its sword free. Its feet wrench away from the pedestal, raining glittering chips of stone down as it advances on Kain. It steps onto the grass, shattering the fragile crystalline fronds beneath a heavy, booted foot.

'Filos ee' ehthros?' it asks again, insistent.

Kain holds both hands up, palms open. 'Translator. Search derivative languages.'

The translator responds. 'Ancient Terran Greek derivation detected. Modifying output to accommodate. Translation complete. Filos ee' ehthros—Friend or enemy?'

'Friend!' cries Kain. The translator echoes him into the ancient language.

The Uher hesitates, elbow pulled back and blade held high. He seems to understand. The blade lowers an inch. A range of emotions plays across the alien's face. 'You are Terran?'

'Yes,' replies Kain, his heart pounding.

'Where am I?' A pause. 'When am I?'

'Inside a monoverse,' says Kain carefully, 'in the 200th year following the creation of the Hegemon.'

The alien's eyes thin to two pale slits. 'Hegemon?'

Kain nods. 'The ruling space authority.'

'Ruling authority?' The Uher shakes his head, his silver eyes spark with gold energy. 'How many years have we been here?'

Kain almost feels sorry for the alien. 'I'm not sure. I only know that the portal orb is thousands of years old. If you are Uher, as I think you are, you've been gone from the galaxy a very long time.'

'Thousands of years? And this Hegemon now rules the space territories?' There is an edge to the alien's voice, his words tainted with some pique Kain can't understand.

'No,' says Kain, backpedalling. 'Not rules. The Hegemon is kind of like an economic government.'

The Uher doesn't seem convinced. His gaze flicks up and away. He takes in the lie of the plain and the statues dotted about.

'Where are the guards?' he asks.

'Guards?' replies Kain. 'There is no-one else here.'

'No one?' The Uher's sudden smile is a wicked sharp-toothed grin that turns Kain cold. The alien swings the sword to point to the other statues. 'My warriors. Release them.'

Kain's heart sinks and for the first time he's not thinking of credits, but of survival. 'Of course. If I can, I will.'

#

The Uher calls himself Moaro and he insists on activating the other statues. Kain knows an outright refusal would be a mistake. He fingers the black pellet in his pocket. He desperately wants to take it—wants to escape the situation. The downer effects of the drug's withdrawal are increasing. Kain's hands sweat and tremors affect his eyes, leaving shadowy ghosts hovering in his periphery.

Hold it together. Don't take it. You need to be clear minded to get out of this. Hold it together.

Kain follows Moaro as the alien inspects each statue. Now, on closer review, Kain notes details he missed earlier. A red light blinks at the feet of some statues, and the button on their chests is obvious now that he knows what to look for.

The scars, weapons and jewels of the statues have also taken on a more sinister aspect. It's as if the fog of his affected eyesight has shown the truth of what the Uher were. They were no benevolent race. Each mark, scar and bounty is a trophy earned by a warrior. Bloodthirsty.

Moaro stops at the tall, lithe statue of a female Uher. Twin blasters are strapped to her stone thighs, and her chin is held high. Arrogance wars against the cold perfection of her face. Cruelty fairly blisters out of her stone eyes. Uneasy, black-induced shadows flutter around her head like dread veils on a corpse bride. Kain shudders and palms the black pellet closer.

No light blinks at this statue's feet. This one is dead. He watches Moaro press his forehead to the cold one of the Uher woman. A growl resonates in the alien's throat, growing to a howl that splinters off the brittle faces of the far mountains. Kain huddles backward, hands over his ears.

Then silence.

Moaro's chest heaves. His chin swivels and the corner of one silver eye locks on Kain. 'She was my sister,' he says. 'We two were the last to fall. We stood back to back on that dread battlefield, our boots soaked in the blood of our enemies.' He pulls away from the statue and looks into its dead eyes. His mouth twists down. 'For you, Syntha, I will finish what we started.'

'Who were you fighting?' whispers Kain, almost too afraid to ask.

Moaro turns. 'Everyone,' he says. 'In my time, power and corruption fed the galaxy. All races came to the Uher wanting our technology to gain supremacy. I saw the danger and, as Lord Overseer, made the decision to end it all. I ordered the collapse of our orbiting star and saw to the destruction of my planet.

'My civilian people perished first. They understood the need and went willingly to their deaths.' He opens his hands to the forest of statues. 'Then, armed with the last of my militia, we turned to the other races, Axxine, Yatsi, Glondian, Kronck...'

His eyes flare again, bright gold flecks against the silver background. 'They resisted but would have fallen if it were not for those slithering vipers, the Isceans. On the last day, in the deep jungles of Amarion-5, they turned our own tech against us. They captured us; cryo-froze us in stone.'

He looks back to his sister. 'And the extreme passage of time has now seen Syntha, the last General of Uher, die. The Isceans shall pay for that. This time, they will be the first to fall.'

Kain's skin crawls. He should never have come here, should never have touched the statues. The desire to take the pellet surges over him again, irresistible. But logic still clings to him by a thread. He holds off, blinking away the ghosts, the tremors and the pain now radiating in his hands. Why the hell did he come alone?

Stupid. Stupid. He can almost hear Shaw laughing at him. '*You have really fecked it up haven't you? And you didn't even go in with a decent weapon...*'

Kain sucks in a breath and squeezes his hands into fists. The weight of the backpack on his shoulders seems distant, but the knowledge of the stunner concealed within it is all too real.

He wants to draw it. He wants to escape. But even addled, his mind recognizes the weapon isn't nearly strong enough to fell the huge Uher Overseer.

Moaro swivels on his heel. 'First we will wake those of my army that remain. Then you must show me the way out of this place,' he says. 'Blood-debts need to be paid.'

Feck. Kain imagines for a moment this huge alien stalking the halls of the University. Imagines him walking in on the University Board, sword swinging. He swallows the urge to laugh recklessly. He swallows again. By God, it's tempting to let the Uher do it. It might not give him the credits he wants, but he would get out of this situation alive.

But, as Moaro's gaze drills down, Kain knows without doubt, that if free, the galaxy will not be a place worth living in. He may be ambitious, but Kain has no desire to see worlds forced to kneel beneath this tyrant's feet.

Thoughts crowd in, painted in half shadows. Kain swipes at the dark shapes that cluster toward him. The black has all but forsaken his body. Nightmares creep closer. It's harder and harder to keep the course of logic.

Need to escape.

Take the pellet. It will help. It's right there, in your hand.

No. I need to stay clear-minded.

You are hardly clear-minded.

Oh god. How the hell do I keep the Uher away from the portal?

But it's no use. He is feck out of ideas.

Kain falls to his knees, biting back frustration through the haze infecting him and the pain that now extends to his elbows. His forearms shake. The agony builds as the black fades further. He clutches his arms to his chest; lets his chin rest on them.

The tall Uher's brow furrows. He leans over Kain. 'Is there something wrong with you, Terran?'

Kain coughs. He tastes bitter bile on the back of his tongue. His organs are revolting against the lack of drugs.

The black. The black. The black.

It calls him.

The addiction…

The wasting…

The destruction, so inevitable.

Destruction.

The word snags in the last clear corner of Kain's brain. Destruction. The seed of an idea, born from the mantra of his weakness, forms.

Kain coughs again. 'I am…unwell.'

Moaro leans in closer and sniffs. 'Your flesh smells of corruption,' he says. The Uher presses a long, pale finger to

Kain's throat. 'Your blood runs rapid.' His frown deepens. 'What is wrong with you?'

Kain huddles in closer to himself. His shoulders begin to shake. The pellet is a small, hard point against the strained tendons of his palm.

Moaro's hand falls on Kain's shoulder. He leans in closer still. His mouth is by Kain's ear.

'Terran?'

Kain moves viper fast. With fragile lucidity and muscles burning, he punches the palm holding the pellet into the Uher's face. The pellet collides with the alien's teeth. The capsule shatters, sending a spray of jet-black fluid across Moaro's long chin. The sweet-honey scent of the drug blossoms into the air.

The Uher rears back and away from him. Moaro wipes a hand across his chin and stares at it. The alien's silver eyes are like two bright coins in the sea of encroaching darkness. Those silver disks turn to Kain, their rims stretched wide in horror.

Moaro leers, his teeth black with the drug-fluid Kain's body would dearly like to possess.

'You wish to maim me with chemicals?' snarls the Uher. 'You wish to stop me?' The alien's face twists, the pale lines hard-edged like a shard of mirror. 'I tolerated you as thanks for releasing me. No more!'

Kain is past caring. All he knows is debilitating pain and a growing darkness. His fingers worry at the glassine ground as his eyes fix on the dimmed sky above—past the shadow of Moaro's sword falling and past the impression of a form behind the alien, knocking the blade aside.

A saviour?

It could just be the downer shadows playing tricks on him.

#

Kain peels open crusted eyes. He is face down on the ground, blue grass tickling his chin as it waves in a gentle breeze. Moaro lies beside him, sprawled dead on the ground. The Uher's throat gapes open to the air, a knife cut scored through both flesh and windpipe. The wide line of dark blood seeps from the yawning wound. His silver eyes stare sightlessly into Kain's.

What the feck happened?

Kain struggles to sit up. He doesn't feel nearly as bad as he expected to without the black to revive him. But then he runs his tongue over the roof of his mouth and tastes a familiar sickly-sweet residue.

'Feel okay, Kain? You should. I squeezed a pellet between your teeth before you woke up,' says a familiar voice.

It's Mercor. He sits with his back rested against the legs of an Uher statue. Across his knees lies Moaro's sword, it's wicked edge still wet with the Uher's blood.

'How did you know?' Kain croaks. His throat feels dry, a side-effect of the black.

Mercor's nose twitches. 'Know what? That you're an addict or that you needed my help here?'

Kain looks at the ground. 'Both.'

Kain pulls his knees to his chest and clamps his arms

around them. His mind is buzzing, high on the recent flush of black. Instead of shadows, light flickers around his vision now. Hypnotic and beautiful. He feels so good. But he can't think clearly, the intake of drug still too recent, and the effects still ascending.

His tongue tingles, fat against his teeth. He manages to form a sentence. 'What happened to Moaro?'

Mercor looks down at the sword sitting across his lap. 'I killed him.'

'How?'

'I just did.' Mercor presses a claw to the blade. He changes the subject and Kain forgets his train of thought.

'Did you know, Kain,' says Mercor, 'that this is an extremely rare and ancient dycerium blade?' He looks back at Kain. 'Did you also know that my people were blacksmiths in the time of the Uher and that their knowledge and skill in the forging of dangerous metals is long lost now?'

Kain can't connect the pieces of information. The air is bright and too distracting.

Mercor pushes his glasses higher on his nose. 'When we started working together, I had the utmost respect for you.' He sniffs. 'But you ruined that the day you were so fecked up on drugs you destroyed our careers. I haven't been able to forgive you for that.'

Kain's attention catches on the slow drip of blood falling from the sword's edge onto the grass.

Fascinating.

Mercor frowns. 'Kain. Look at me.'

Kain looks up, slowly. Interesting. Mercor's fur is gold in this light. Suddenly the thought seems funny. No. Rats are shit-brown in colour, not gold. Kain giggles.

'Are you listening to me?' asks Mercor.

Kain leans in to look at the grass. Up close he can see the patterns of its crystal makeup.

'Kain?'

Kain breaks off a piece and licks it. No taste.

Mercor sighs.

He seems upset with me, thinks Kain. But why?

Mercor gets to his feet, the sword cradled in his palms. His rat-eyes look big behind the lenses of his glasses. Another detail Kain finds amusing.

The Yasti lifts the sword. 'This weapon is my future, Kain. With it I can rediscover the dycerium forging process and use the metal and method to create indestructible hull-skins for space vessels. Sooner than Shaw and his bunch of monkeys.'

Something catches in Kain's mind; a light-rimmed recollection of dreams. 'No. You can't have anything. Everything here is mine…for me.'

Mercor's lips twist into an angry knot. 'You're a selfish bastard and you deserve what you get. Have no fear, Kain. I'll only take the sword. The rest is yours.' Mercor digs into his lab-coat pocket. 'And these also, for as long as they last. Good luck to you. I hope for your sake you choke on them for I'll not return here to help you.'

The Yasti throws a plastic bag to Kain. It lands on the ground, spilling black pellets through the grass. All thoughts of ownership flee as Kain grasps for them.

I need them. It's okay. I am in control…

Kain counts the pellets as he finds them. One. Two. Three. He barely notices Mercor walking away. He doesn't say goodbye.

All is good.

Kain doesn't even look up when a burst of power flux blossoms across the sky, signalling Mercor's departure and the orb's portal closing.

Because his mind is a cradle of light, held in the thrall of the black.

END

1545 hours: The Hunter Arrives

Cordelia Bane

Cordelia Bane eased into the Zoo, cat-like on silent feet, and careful not to disturb anyone. It looked like Clare O'Malley wasn't here, yet. Almost 1600. Unlike her to be late. Well, this late.

Cordelia scanned the room again. A huge Aquanorian with ivory and teal facial tentacles hulked behind the bar, polishing glasses. But the public space was half-empty and smelled faintly of vomit and old beer. The more recent smell of strong disinfectant overlay it all. Along one wall, several habipods waited for aliens who required special atmospheres. Only one was taken; the alien obscured by a dense bluish gas.

The rest of the room was filled with basic metal tables and chairs. Most occupied by Dirtys, along with a couple of Kroncks, a Yasti, a Glondian, and an Iscean.

Definitely no Clare. No-one else paid any attention to Cordelia. Hardly surprising given she was muffled to the eyebrows in her camouflaging, chametek coat. As long as she didn't brush anyone, they wouldn't see her.

One of the corner booths was sheltered and had a clear view of the Zoo's occupants. The Zoo was reputed to be a good place to find work. If one wasn't fussy. And Cordelia couldn't afford to be fussy—too many debts owed to the wrong people. Bounty-hunting was good money, and she was one of the best, but it was a competitive industry. The Underground Banker had put a deadline on her debt. One more week and a kill order bounty would be listed for one Cordelia Bane.

She needed every job she could get. Clare was usually a good source of courier work, at least. Better than nothing, even if the pay wasn't great.

Should she wait here or go back to the Customs entry point where Clare would have to be stamped aboard the Asteri? Hmm. More likely to be bumped into if someone tried to take her booth here in the Zoo. At the Customs point she could lurk, unnoticed. And she preferred to be unnoticed until she had the lie of the land.

She headed out.

At the docking entry she flipped back her chametek jacket hood and switched off the invisibility camouflage.

The young Grey Guard lieutenant—Ori Bligh—who'd logged Cordelia onto the station, glanced up from her desk. 'You're back fast. Leaving already?'

'Got a friend due in.'

Lieutenant Bligh checked the bank of screens on the wall beside her desk. 'Name?'

'Clare O'Malley. Not sure of the ship's ID, though.' Cordelia blinked and activated her ocular implant, in turn switching on the lie-detector mod chip installed in her prefrontal cortex.

'Nothing yet. When was she due?'

'Couple of hours ago.' Cordelia frowned.

'Where's she coming from?'

'Raspberry Station.'

Bligh's eyes widened. 'Ah. Just saw on the holo-news. There's been an incident out that way.'

The truth of that statement pinged through the lie-detector mod.

'Shit!' Cordelia sighed. 'Knowing Clare, she's involved. What happened?'

Bligh shook her head. 'Don't know the details. Only that it involved the governor of the station and a local criminal. Someone called The Baggerman.'

Another truthful statement, according to the lie-detector chip. But a criminal? Cordelia swallowed. What was Clare mixed up in?

'Never heard of a Baggerman,' Cordelia said. 'But I don't know that sector well. Anything else?'

The lieutenant tapped her screen. 'Hegemon Core computer reports don't have anything mentioning a Clare O'Malley. Daresay your friend will tell you when she gets here.'

'If she gets here,' Cordelia said darkly. 'I might go scout the station. See if she's slipped in without making it to your list. If you hear from her, buzz my comms?' She flicked her comms link signal to the Grey Guard's network.

Bligh nodded. 'Will do.'

Truth. And she hadn't even asked for a bribe. Unusual for a Grey Guard out this part of Hegemon-controlled space.

Cordelia activated the chametek coat and stalked off. Clare had better be alright. There weren't many people in this galaxy Cordelia liked and trusted. And she'd lost too much to the criminal syndicates already.

What the hell had happened at Raspberry Station?

Raspberries and Rum

Aiki Flinthart

A Mac and The Baggerman Tale

Current year

'Clare O'Malley why aren't you dressed?' Malia put her hands on her generous hips and glared.

Clare looked down at herself. Had she forgotten to put on a shirt again? Nope. All there. Grey shirt. Grey cargo pants. Chunky-soled boots with inbuilt anti-grav mag-unit. Belt with stunner holstered and hanging at the appropriately jaunty angle on her hip.

Malia sighed and scrubbed a hand over her face, careful

not to smear her scarlet lipstick. 'I mean, why aren't you dressed as a pirate?'

Clare checked again. 'I am. This is my pirate outfit. I'm a pirate. It's what I always wear.' She plucked at the utilitarian shirt. 'Except for when I wear blue, which I also like. Or the exosuit, which I don't like, but which is useful when boarding a ship from the outside.'

'Gah!' Malia drove long fingers into her elaborately-curled raspberry-pink hair, putting into disarray what must have taken the beauty-bot at least an hour to create. 'You're impossible. Look.' She indicated her ridiculous black corset, thigh-high boots and floofy-sleeved indigo blouse. 'Pirate. See?'

'No. I see a stupid mock-eighteenth-century Earth costume that bears little resemblance to what pirates actually wore in those days. And don't get me started on what women wore.'

Malia snatched up a broad-brimmed hat and brandished it. It had a long, fluffy blue-dyed artificial feather. 'I have the *hat.* And the eyepatch and everything. I'm a pirate. You aren't. You're a...' She scowled. 'What do you call yourself again?'

'LOOPER.' Clare grinned. 'Liberator Of Other People's Extraneous Riches.'

'Oh, for...Get into your costume or we can't go to the party. And the governor's insisting that *everyone* on Raspberry Station attends.'

'Very fairy godmother of you. Will there be glass slippers to go with the wooden peg-legs?' Clare raised one brow.

Mal returned a blank look. Clearly not a fairytale reader.

Clare tried reason instead—not, traditionally, her strong point. 'So you're saying I can't go as a pirate, to a pirate-themed party?'

'I'm saying you can't go as *yourself* to a pirate-themed party being held by Governor Gera. The governor of this space station. The governor whose pleasure-yacht you held up two weeks ago, who impounded your ship, and who still has a shoot-on-sight order out for you, because you escaped, pissing him off.' Mal pointed to the outstanding warrant holo that hung on permanent display on her wall.

It was an image of Clare taken in mid-snarl, so it was hardly flattering.

'I like that holo,' Clare said stoutly. 'Gives me the right air of ruthlessness needed to be respected in piratey-thiefy-mercenary circles.'

Mal sniffed. 'Pity The Baggerman didn't think so.' She wagged a finger. 'Admit it. You overreached yourself trying to impress the biggest criminal in the sector. Should have run with the cargo from your first job instead of trying to steal the governor's yacht.'

'Meh.' Clare waved away the mistake. 'The Baggerman's just in a bad mood. He's had it in for everyone since his chief scientist liberated some valuable tech and disappeared three months ago.'

'Really?' Mal smoothed the front of her corset several times and checked the fall of her skirt. 'Disappeared, huh? Why would a criminal employ a scientist?'

Clare shrugged. 'Good thieves need good tech. The Baggerman has a whole research and development branch and makes a fortune selling the legal stuff to the Hegemon as a front for all the illegal stuff.'

Mal tut-tutted. 'Well, all I know is that if you'd stayed away from Governor Gera's yacht you wouldn't be in this mess.' She scolded like the mother Clare never had and never wanted. 'You'd have your precious flip-ship, with interest, and you wouldn't have The Baggerman and his flunkies breathing down your neck for the guild membership fee.'

'I know, I know,' Clare said. 'I'd also already be on Catterman IV, wallowing in unnatural luxury. You've said all this before.'

'Well, hopefully the governor will lose interest in shooting you.'

Clare shrugged. It had been two weeks. He wasn't showing signs of disinterest yet. He must suspect her of knowing where more booty was hidden. Which would explain why he had every bounty hunter in the Hegemon looking; scouring every backwater village on every planet, station and asteroid. He knew she was still around. After all, he had her damned ship. Lucky he didn't think to look on his own space station.

Hiding in plain sight: Pirate101.

'What's so important about your moth-holed old ship that you'll go to this much trouble to get it back, anyway? Or is it the cargo?' Mal said, eyes narrowing. 'You've camped on my couch for two weeks. I think I deserve an explanation. If I didn't owe you for getting me this job, I'd have kicked you out, already. You're the messiest roommate ever.' She gestured at the stark white furniture and bare walls. Over every surface lay draped various articles of grey clothing, shoes, odd bits of tech, and unrecycled dishes. Drawers stood open. Cupboard doors ajar. Cushions lay askew. A longsleeved blouse, corset, and skirt were lying on Clare's bed.

'OK, the messy roommate I'll own up to. But the *De Lune* has earned every one of those holes, thank you.' Clare smiled. 'And, as for my cargo, all I can say is that it's something with the potential to destroy everything, forever.'

'Well, that was irritatingly-vague.' Malia pursed her lips. 'And hyperbolic at the same time. Impressive.'

Lifting the floofy-sleeved, dove-grey shirt from the bed, Clare shook it. 'I'm good that way.'

'If the *De Lune*'s cargo's that important, then surely the Governor found it when his men searched the *De Lune*?' Malia re-arranged the set of her breasts in the corset, grimacing, wriggling, and prodding at her cleavage.

Clare chuckled, low in her throat. 'Highly unlikely. And yes, it's important enough to risk everything for. Basically, it's something that means this Governor and The Baggerman will both be off my back—and I'll never have to wear an outfit this ridiculous again.' She wrinkled her nose at the red corset and black, ruffled skirt still on the bed. 'Really? Me. In a skirt?'

'Fine. Don't tell me. And yes,' Mal said briskly, holding up the offending item.

'I hate them.'

'I know.' She pursed her lips. 'But it's more feminine.'

'An outdated term I also hate.' Clare shucked her shirt and yanked on the big-sleeved one. 'This is a nice colour but the sleeves are too floppy. They'll get in the way.' She waggled her arms to demonstrate. 'Still, they do hide my nano-carbon throwing knives nicely.' She adjusted the wrist-strap and tugged the sleeve down.

Mal ignored that and handed over the skirt. 'You're supposed to take your pants off, you know.'

'Tough.' Clare settled the skirt on her hips. She did take the stunner pistol off. Security wouldn't let her near the Governor with it, anyway. Malia could get away with her imitation flintlock stunner. That would give them a decent weapon, at least.

Malia straightened the shirt-collar and ran a hand over Clare's buzzcut hair. 'I wish you'd grow your hair.' She settled a wig over Clare's head. 'Changes how you look completely.'

'Nope,' Clare returned, pushing the curling black mess back from her eyes.

'Here.' Mal held out two hand-sized blobs of something that looked like flesh-coloured jelly.

Clare took them and squeezed dubiously. 'What are these?'

Mal pointed at her chest.

'Oh, for…' Clare sighed and shoved them inside the shirt, repositioning her own minor assets for best display at the top.

Mal laughed. 'Well, you do look like a woman now. He'll never recognise you.'

Clare sent her an ironic look.

'Oh! That reminds me.' Mal pushed Clare down in front of the beauty-bot. 'Makeup.'

'No!' She tried to rise. Mal pressed down on her shoulders, surprisingly strong for a woman who spent her days doing rudimentary data maintenance and programming checks on the station's computers.

'Yes,' she said. 'Otherwise the face-rec software will spot you the minute you stand dramatically in the doorway of the ballroom—hair or no hair.'

'Makeup won't fool face-rec software,' Clare protested.

'My beauty-bot will.' Malia patted the mirror and touched the programming screen. 'I'm a genius.'

Clare groaned and closed her eyes.

#

'I look ridiculous,' Clare muttered, adjusting the eyepatch. At least Mal'd had the sense to include a heads-up display in it—along with other useful tech—so the security cameras in the room were obvious. Then again, everyone else was wearing eyepatches too, undoubtedly with the same options. Someone had made a killing on pirate accessories. Clare spent a moment regretting it hadn't been her.

'We all look ridiculous,' Malia returned. 'I suspect Governor Gera did this because he has a wicked-sharp sense of humour and he likes to make people feel silly.'

'He succeeded, then,' Clare muttered, snatching a drink

from a passing server-bot. She'd managed to stay out of Gera's way on this large station. But he'd insisted on full attendance at this shindig, and she was sick of the inside of Mal's quarters. It would be interesting to finally see him. He hadn't been on his yacht when she tried to steal it. Unfortunate, because ransom was a much more lucrative game than just theft.

Malia's obligatory scarlet, shoulder-parrot squawked, flapped its wings and generally looked quite realistic—until the head rotated the full 360 degrees and its eyes flashed a particularly demonic shade of red.

'Polly says the room is alarmed with two backup systems in place and twenty Grey Guardsmen disguised as pirates. And I found out earlier that the governor's installed an emergency lockdown protocol that will switch off the gravity or evacuate the air if he gives the command word.'

'Useful bird. Evacuate the air? Harsh. Do you know what the command word is?'

'No.' Mal grimaced. 'Couldn't hack into that. The gov has his private files on a stand-alone system.'

'Huh.' Clare eyed the governor's broad back in its red velvet and white lace coat. 'Smart man.'

Malia drifted over to the refreshments table and picked up a canape, sniffing it suspiciously before she nibbled. 'I don't like this, Clare.'

'Don't eat it then. It's just protein tank paste made to look like shrimp, anyway.'

Mal rolled her eyes and waved the fake shrimp at the room. 'I mean *this*. It feels like a trap.'

Clare chuckled. 'Of course it's a trap. But you have to admire his sense of style. Luring out a pirate by filling the room with pirates. It has...flair.'

'Why didn't they search us for weapons at the door?' She glanced over her shoulder at the fake weathered-timber doorway at the entrance.

'They did,' Clare said, watching the crowd shift. 'Didn't you feel the tingler?'

'What?' Mal's dark eyes widened and one hand patted the mock flintlock-come-stunner pistol at her hip.

'Don't check it, you idiot. The tingler deactivated it as we came in. But Polly is still working. Just get her to network with it and hit the internal reset breaker.'

'Oh,' Malia flushed pink beneath the makeup, 'of course. Not used to this cloak-and-dagger stuff.'

'Clearly.' Clare jerked her chin at the obs lounge area—a section devoted to uncomfortable-looking lurid orange seating and dominated by a huge clear-carbon window that currently overlooked the planet below. 'I'm going to eavesdrop on the gov.'

'You're mad,' Malia said in tones of despair. 'I told you this was a bad idea. You'll be arrested and spaced if you go near him.'

'Oh no,' she said mildly. 'Really? Relax Mal. You do your bit and I'll do mine. With even a little luck I'll have my ship back and the money for The Baggerman before the end of this tedious event.'

'Are you going to tell me what the whole plan is?' Mal

nibbled at her shrimp and screwed up her nose.

'Nope.' Clare kissed her cheek and whispered in her ear. 'Trust me, you don't want to know. Just listen in to our conversation on your comms and wait for my signal.' She snaffled two fresh drinks and sauntered away, leaving Mal spitting the fake shrimp out into a fake palm tree pot.

#

The governor stood before the huge observation window, chatting to someone who might possibly be a woman. It was hard to tell beneath the wig, makeup, eyepatch, parrot, and monkey.

Clare stoically ignored the two Grey Guardsmen, dressed in matching striped shirts and black headscarves, who stood protectively near the governor.

The governor turned. Clare coughed. Pirates and governors are not supposed to know each other—either socially or carnally. And she knew him in both senses. The near future would contain complications. Possibly complications involving stunners and incarceration.

But for who, that was the question?

Once she could breathe again, she waited and stared idly out the window.

The station had now rotated and the colony planet was no longer visible. Dominating the view was the massive, faintly-pink gas cloud known as The Raspberry. It looked nothing like a raspberry, but apparently was stuffed full of ethyl formate—

the gas that gave raspberries their flavour and rum its smell—
and a bunch of interesting dust.

Clare thought and sipped her drink. Raspberries, rum, and
dust.

She turned her attention to the governor's huge, sleek
pleasure yacht—all shiny silver with pointless gold
highlights—which dangled alluringly out in the void, tethered
to the station only by a flexible boarding tube and a fuel line.
Behind it, floated her rather battered little flip-ship, *De Lune*;
all dulled metal and patched meteorite holes. No place like
home.

Finally, there was a pause in the painfully-awkward, flirty
conversation between the governor and his pet pirate wench.

'So, Don,' Clare said cheerfully, boarding the
conversational boat in an appropriately-piratical fashion,
'how's things? You're looking well.'

The governor swung about and swept an elaborate bow,
feathered hat brushing the floor, black wig dripping curls over
his broad shoulders. 'That's Governor Gera to you, my good
lady.' When he straightened, his one visible black eye glittered
in a thoroughly roguish and irritating way.

She handed him the second drink she'd brought.
Something virulently-green and reeking of rum, in a fake half-
coconut.

He brought her fingers to his lips and kissed her knuckles.
'And you are?'

Off to one side, the possibly-woman he'd been chatting
with sighed and adjusted her corset, squeezing up her jiggling

breasts and sending Clare a sidelong glower for good measure. He had that effect on females. And quite a few males. Even a few aliens of uncertain gender.

Clare withdrew her hand. 'I'm the one you threw the party for. And I'm bored. So let's get on with it, shall we?'

The two Grey Guardsmen loomed closer. The governor waved them languidly away.

He peered closer, his grin turning raffish. 'Clare? Is that you? Well, well. I didn't recognise you under the makeup and hair. Can't say it suits you.'

'At least we agree on that,' she snapped. 'Now, you're going to give back my ship.'

He swallowed deeply from his drink and studied her thoughtfully. His dark eye twinkled.

'Do you like my space station?' He gestured at the obs lounge—as if she'd somehow missed the palm trees, pile of white sand, and half-buried wooden trunk full of overly-glittery coins and jewellery.

'I did before you filled it with chattering pirates and gene-modified monkeys.' She leaned in and murmured, 'In case you can't tell, the monkeys are the ones eating canapes and talking about the hideous price of rare earths and the latest model flipships. The pirates are climbing trees, throwing fruit, and chittering at people. No, wait.' She smiled brightly. 'The other way around.'

He grimaced. 'You may have a point. They are a bit...'

'Dull, I think is the word you're looking for. At least compared to the people you had as crew last time I saw you.'

She cocked her head. 'How in the great void did you end up here, Don Geramaggio? This isn't you.'

He downed the rest of the drink, tossed the coconut aside, and shoved his hands into his pockets. 'I got bored.'

She gaped. 'You? I heard you were running the Calibrian Loop and smuggling rare earth ore by the tonne from Bakatar to Calibria. That must have made you a fortune.'

With a shrug, he laughed, but there was an edge of uneasiness to it. 'That was the problem. I had too much money.' He sent her an ironic look. 'Made me a target for pirates, would you believe.'

She sputtered her drink, spraying the purple rum concoction over a nearby parrot-camera. The machine squawked and began to smoke gently.

'So,' she said, 'what? You decided to go into politics? I hate to tell you, but—'

'Yes, yes.' He waved a dismissive hand. 'I know. Politicians are worse pirates than pirates. Yawn. I didn't exactly have a choice, as it happens.'

'Huh?'

He scratched at the ridiculous curled wig and shifted his eyepatch to one side. His one blue and one black eye both fixed on her and he leaned closer. 'The Baggerman.'

She sprayed alcohol on him this time, coughed, apologised, and patted down his damp white shirt with her floppy sleeve. Well, at least it had some use.

'Um…' She cleared her throat. 'What about him?'

Don's broad shoulders drooped. 'He set me up here.

Believe me, running a space station this size – any size – was not my retirement plan. Two months ago, his ships hijacked me in the Loop and I had to bargain my way out or…' He drew his finger dramatically across his throat and made a noise like walking on broken glass.

The Grey Guardsmen sidled closer.

Ahhhh. Things were about to get…interesting. She shifted, casual-like, so she could see the room. In one corner—where the back exit lay—a couple of people used soft mallets to hit what looked like giant kitchen pots, producing surprisingly-pleasant, bell-like notes.

Between her and the main door milled a hundred or more over-jolly pirates, glittering with faux jewels and faux gold teeth, and faux bonhomie. Or maybe not. Given the wealth of this system, the jewels and teeth could be real.

The point was, her escape routes were blocked.

'So,' she mused, swigging on her liver-dissolving drink again, 'The Baggerman.'

Don started and raised a brow. 'What about him?'

'Short, blond, bit paunchy? With a penchant for snorting powdered black so his nostrils are a delightful shade of dark purple?'

Don grimaced. 'Can't say I got a good look up his nostrils, but the rest of that sounds more like his offsider, Mac. Never saw The Baggerman. Too busy having my face ground into the decking plate.'

'Ah.' Well, clearly he had been in close proximity to The Baggerman. No-one knew what he looked like, and only a lucky few had survived seeing Mac, his punch-happy right-hand man.

She cocked her head and put her drink down. 'Would you like to get out of here?'

He gave her a bemused look. 'Er...you do know you've walked into a trap, don't you?' He leaned closer, his breath sweet and sour with rum punch. 'The Baggerman's got the Grey Guards in his pocket in this sector. As much as I'd like to, I can't call them off. I have to finger you.'

She leered and he flushed and muttered, 'Not *that* kind of fingering.'

Laughing, she patted his cheek. 'You're way too easy. In every sense of the word.' His flush deepened. She added, 'Let's see if we can come to some mutually-beneficial arrangement. You have something I want.'

She gave him her best vampy smile. 'I'll bet I have something you want.' Now he was a lovely shade of scarlet and she chuckled again. 'Wow. It's hard to get away from the double entendres once you start down that path, huh?'

He cleared his throat. 'I don't think you have anything I...er...want.'

'Not even a shiny space station?' she whispered.

His mouth gaped and his eyes darted from side to side. 'I...er...already have one of those.'

'Maybe,' she said coyly. 'Maybe not. *Captain Hook*.' She stamped hard on the decking plate, activating her boots' mag-unit. Screams broke out.

Clare smiled as everyone, except herself, rose into the air.

Don yelped, arms flailing, hands grasping as he floated gently toward the ceiling. Clare dodged his grip and glanced at the rest of the room in satisfaction.

Apparently "Captain Hook" *was* the gravity-shut-down code word. He was so predictable. Always identifying with the underdog in every story.

Don rotated in an awkward, aerial ballet. Clare clunked across the floor, her mag-boots sticking like tar, and yanked off her eyepatch. Ducking Don's foot she tapped the eyepatch to his wrist then swayed out of reach before he could react.

His eyelids drooped and he took long, slow blinks. 'Wha...wha'dyoudo...?'

'Fulfilling my piratey To Do list. Drink spiked? Check.' Waggling the eyepatch at him, she grinned. 'Copy of your wrist ID chip taken? Check. You just hang here while I go and get my ship back, huh?'

She hurried towards the main entrance. A small bubble of mirth escaped as she pushed floating people, spinning them ungently into each other for maximum chaos. Skirts flew, monkeys and parrots squawked; people clung to trees, palm leaves, and each other in red-faced anger and laughter.

People, drinks and treasure drifted toward the outer walls as centrifugal force took over in the slowly-rotating station. The marimba band continued to play, their equipment bolted to the floor.

Clare grinned.

One of the Grey Guardsmen—trained in zero-gee fighting—pushed off a wall and arrowed toward her. Another came in from a different angle, aiming for where she would be if she dodged sideways.

At the last second, Clare pulled herself to the floor and let the first sail over her head. He ploughed into the cushioned bosom of a matronly pirate whose skirts floated around her head. She clung to him, screaming, pressing his face into her chest.

The second man floated past, gasping, coughing, and rubbing green rum punch from his eyes. Not far away, Malia held an empty jug. She gave Clare a thumbs-up then rebounded deliberately off another Grey Guardsman.

A third she shot with her re-activated flintlock-stunner. She seemed to be enjoying herself.

Clare bolted before any more of the Grey came after her. She slammed and locked both outer door and the airlock door, resisting the urge to see if *crocodile* was the command for venting the air. After all, Malia was still in there. And Don wasn't such a bad guy. Opportunistic, but what good thief wasn't?

Humming a jaunty pirate tune, she hurried through the empty corridors. Since everyone had been at the party, she probably had a good ten minutes. The null gravity wasn't going to stop any time soon with Don safely sedated. He was probably the only one who knew the restoration command.

Only five minutes walk away, was the restricted section of the station that housed the governor's quarters. And the private dock connected directly to his yacht, and the *De Lune*.

So close, now!

#

She was at the governor's door when weight dragged at her body again. She grunted and flexed her knees, pushing upright with a groan. Gravity was a bitch. Knocking her heels together switched off the mag-boots.

A strident alarm shrilled through the station. Damn. Don must have woken up early. Time to move things along. She swiped the eyepatch over the ID reader. Sweat pricked under her arms and her heartrate tripled.

The red light flashed to green and the door swooshed dramatically open—just as the emergency claxons switched to red alert and airlock doors started slamming up and down the shiny-metal corridors.

Clare slipped into Don's quarters. The door snapped shut and sealed itself against air loss with a satisfying hiss. She kissed her fingertips to the idiot who'd punched the red alert button, effectively locking everyone in place—including those trying to reach her.

A quick survey of the governor's quarters made her grin. Don had clearly done his best to bring some life into the place, but all the exotic tapestried blankets and bizarre holos of his favourite alien music bands couldn't hide the prissy, do-gooder bones of the place. All sharp lines and walls in varying shades of matte beige.

She collected his stunner from its stand on a slick beige dining table and tucked the weapon into her belt. Then she headed for the private exit and the boarding tube to his yacht. The door still showed green. Allowing access to ships for escape from an emergency. Smart. Convenient.

Clare paused, frowning. A little *too* convenient? This had all been very easy. No. She was being paranoid. Nothing ventured, nothing caught—said the virgin to the whore. She opened the airlock and propelled herself along the null-grav boarding tube to the yacht.

Her heart thudded. Beyond the yacht lay the *De Lune* and beyond that lay the freedom of the Great Black.

Once inside, she glanced through the observation window toward the station, and grinned. The rotating central spike had turned, so she couldn't see into the party-room she'd left behind, but a dozen or more small craft had disengaged from the station airlocks and were either tiny specks speeding into the Great Black, or floating a few hundred metres away, waiting for the all-clear to return. After all, no-one would know what caused the red alert. Could be biological, tech malfunctions, or just a false alarm.

But none of the craft were heading her way, which meant the Grey Guards hadn't been alerted—or hadn't got to their scoutships in time and were now in lockdown as well.

Just a few more minutes and the greatest sting of the millennia would be written up against her name.

The hiss and clang of an external airlock echoed through the vessel.

Clare turned and froze. 'Ah! You made it, then,' she said.

Malia touched a tab on the side of her exosuit and the

faceplate and helmet module concertina'd smoothly back into the neck. She patted herself down, the shiny silver material crinkling beneath her gloved hands.

With a shudder, she released a sigh. 'I hate these things. And I hate being out there in the black with nothing but thin material between me and nothing.'

'So, the suit was in the airlock of the obs room as planned?'

She nodded.

'And the push across to the yacht?' Clare glanced out the window again. Still no pursuit craft. 'No-one saw you? None of the Grey followed?'

Malia shook her head.

'And the airlock door to the yacht?' Clare raised one brow. 'No problems getting in?'

Malia shrugged. 'It was already open. Thought you'd done it.'

'Ahhh.' Clare smiled serenely. 'I thought this was going too smoothly.'

'What? What?' Malia swung around, eyes wild and darting to every corner of the yacht's gleaming, curved halls.

Clare patted her arm again. 'Never mind. Let's keep going. We need to get down to the room I was held in when the governor's crew took me prisoner. Then over to the *De Lune.*' She spun on one heel and strode down the arcing silver corridor toward the guest rooms. Malia's heavy footsteps hurried after her.

Inside the luxurious guest quarters, Clare made a beeline

for one wall. She pulled a throwing knife from inside one ridiculous sleeve and levered at a decorative panel of abstract colours and shapes. It popped free, exposing a maintenance space behind—full of tubes and incomprehensible wires. She slipped a hand in and withdrew a small, burnished-steel container with a bioscan-secured, vac-sealed lid.

She turned around. 'And now we—' She stared at the small black device pointed squarely at her chest.

'Hand it over,' Malia said, all traces of brainless fluster gone. Her jaw was sharp, her eyes flint-hard, her hand steady.

'What is that, exactly?' Clare pointed at the small black item.

'Detonator,' Malia said. 'For the shape-charges in the fake boobs I gave you, earlier. The ones you so obligingly shoved into your shirt. You try anything funny and I will blow you to pieces.'

'Clever.'

Malia smirked. 'I know. Now. Put the container and knife on that table and back away.'

Clare hesitated, her heart pounding so loud she could barely hear. Crunch time. She did as instructed, backing away with her hands at shoulder height.

Eyes narrowed, Malia sidled to the table and snuck a quick peek at the container. Her lips pressed thin. 'Unlock it.'

'It's keyed to The Baggerman's biocode.'

Malia swore.

Repressing a smile, Clare added, 'So I take it you're *not* The Baggerman, then?'

'Of course I'm fecking not The Baggerman,' Malia snapped. 'No-one but his dickhead offsider, Mac, has ever seen The Baggerman.' She swore again and dug her free hand inside her exosuit, pulling out a matching steel container from between her breasts.

'Impressive,' Clare murmured. 'Mine aren't big enough to hide something that large.'

Malia snorted. 'Funny how people equate big boobs with small brains.' Her eyes glittered. 'Suits me, though. Makes it easy to trick people.' She sneered and raked Clare with a scornful look. 'Idiots, especially.'

'Ouch,' Clare said, mildly. 'Now what?'

'Now that I have both parts of the catalyst, I'll reverse engineer them and sell the formula to the highest bidder. Most likely the Hegemon.'

'Even though they can be weaponised to destroy entire solar systems?'

With a careless shrug, Malia said, 'As long as it's not mine, and I'm paid, what do I care?'

'So,' Clare said, folding her arms, 'you've been playing the long game these last two, no—four months? You came to me with a sob-story about having no job two months ago so I'd get you a position on this station. You knew then that The Baggerman would use me as a courier for one half of this catalyst, didn't you?'

'Of course.' Malia shrugged. 'You were his favourite courier. I was one of his pet scientists. The one who left. When my team invented this, I knew it was too good an opportunity.

And you were such a sucker.' She batted her fake eyelashes and made a moue with her painted lips. 'Then it was a simple enough task to take a sample of the easy-to-make half of the catalyst.' She tapped the two steel containers. 'But The Baggerman kept the other half and the full formula under tight security.'

A faint vibration trembled through the deck. Clare shuffled her feet and cleared her throat to distract Malia.

'What are you going to do with me?'

Malia gathered up the two containers and tucked one into each pocket on her hip, so they bulged like old-fashioned panniers. 'You can stay locked up here. The governor will take care of you. I'll take the *De Lune* and go start a new life.' Her mouth twisted. 'One where I control the money, not arseholes like The Baggerman.'

'Oh, I don't know, The Baggerman's not that bad. Doesn't like you, I know that. After all, you did steal from your own teammates. The rare-earth agglomeration catalyst wasn't even your invention.'

'So? The Baggerman's not exactly a white-knight of chivalry, even if he likes to think he's a modern day Robin Hood. He was too scared. He wanted to destroy the formula!' Malia made a disparaging noise. 'Waste of an opportunity to get stinking rich.'

'True,' Clare said. 'True.' She eased one hand toward the other throwing knives strapped to her wrist.

'Oh, no you don't.' Malia gestured with the detonator. 'Get into the bathroom. You can come out when I'm gone.

You're stupid, and messy, but I don't want to hurt you.'

'How kind.' She sauntered into the bathroom. The door slid closed and the strong smell of burning electronics suggested Malia had fried the operation circuit.

Clare wasted no time removing the possibly-explosive breasts. She placed them in the waste disposal unit, hoping the molecular disintegration process wouldn't detonate them. Holding her breath, she backed away.

Nothing happened, so she released the breath and leaned against the wall, waiting.

#

A minute or two later, the door ground reluctantly open and she lifted her brows. 'You took your time. She's probably already cast off in the *De Lune.*'

Don Geramaggio shrugged sheepishly. 'Sorry. *Someone* drugged my drink a bit too much.'

Clare chuckled. 'Couldn't resist.'

He glanced around the empty room. 'So it was her who stole it from Baggerman?'

'Yep. I wasn't a hundred percent sure. Hence the setup. I searched her rooms and found nothing. But she very carefully never asked how I escaped from the governor's yacht, so I figured she must still be waiting for me to lead her to the second part.'

'Looks like it worked.' He grinned. 'Now we just have to get her back. Then The Baggerman will be happy and I can get out of this boring job.'

Clare thumped him on the shoulder. 'Don't speak too soon. C'mon. Let's put this sweet ship of yours to the test. Get close but not too close.'

He led the way to the bridge. In its gleaming, glowing expanse, waited the captain and copilot chairs: plush matte grey and maroon confections made of real leather. Don sank into the captain's chair and swiped his wrist-ID over the console. The controls sprang to life and a sultry female voice answered his command to disengage from the station.

Clare relaxed into the copilot chair. The rich smell of leather and newness enveloped her.

'Not bad,' she said. 'Tell the ship to follow *De Lune* and fire a few shots off her bow. We want her to head that way.' She pointed toward The Raspberry gas cloud nebula and leaned back, smiling in anticipation.

Don gave the command. 'The ship's name is *Il mia*, by the way.'

Snorting a laugh, Clare nodded. '*Mine*, huh? That figures. Don't get too cocky. If you're lucky and this works, The Baggerman might even let you keep your head.'

He cleared his throat and ran his finger inside the collar of his poofy-sleeved shirt. He still wore the long black wig and looked ridiculous on the bridge of a flip-yacht.

The *Il mia* banked smoothly and accelerated after the rapidly-retreating dot of the *De Lune.* Clare gripped the arms of her seat and leaned forward. Two streaks of green laser light arrowed past the little flipship in eerie silence. The *De Lune* jerked and rolled sideways.

'Again. I want her aimed at 280 mark 40.'

Don frowned and stared out the giant front window at the glittering expanse of darkness, stars, and dust. 'That'll take her straight into The Raspberry. It'll be hard to follow. The *Il Mia*'s instruments are fancy, but not scientific. They aren't rated for navigation in a dust cloud of that density. Lots of interference.'

'Leave that to me,' Clare said grimly. 'And tell *Mia* to demand surrender. May as well give her one last chance.'

'Last chance?'

'Just do it.'

Don gave the order.

The *Lune* shot two feeble blasts backward at *Mia*. The energy bounced harmlessly off her shields.

'I'll take that as a No, then,' Clare muttered.

Mia returned fire, each shot driving the little flipship closer toward the dustcloud.

'The second she disappears from visual and sensors, shoot at her most probable current location,' she ordered.

'*At* her location?' Don said, his brows practically to his hairline. 'I thought you wanted to take whatever she stole back to The Baggerman.'

'Change of plans. The Baggerman's orders.'

He opened his mouth and shut it again at her cool look. Pale, he gave the instruction. 'You know I'm not much of a killer.'

'Me neither.' She gave a tight smile. 'Consider it more of

a scientific experiment.'

The *Lune* vanished into the thick dust. A brilliant flash of energy erupted from the *Mia*'s gun ports.

Clare leapt from her seat. 'Get us away! Get us out of range. Quick!'

Don stammered out the command and the *Mia* accelerated into an inverted loop back the way they'd come. Clare punched up a visual from the rear sensors and threw it onto the front screen.

'What the…' Don gasped, his face as grey as his seat.

The Raspberry cloud sparkled. Energy coruscated and leapt, dancing from dust mote to dust mote in a display of fireworks a billion kilometres across.

'Get us further away.'

Don nodded and the image blurred for a second as the *Mia* pushed her sublight engines to the limit.

The Raspberry vanished.

Don rose, his mouth agape. 'What? Where?' He pointed at the empty expanse.

No. Not totally empty. The nebula still existed, but it now contained much less dust and several small planetoids that hadn't been there before.

'Ha ha!' Clare did a little dance and caught Don's hands. 'It works!'

'Wha…?' He was still staring open-mouthed at the emptiness. 'You blew up the *De Lune*. You loved that ship. And you killed Malia. And you vanished an entire *nebula*. Okay, it was a small one, but still. What the feck *was* that?'

She pinched his white cheek. 'Told you. Scientific experiment. Malia was a scientist. She broke contract with The Baggerman and stole one third of a catalyst designed to reduce clouds of cosmic dust to useful components—rare earths, especially. She'd hidden it somewhere, waiting until she could get hold of the other third and the formula.'

Clare pointed to herself. 'Hence my dummy courier run. My job was to draw her out of hiding—with her portion.'

'Thirds? You said you had one part and she had the other. Where was the last part?'

She shrugged. 'It needs a burst of energy and the presence of organic matter to activate it. Malia *was* the third part. We needed to know if it worked on a large scale. She volunteered—sort of.'

Don sank down into his chair with a thud. 'And I thought The Baggerman was a ruthless bastard.'

'Well,' Clare smiled. 'She did intend to let the Hegemon weaponise it. And, hey, at least now you're free to go back to smuggling.'

He grimaced and pointed at the empty space outside. 'You've just cut the guts out of the rare earth market.'

'Nah. The Baggerman's not stupid enough to do that. He never intended to release it.'

'Do I get to keep the yacht?' He lifted hopeful eyes to hers.

'What do you think?' Clare patted the arm of her seat and looked around possessively. 'This baby is *my* reward for a job well done.'

His shoulders slumped. 'Thought not. Fine. Drop me off

at the station and I'll get my ship out of mothballs.'

She laughed and, when the ship docked, gave him a deep, passionate kiss that left them both panting. When he reached for her again, she pushed him out the airlock, into the boarding tube. He tumbled his way back to the station, swearing at her.

Finally, she wandered back to the bridge and took the captain's chair, sighing in satisfaction.

Light footsteps sounded and the leather of the co-pilot's chair creaked beneath the newcomer's lean backside.

'Where to, Boss? Back to the office?'

Clare glanced over at Mac and grinned. 'I'd forgotten how much fun it is out in the field. Running the show is dull. I'm not ready to go back to being The Baggerman, yet.'

He rolled his ice-blue eyes and sighed. 'I did hear you describe me as short and paunchy, you know.' He patted his flat, muscular stomach and sent her a lazy smile. 'And I haven't snorted black since I met you five years ago.'

She grabbed his shirtfront and hauled him close for a kiss. 'Just acting, lover. Now that we've stopped a psychopath from destroying the galaxy, I think we deserve a drink and I'm late to meet Cordy Bane. Let's go to the Zoo.'

END

1630 hours: Old Friends and New

Cordelia Bane

Cordelia's comms finally buzzed with a message from Clare saying she was at the Zoo. A rush of relief washed through Cordelia. She didn't have many friends in this fecking galaxy. She headed straight for the bar.

The Zoo was busy this time of the day. Close to evening meal hour and Asteri's refectory was right next door. A quiet rumble of conversation filled the darkened space—conversations spoken by all manner of aliens drinking all types of the barkeeper's rainbow-coloured drinks.

Cordelia edged past a Kronck and up to the bar. But instead of finding the huge Aquanorian's presence lingering there, another stood in his place. A grey-and-white furred caninoid of some kind. The alien's black lips peeled back in a friendly, although decidedly carnivorous, smile.

'Howdy,' he growled in a base-tone voice. 'What can I get you, ma'am?'

Cordelia tipped her chin. 'Where's the normal barkeeper?'

The caninoid grimaced, his sharp top teeth pressing down on his bottom lip. 'Absinthe? He's off helping a young Terran woman give birth to her pup. She's having a hard time of it apparently, and Absinthe's the best midwife we've got on board the station. He likes pups. Always has. No idea why, myself.'

Cordelia pursed her lips. Childbirth? She'd take a bloody bounty-hunt in place of that anytime.

The bartender shook his head. 'I swear Ab spends more time off helping Asteri Station folk sort out their stupid mistakes than he does filling glasses.' He offered a paw. 'Anyhow, I'm Vell—Asteri Station's substitute bartender. And I mix a mean fireon water if I can interest you in a drink.'

Cordelia's estimation of Vell rose. A bartender who read customers well. Fireon water was her favourite. She shook his paw.

'Done,' she said, and swiped her wrist implant over the credit reader.

#

Clare O'Malley was waiting in a booth by the last habipod. Lieutenant Bligh from the Customs point was also there, chatting quietly with her. A glass of expensive-smelling gin sat on the table in front of the Grey Guard.

Cordelia slid into the booth. 'You've a terrible habit of making friends with the locals, O'Malley. Thought we were having some quality time.'

Clare, dressed in her signature grey pants and vest, smiled her best debonair smile. 'Cordy!'

'I can go,' Bligh picked up her glass as though to toss the rest into her mouth in one hit.

With a shake of her head, Cordelia sipped her own drink, revelling in the icy burn. 'All good, kiddo. O'Malley can't help making friends and I suck at it.'

In truth, she had hoped to broach the topic of quick, well-paid work with Clare—and what to do about the Underground Banker—but it could wait an hour or so. And making friends with a Grey Guard lieutenant out this neck of the woods could come in handy.

'Bout time you got here,' Clare said.

'And you.' Cordelia eyed her friend narrowly. 'I hear there was trouble at the Raspberry. What'd you do? Care to share?'

'Nope. There are some things you're best off not knowing.' Clare sent a significant glance toward Bligh.

'Nothing to do with the bounty I turned down on you two weeks ago?' She had no idea what Clare did for a living apart from running a courier business and suspected she shouldn't ask.

'That was just a misunderstanding,' Clare said airily. 'All sorted now.' She pointed at the Grey Guard. 'Cordy, this is Lieutenant Ori Bligh. She's just newly arrived from the Inner Systems. Still wet behind the ears.'

'We've met.' Cordelia raised her eyebrows at Ori. 'Why come to a shithole station like this?'

The lieutenant frowned and swirled her drink. After a pause, she said, 'To bring justice and order to the Outer Systems. To catch criminals.'

Cordelia laughed out loud. She didn't need the lie-detector turned on for *that* perfect Grey Guard Academy answer. The kid was clearly hiding something.

'Well,' she said, watching the lieutenant closely, 'you're working for the wrong crew to do that. Should've become a bounty hunter. The Hegemon aren't clever enough to stop the feckers roaming this part of space.'

Bligh's brow furrowed. 'You have a problem with the Grey Guard?'

'None.' Cordelia placed her glass on the scarred tabletop. 'No offense, but your lot just aren't the best when it comes to protecting innocents and catching criminals.'

'Cordy,' warned Clare, her eyes gleaming with amusement. 'Stop it. Play nice. Ori's alright.' She pressed a hand to Ori's arm. 'Forgive Cordy. She has history with the worst kind of criminals in this sector. It's made her hard and sour.'

Cordelia grinned and took a sip of her drink. The fire and frost mix burned on its slide down her throat. A mix of pain and pleasure. Just like life.

Bligh cocked her head. 'Who exactly are the worst in this sector then? I thought bounty hunters worked for the criminal syndicates.'

Clare's eyes widened. Cordelia ground her teeth and tried not to think worse of the kid.

'Some do,' Clare said, 'but not Cordy.' She glanced at Cordelia. 'You want to tell her about the Chancer Brothers Crime Syndicate, or should I?'

'That one's mine, I think.' Cordelia sighed.

Credits, Honour, and Decency

Pamela Jeffs

25 years ago

I messed up. I'd dropped my bag. The medicine vial Gregor gave me for my brother lies shattered in the bottom of it and its too dangerous to go back for another.

I slither down the rusted corrugated iron wall at the front of our shack. Its touch at my back bleeds cold through the thin skin of my patchwork shirt. Mutterings inside the house grow louder. I press my chin to my chest and squeeze my eyes shut, biting back tears. Then Tomas's screaming begins—a sickening sound to come from a ten-year-old.

My brother is one of twelve hundred children who fell victim to a gas leak in the illegal dycerium mine last month.

The semi-rare metal is used to make indestructible hulls for space vessels. But the toll on miners is high and illegal mines make more profits than safe ones.

And now Tomas's awareness is splintered. One minute he's lucid, the next haunted by bleak prophecies of doom. Most the other children are already dead. Twisted. Emaciated. Bloody-mouthed, having chewed through their own lips.

His screams become punctuated with hoarse, desperate words.

'The predator...it's coming. The kid is dead! Are you *listening* to me, Cordy? Gregor? He died! And so will the teacher...'

His ravings make no sense. I steel my heart to his anguish. I try instead to focus on the watercolour sunset as it soaks into darkness over the mine's cloaking dome. The blood red tones highlight the electrified mesh but the distant vista beyond it is blurred.

I often wonder what's past that fence. Past that horizon.

Other miners, dressed in rags no better than my own, hurry by on their way home from the afternoon shift. Their eyes remain firmly fixed on the road ahead, ears blocked to the sound of my brother's wailing.

It is an all too familiar state of affairs in this place. My neighbours are not without compassion, but they can't help. No rescue to be found from that quarter.

In my eighteen years, only Gregor, now in the position of East Gate security guard, has ever stood by Tomas and me. Gregor is my adopted brother. Or was years ago when my parents took him in after his own family was killed. That was back before he saved a guard's life and was gifted employment by the Chancer Brothers Crime Syndicate.

Maybe he feels guilty that he got out of the mine and we didn't, and that's why he sneaks Tomas meds from the guards' supplies.

But I've wasted this last dose, and there is nothing I can do about it now but wait out my brother's episode.

If we could get off-planet I'd have a chance of saving Tomas. But we've no credits, and even Gregor demands credits every time I ask him to let us go.

Credits. The only source of power in the galaxy.

Or so my father used to tell me.

I'm Terran, but was born in this stinking off-world mining camp. And there's no way off Aureehn—this asteroid moon of black and silver rock—unless you have a shitload of credits to bribe the guards with. I ain't got access to that.

The Syndicate own us. My father's gambling debts brought him and Mother here. Together they died in this place, and my brother will, too.

#

With darkness comes Tomas's silence. I rise, brushing rock dust off the seat of my pants. The door to the shack opens to my touch with a quiet screech. A wash of smells rolls past me: body odour, fear and piss. The smell of my baby brother.

I step across the threshold and into the sparse room.

Tomas lies on the pallet where I left him. The light of the ceiling's single glow-bar reveals his small, thin body lying twisted in sweat-soaked sheets. His eyes are closed, Exhaustion has taken him down into the oblivion of sleep.

I gently place my bag on the side table and untangle his limbs. He looks peaceful as I lay him out straight, kiss his forehead and cover him over. The dead slumber is a kindness to him.

My stomach grumbles. I haven't eaten since breakfast. On the ore sorting belts, where I'm stationed, we aren't allowed to stop for lunch. It's all about efficiency and production for the Syndicate.

I press the griddle on and rummage in the cupboard. The single, blackened pot we own, clanks as it hits the hotplate. Water hisses as it hits the saucepan's base. I drop three sanitiser pellets into it. They fizz, taking with them the toxic, heavy metals and cleaning the water for consumption.

I pry three standard issue gruel pellets from the packet tabs and drop them in. They dance in the water, expanding. Soon they fill the pot, disintegrating to form a thick green paste. Mum told me once that it tastes like old earth chicken, but who can really tell. Chickens don't exist here.

I spoon some into the bowl, leaving the greater portion for Tomas waiting until he wakes. I take a bite.

A knock raps at the door. Furtive. I put down my bowl, cover the pot and slide over. It's late for people to be knocking. I open the door a crack to see Gregor standing in the shadows.

'Cordelia! Let me in, quickly!' he hisses.

I step back and he enters. He eases the door shut and stands for a moment, eyebrows furrowed over his nose and lips pressed tightly together. His green eyes dart from left to right. Sweat slicks his forehead as he surveys the darker parts of the room. He takes a shuddering breath and finally his gaze falls on me.

'Get your things together. We've got to leave now.'

Gregor is usually the epitome of calm confidence. I've never seen him so rattled before.

'What's going on?'

His nostrils pinch together. 'The Syndicate has classified this planet as mined out.'

'So they're moving us on?'

'No.' He runs a calloused hand through his grey hair, a colour that makes him look a lot older than his twenty years. 'We've been issued with termination orders. In the next half hour, all miners will be herded to the valley diggings and vaporized.'

My breath hitches. 'Why would they do that?'

Gregor shakes his head. 'Miners are dispensable. This mine's no longer profitable and it's too expensive to ship you all off world. It's done. And you're done if you don't come with mc now.'

'But I ain't got credits to pay you with.'

'Don't worry about that. Let's just go.'

Gregor has never lied to me so I do as he says. I gather up my bag and throw all the food and sanitiser pellets I have into it. I turn to Tomas.

'Help me get him up,' I say.

Gregor shakes his head. 'Sorry Cordy. He'll have to say. I only got room for one extra on the ship.' .

'What? How can you say that? He's only ten years old.' I back away from Gregor. 'I ain't leaving him here.'

Gregor's teeth grind together. He leans in close, imploring me. 'Tomas is done for. There are no more meds and without them he'll last a week at best. But I'm not heartless. I won't leave him to *them.*'

I square my shoulders. 'I'm not leaving my brother.'

Gregor straightens. 'Cordy, please. You're a fool if you stay.'

A cough sounds out behind me. I turn. Tomas's eyes are open. Clear. Lucid. He lifts a weak hand.

His voice is a raw whisper. 'Cordy?' He coughs again.

Alarms blare out in the street. I suck in a breath, my chest tight. I kneel by Tomas's pallet and take his hand. 'Hush. It's okay.'

Tomas's eyes close then open. Even at ten, he is smarter than I sometimes give him credit for. His gaze turns to Gregor. 'Will it hurt when they kill me, Greg?'

'They won't!' I whisper, squeezing his hand. But we both know I'm lying. If we have learnt anything in our short lives, it's to know that death in this place is inevitable. I push my tongue to the roof of my mouth to bite back tears.

Gregor kneels next to me and presses a hand to Tomas's forehead. His voice is gentle. 'I won't ever let them touch you.' He pulls out a blue capsule from his breast pocket. 'See.

I got you a special weapon. A new pill. It makes you invisible. The guards won't see you.'

I glare at Gregor. 'Don't you dare give him that.'

His eyes fix on mine. They shimmer with unshed tears and I realise that he loves Tomas, too. He is making the hard choice—the best choice.

He's giving my little brother a kind way out.

I look at Tomas. His cheeks, sunken and drawn, are dark shadows beneath haunted eyes—eyes struggling to remain logical for me. And I know Gregor is right. I hate him for it; and the world for the decision I'm forced to make.

'It's okay, Tom,' I say, the words tasting like bile. 'Greg's telling the truth. Take the medicine and you'll be safe.'

'Okay Cordy,' he whispers.

#

Tomas lies still on the pallet. His eyes are closed, his thin chest still. My heart hurts but my tears refuse to fall. I let his small hand slip from mine and arrange it neatly next to his leg.

He is gone.

I turn. Gregor's face is a sickly shade of grey, his lips thin lines of grief. He doesn't look at me as he points to a plank on the floor.

'Third from the centre. It's loose,' he says. 'Open it. Take out what's inside.'

Numb, I don't argue. Gregor turns away, glancing out the grimy windowpane overlooking the street. The board comes away easily. Inside is an oilpaper-wrapped package.

Gregor's head swivels, his chin and left eye illuminated by the light from the window. 'It was your dad's contingency plan. The way he was going to try and get us out of this place. Now it's yours.'

I unwrap the package. The paper falls away. A rolled jacket unravels from within. I touch it and the colour of the fabric shifts, muted grey to skin tones.

'A chametek jacket,' whispers Gregor. 'Old, but it works...' He approaches. His fingers stroke the fabric reverently. 'These are rare, Cordy. It'll help us get you out— keep you safe.'

I bare my teeth. 'Just like you kept Tomas safe?'

'I did the best I could for him.'

I scowl. He's right, but my heartache is still too raw. I shrug the coat on and pull the hood over my head. The cut of the garment feels worn, as if it were moulded around larger shoulders than mine. My father's, I guess.

I immediately feel safer within its embrace. It drapes almost to the ground.

The fabric across my shoulders thrums with the energy. Gregor taps the shoulder pad.

'The power-threads in the weave work colour change and environmental mirror functions. It'll pretty much render you invisible.' He reaches over and presses a button on the cuff. A wash of warmth curls over my skin and Gregor's lips peel back in a grin. 'It works! I can't see you!'

'A special medicine to make me invisible,' I mutter.

Gregor ignores me. 'Stay close,' he whispers. He opens the door to the shack and peers down the street. 'It's clear,' he says and heads left, down the worn path toward the guards' quarters.

I take one last glance at Tomas as the door swings shut behind me. My vision blurs with tears, but I don't have time to cry. I blink. At least my brother is at peace.

Outside, the alarms are louder, more insistent. A voice, genderless, barks over the community comms system.

'All miners to assemble at the valley entrance immediately.'

Gregor marches, straight-backed at my side, his sleek, silver disruptor in his hand. Tears streak my cheeks but I don't dare make a sound. I focus on my father's coat and how it holds me in its embrace, keeping me protected. Keeping me invisible.

Gregor stalks on, a predator. To any observers he would seem alone, just another guard looking to round up stragglers.

We turn a corner. Just ahead a group of guards are knocking on doors. Out of one house, they drag an older man. Thin and grey-skinned, he is obviously a gas victim like Tomas. He stumbles to a stop in front of three armed guards.

A sizzle of disruptor fire cracks out. The miner straightens suddenly and grunts. Then he pitches forward into the street. I suppress a cry. Gregor leads us down another path away from the scene.

'Stay strong, Cordy,' he whispers. 'Not far now.'

I bite my lip and taste blood. I keep walking, now thankful

for the kindness in the capsule Gregor gifted Tomas.

#

The track to the ship hanger is free of people. Red halo lights fixed to the top of the signal towers illuminate the distant flight pad—great red eyes, chasing away the darkness. Six vessels of various sizes are lined up ready for take-off. Security craft, ore haulers and zoomers.

No people carriers though. No others except paid staff are expected to leave Aureehn alive.

The rugged, black tarmac is hot beneath the bare pads of my feet. The air smells bitter with the scents of oil and grease.

I look up. The cloaking dome overhead has been deactivated too. I trot to keep up with Gregor as he heads for the smallest vessel. It's a two-seater security zoomer with fake Hegemon registration numbers painted in a bold black on its silvered side—the Syndicate's trick to avoiding closer inspection by authorities on deep space runs. I resist the urge to spit at the lie it is.

Gregor presses the access hatch override on the vessel's entrance pillar. A series of green lights blink on and the door slides up. Two black seats wait inside. Welcoming. Warm.

I move into the co-pilot's seat. My jacket whispers as it passes across the metal console. The colours of it ripple, refracting light to replicate the cockpit surrounds.

'I just have to untether the rotor anchor,' says Gregor. 'I'll be back in a sec.'

I settle down deeper into my seat. Sensor equipment beeps quietly around me. I glance at it. The skies above the planet are clear. Our getaway should be good.

Voices rise at the rear of the ship. Gregor's base tone is highlighted against a lighter, female voice. I lean towards the open door and listen.

'What are you doing here?' asks the voice.

Gregor sounds confident. 'Prepping the ship for evac, Kerrin. What are you doing here?'

'You're meant to be out at the valley. I know because I wrote the roster up, myself.'

Silence.

'What are you hiding, Gregor?'

'Nothing. I'm prepping the ship.'

I can almost hear the woman's shrug.

'Well, you won't mind then if I have a look inside.'

'Not at all. Go right ahead.'

Booted footsteps head toward the door. I slither back into my seat and press myself as close as I can to the side wall. The metal struts push painfully into my elbow. I ignore the discomfort and try to keep myself small.

Guard Kerrin crosses into view. Her black uniform is pressed crisp, the silver buckles at her waist gleam bright. I recognise her by the non-standard issue dagger she carries sheathed in a leather holster at her side. Gregor's told me before that she likes to cut people's ears off with it.

Her slim, pinched face—made more severe by tightly-bound blonde hair—leers into the cockpit. Her mud-brown eyes rake across the interior and nostrils widen as she sniffs. She will find me, I'm sure. Her head turns to look in the cargo carrier behind the pilot's seat.

My foot slips free of my jacket. Desperately, I pull it back but Kerrin senses the movement. Her dagger flies toward me. The blade pierces the fabric of my jacket, slicing across my cheek as it passes by.

Somehow, I manage not to flinch or gasp.

The blade embeds itself with a high-pitched *twang* in the hull next to my ear. It sits there, vibrating. I don't dare move. Kerrin's eyes are pinned to my hiding spot but she sees nothing.

Then Gregor pushes past her. He reaches over me and pulls the dagger free. He frowns at the blood wetting its edge and covertly wipes it on his black sleeve before turning back to Kerrin.

'Jumping at shadows?' he says.

Kerrin presses her lips together. 'Something moved in there.'

'Yeah,' he says, sympathetically. 'They never can quite clean out the vermin from these ships.' He hands the dagger, handle first, to her.

Kerrin doesn't look convinced but she takes her weapon. 'All right, then. You win. But no more of this. Get down to the valley. The crew will want your help.'

'I'll just finish up here then I'll head down.'

'Didn't you hear me?' says Kerrin. 'Get down there now, or I'll shoot you for being a deserter.'

'I said I'll be along.'

Kerrin's hand falls to rest on the handle of her disruptor. Gregor's moves to his own.

Moments pass.

I hold my breath. Something seems to shift, a small dilation in time. One moment weapons are holstered, next they are in hands, firing.

Two bolts of blue electricity crackle out of the barrels. One flies toward Gregor, but he moves faster than seems possible. It misses. His shot flies true. It batters into Kerrin's chest. Her disruptor is flung wide and she falls backwards, arms splayed out, onto the tarmac.

'You bastard,' are her last words.

I have never seen someone shot before. My own wound is a distant annoyance as I watch the blood leak out of the woman's nose.

Gregor steps into the cockpit and pulls my hood back. My reflection is painted in his eyes, the cut down the side of my cheek and the sheet of blood that has coloured my chin scarlet.

He twists my face toward the light. 'Thank god she missed you. A few stitches and you'll be all right.'

All right? My chest tightens as I think of Tomas lying cold and alone back on his pallet. My stomach roils with nausea. No. I don't think I will ever be all right again.

He releases me, and turns to plug in co-ordinates into the navi-comp. 'I've set us a course for Earth. We can get accommodation and work.'

He presses an earbud into my hand. 'This is a translator

bud. All free Hegemon citizens have some version of one. This will have to do until we can sort you out an implant.'

'I can never repay you for any of this,' I whisper.

Gregor glances at me. He smiles a wicked grin. 'Hell. Maybe one day you'll fall in love with me and agree to marry me. Then we can call it even.'

'Marry you?' His words shock me. I've never looked at him in that way before. But then everything falls into place. His help, his desire to save me. All this time Gregor has loved me in more ways than one. How did I miss it?

I grasp his hand. He squeezes back. He presses the autopilot button on the console and the engines whir to life. The reflection of the booster's light illuminates Gregor's face.

Maybe, just maybe, I could love him back too. He is a good, decent and honourable man. Maybe a good life is possible after all the heartbreak of this place.

Gregor lets go of my hand. I turn to look out the side window. In the distance, disruptor fire flickers in the valley. I can't hear the cries of my neighbours, but I know they are out there dying. Just another heartbreak to leave behind.

'Cordy?'

I turn. Gregor is staring at me, his eyes wide.

'What's wrong?' I ask.

His mouth works, but no sound comes out. He coughs and blood dribbles down his chin. The scene doesn't make sense.

Then I look down. The point of a dagger protrudes from the centre of his chest. Kerrin's dagger. My heart drops into my stomach.

'No…no! Gregor!' I sob as he slumps forward, his blood splattering across the console.

I shift my gaze. The door hatch is still open. Kerrin sits upright on the tarmac, her arm extended from throwing the blade.

She sees me too. Her mouth stretches into a fierce grin— a rictus of victory. She pulls her shirt aside to reveal a weapons-protection vest concealed beneath it.

'You're next, little bitch,' she snarls.

In that moment I realize that it doesn't pay to be honourable or decent. Life will always find a way to tear you down.

Before I think, Gregor's disruptor is in my hand. One small squeeze. I grit my teeth as Kerrin's head disintegrates into a bloody cloud of corrupted flesh.

I sit for a moment in the silence. Alone. The slow *drip, drip* of Gregor's blood on the console sounds like thunder in the cockpit. I need the sound to stop.

I draw the dagger from his chest and wipe it clean. It will stay with me, now. A reminder, just in case I ever need it.

I gather Gregor's still warm corpse in my arms. I hold him close as the navi-comp beeps.

'Course set and acquired,' it states in its monotone voice. The door groans closed and seals my future in a hiss of air. My future without Tomas or Gregor. Without anyone of honour or decency.

The ship vibrates as the sublight engines roar to full power. The engines' flux overflow burgeons outwards.

I feel nothing as I watch Kerrin's corpse burn on the tarmac below.

Something inside of me has broken.

END

1700 hours: New Thoughts

Ori Bligh

'Well, that was moderately depressing, Cordy,' Clare said, throwing back her third drink.

Ori debated another gin and decided against it. Finding her way back to her room was going to be tricky enough as it was. And she didn't know these women well enough to trust them if she drank too much. It sounded like she ought to arrest both right then, but neither had committed any crime on Asteri Station. Yet. And both could be useful sources of information going forward.

Especially since she was stuck here for three years. She suppressed the urge to swear and sighed, oppressed by the weight of knowledge unlearned; things unknown that could make or break her time here. This place. These people. They were very different to the rule-abiding Inner Systems rich families she'd grown up around.

And yet, not bad people, as far as she could tell. So far. No-one knew much about the past of the regular barkeeper, Absinthe, but he was like a mother to everyone on the station. And Zev swore up a storm but seemed to work all hours to keep the place running. Cordy was a bounty hunter, of all things, but understandably had a violent dislike of child-killers.

Clare slapped her palms on the table, startling Ori from her fog of depression.

'We need food to soak up all this booze,' Clare stated. 'I'll go next door. Back soon.' She slipped out of the booth and strolled away.

Ori stared moodily into her empty glass. She slid Cordy a look beneath her lashes.

'Do you really think people have no honour or decency?'

Cordy shrugged one shoulder. 'In my line of work, you don't see many of the good guys.' She stroked the scar on her cheek. 'But who knows. Years ago, folk didn't trust cyborgs and now no-one even blinks if someone has their whole fecking head replaced.'

Ori smiled faintly. 'True. My Grey Guards Academy Psych lecturer told a story about how they used to treat cyborgs a couple of hundred years ago on Ballinor-3. Nasty stuff.' She shivered. 'Humans can be pretty cruel to each other.'

'I know.' Cordy's lips pressed tight.

Ori cocked her head. 'But this one guy—cyborg, actually…well, I always thought maybe he had a good reason for what he did.'

Sitting back, Cordy nodded as Clare returned with a tray piled high with food.

'I'd be interested to hear what an Inner Systems kid thinks is a good reason to treat someone badly.'

Ori bit back a hot reply.

'Be nice, Cordy,' Clare said. 'Let her tell the story. Might just melt your cold, cold heart.'

Cordy laughed.

A Window to the Soul

Aiki Flinthart

200 years ago

'You gotta be pretty close, now, Jeff?' Mike winked, man-to-man, inviting uncomfortable friendliness. He leaned over his shop counter, a rarity who would ignore the eyepatch and look Jeff in his functioning eye—which was even more unsettling. 'That woman of yours must be something else, the effort you've gone to for that house of hers. Must be nearly finished?'

Jeff shrugged, letting his lack of reply be swallowed by the distant rumble of a shuttle taking off from the Ballinor-3 spaceport a few klicks away.

The demolitions warehouse rattled. Dust drifted from the

ceiling and settled on Mike's shoulders and sweaty-shiny scalp. The bitter smell of flipship grey fuel burned Jeff's throat.

He looked toward the back of the building, his skin prickling. It was true he could deny Zoe nothing. She'd held his heart to ransom from the moment they'd met. Why else would he be spending all this time and effort?

The rumbling faded and Mike scrubbed a yawn from his round face. Jeff forced a polite smile and controlled the urge to demand what he knew must be somewhere in the yard. The demolition notice had been on the bulletins yesterday and Mike was always first onto a site.

A saner man wouldn't have left it to chance; would have gone to the demolition, himself. Sought closure, perhaps. But Jeff couldn't see the place again and stay focussed. The memories weighed too much and there was too much at stake. He absently stroked the scars on his chest.

There was little point in looking backward, anyway. The way to escape from one world to the next lay forward, always. He'd learned that long ago.

And now the final pieces were close. The next world was almost in his grasp.

Mike cleared his throat and jerked his chin. 'Well, security windows are back there. Just got some new stock in, too. Long as you don't mind where we got 'em.' He brayed a laugh.

'Something wrong with them?' Jeff's fingers curled into fists. He wasn't willing to play games with his vision of Zoe's house. Had it been compromised? Had someone else seen what he saw in those windows? Seen their potential?

Zoe and Elya were vital to his future. To his dream of freedom. He'd do whatever it took.

The question was waved aside with a hasty hand. 'Nah, nah, mate. All in good condition. Just what you're after. They won't stay in the yard long, that's for sure.'

'So?'

Mike's skin flushed darker and his eyes slid away. He shrugged. 'Y'know. They're from the old psych hospital, up on Greene Street. The one where all the uptown folk sent their crazies when the gene modding didn't take or went wrong.' He shuddered.

'Got cleared out last week. Saw some of the last ones gettin' carted away. Made me glad I'm too poor to afford gene mods. Don't seem right, lockin' 'em up, though. Not like it's their fault.'

He leaned closer and whispered. 'Heard they was doing experiments on 'em, y'know. Makin' some into cyborgs to try and fix the mods gone wrong.' He grimaced.

Jeff kept his composure. Was that all? Hardly the worst he'd heard. Not exactly news that cyborgs were feared, even while they were necessary. The rich might be able to afford re-grows, but the poor could not.

'Not that there's anything wrong with cyborgs.' Mike's gaze flickered over Jeff's eyepatch and he hurried on. 'But I heard the Hegemon scientists were using the inmates as human testers for the latest model flipdrive. The one they're makin' ta try and fix the flip psychosis pandemic. But those poor joes never came back.' He spread his arms wide. 'Lost in the flipvoid somewhere.'

'Rumours,' Jeff said, relaxing. If Mike didn't know what had happened, no-one did. 'Unlikely to be true. If they were poor folk, they could disappear without anyone complaining. But people related to the uptowners? No way.'

'They stuck 'em in that place, didn't they? Mebbe they were glad to be rid of 'em. Uptowners. Pfah!'

Jeff had no comfortable reply so he kept silent. They were glad. He remembered that. If he could ache for what he'd lost, he would, but his heart was dull and steady. Mechanical in its rhythm. Unhurried.

Mike cleared his throat again and put on his business face like he'd just remembered Zoe and Jeff were building amongst the uptowners.

'But the windows are good. They're what you want. Unbreakable glass. You said that little lady of yours was worried about break-ins. That's what you need, innit?'

Jeff nodded. Zoe had decided to move again so she and Elya would be safe. She was a product of the spaceport backstreets; hand to mouth, eye for an eye, knife to heart.

An intruder's knife to her mother's heart and father's eye. Zoe's eye to replace it. Her father's hand to Zoe's mouth, to stifle her screams.

It had taken Jeff years to win her trust. Then Elya's birth, to an unnamed father five years before, fired her protective instincts and she'd begun to rely on him, to look to him. They'd worked hard. Saved every cent. Moved four times. Her always seeking a higher fence, a stronger gate, a safer neighbourhood.

Him, waiting for the right moment.

Finally, she'd bought the worst house on the best street. Surrounded by neighbours with drones that fired lasers at anything that moved; security that arrived with flashing lights and sirens at any hour; gene-modified Hell-hounds patrolling neat-manicured yards hidden behind electrified walls as tall as trees.

Nothing would do but for her house to equal theirs. To be lesser would be to paint a target for thieves and murderers, Zoe claimed. As though thieves and murderers were only ever outside the walls.

So, Jeff rebuilt; painstakingly, purposefully, patiently. Almost every wall had now been removed. He could have put in digital windows, but he'd persuaded her to get real ones. It hadn't been hard. She'd grown up surrounded by the close-walled, garbage-carpeted concrete and steel slums. She wanted Elya to see the dust blue sky over Ballinor-3.

And now the right windows were available.

'There's two doors, as well,' Mike said. 'If you want 'em.'

Nodding, Jeff picked his way through rough-stacked piles of posts, wall insulation, and random oxidising parts for obsolete flipships.

A graveyard of pasts through which others, like him, rummaged for materials to build a new future—one stripped of painful memories and hollow promises.

The windows were piled neatly in one corner, with a clear

space around them. Large, square, and so thick they were faintly blue. A lot like the windows for short trip sublight transport shuttles.

His laser scanner confirmed they were exactly the right size for the spaces. A count showed there were exactly enough to fill every gap in the house walls. His lucky day. He smiled wryly.

With a glance around, Jeff collected a steel bar and smashed it against the glass with all his considerable strength. Not even a chip or a star. And their frames were solid, too.

Perfect.

As he turned to head back to the front desk, movement flickered on the edge of his one-eyed vision. He scanned, enhanced sight looking even beyond the infrared and ultraviolet ranges. He stared at the almost-skeletal image reflected in the dusty window, nodded, and moved away.

#

Back at the house, Zoe and Elya were there, chatting with a pastel-clad, diamond-decked neighbour. All white-toothed smiles and cooing words.

Zoe's dark hair was shorn fashionably in zigzag designs, leaving stripes of pale scalp showing. A small personal carry-bag lay strapped along one forearm. It held everything she considered important, though she'd never let him see the contents and it would be rude to ask.

He didn't need to, anyway. He knew what was in it.

His bag held nothing. His ID-finance chip was embedded in one wrist. A comms chip behind his ear. he had no need of anything else.

Almost.

Elya waved at Jeff, hung off Zoe's hand and sighed heavily. Zoe and the neighbour smiled down at the child. Zoe and Elya lived temporarily in a nearby secure hotel and visited every week but Zoe was doing her best to ingratiate herself with the family next door.

Jeff smiled at Elya, ignored both the women and paused at the gate, assessing the worksite. The house was merely interlocking metal skeletons; like the bones of android hands curled, claws embedded in the silcrete floor, caging the empty spaces inside. Once the windows were installed, he could call in the spraycrete contractor to put flesh on the bones. Then the outer, solar-gathering skin. Then the house would be alive.

A body, ready to hold souls.

He nodded to Zoe and the stiff-faced woman who smelled cloyingly of roses and whose name he still didn't know. The woman's knife-blue eyes sliced through him and away. Her lip curled.

Zoe hastened into speech, her voice pitched low, the spaceport beggar accent creeping in as it did when she was stressed. Jeff let a surge of bitterness go and pretended not to hear. He'd heard all her lies about his origin before. If it made her happy to pretend, then it didn't matter. Not for much longer, anyway.

Methodically, he unloaded the windows and began bolting

them to the frame. Zoe finished her conversation with an airy wave and hastened over, Elya skipping by her side, chattering in her usual excitable fashion.

'Hush, sweetie,' Zoe said, kissing her daughter's forehead. 'I just need to talk with Jeff for a moment. Go play, but be careful!'

'Yes, mama!' Elya ran toward the house, her long dark hair flying.

Zoe turned to him, serious, focussed. 'They're unbreakable?' She wore a fitted skinsuit that changed colour and patterns to suit her mood. Matte grey with flashes of burnt red came and went over her chest and stomach. A sure sign she was having trouble controlling some strong emotion.

His skinsuit was pale grey. As always. He didn't need to look to check. Emotions were easy to manage if you had a good enough reason. And the right training.

He'd warned her that she didn't have the training the children of the rich got. The methods that taught them to suppress their emotions so they could present a pastel-perfect, glittering surface to the world. She was determined to learn. To fit in. To take—by any means—what she felt her birthplace deprived her of.

'Yes, the windows are unbreakable,' he confirmed, waiting, watching beneath his lashes.

'That bitch,' she said, her fingers becoming claws as she glanced back over her shoulder, 'said there were two attempted break-ins around the corner last week.'

'You and Elya will be safe, here.'

'And you,' she put in sharply, frowning.

He inclined his head.

She folded her arms and glanced at the neighbouring house. 'I hate the way she looks at me. All pretence. And at you like you're…nothing. All of them do it.'

'It doesn't matter,' he said, bolting a window to the frame with a final twist of the socketwrench.

She tilted her head, frowning. 'Don't you mind that they look down on us?'

Jeff shrugged. 'They were born to privilege. I'm a cyborg. You worked your way up from the slums. It's inevitable that they think less of you. Whether it's because of me or your background is irrelevant. They can't help it.'

Her mismatched eyes flashed and her lips pressed thin. He'd pay for that dig at her, later, but it was one of his few indulgences. As long as she needed him, he'd be reasonably safe.

He stood back and inspected his handiwork. Once the house was done, though…

A pair of grey eyes stared back at him from the window. The face bearing them was hollow-cheeked and dark-shadowed. He touched his eyepatch and shook his head, banishing the illusion.

Not yet. Not yet.

'You won't leave us, will you?' Zoe asked. One hand fiddled with something inside the wrist-bag, pushing its bulge through the pale fabric.

'You know I won't,' he replied. 'I couldn't.'

Elya ran over, her cheeks pink, face alight, breath coming in gasps. She'd been basking in Zoe's inattention and swinging like a tree-rat from the house frame.

'Jeff!' She threw her arms around his leg and squeezed as tight as her plump little arms could. Jeff barely felt it, but smiled and stroked her waist-length hair. She tilted up her chin. 'Which one's my room?'

He pointed at the middle-sized of the three bedrooms. She pattered away and paced the room with adult solemnity, muttering to herself and holding her hands apart to check distances.

'She'll be safe, won't she?' Zoe stared at her daughter and chewed on her lip. Elya was her heart and soul. The one crack in the armour she wore against the world. The one chance he had of success.

'She'll be safe,' he said, truthfully.

'Good, because I have no credit left. This house has to be perfect. Right.' She dusted imaginary debris off her hands. 'Comms me when you're done and the spraycrete is in. I'll come inspect again when it's at lockup stage.'

Jeff nodded. She called Elya and strode away. Elya looked back and waved. Jeff raised a hand.

#

Finishing to lockup didn't take him long. His body didn't tire much. Nor did his mind. Especially not when the house was so close to completion. When the crete had set and the solarskin was stretched and fixed, Zoe and Elya returned, as promised.

The front and rear doors were also from the old hospital. Thick, solid, with a small square window to match the others. With those in place and the security system wired in, the house was a bunker.

Jeff had been careful to never lock himself in over the last week. Until the electronic locks were properly coded it was impossible to get out.

Zoe paused just inside the high front fence, hands on her cheeks, face flushed. Her skinsuit blushed to match. From the purpling horizon, the sunset threw bloody light across her face.

The house's programming had selected an old Earth landscape image to project onto the external solarskin. It was like looking at rolling hills punctured by portals to soulless darkness.

Jeff gestured and the lights inside blinked on. Each room had its own wallskin. They all showed plain grey, awaiting life at the hands of their owner.

Zoe strode toward the open front door. Elya dashed after, but Jeff grabbed her arm to hold her back.

'Give her a moment,' he said. 'She's been working toward this since we met, ten years ago. Let her have a little time.'

Elya cocked her head and looked up. 'Where did she find you? You never said.'

He hesitated, but this was the right time. His moment as well as Zoe's. The door closed behind her, snicking shut with a satisfying click. Secure.

Through the living area window, he saw the wallskins

flicker and change. First to a seascape with raging waves, then pale green desert sands, then settling to a vast view of golden grasslands.

Her illusion of freedom locked behind her desire for security, gained at unspeakable cost.

The cost of his heart.

'Well?' Elya tugged at his hand.

He smiled thinly. 'We met when your mother found me escaping a place where I was being held prisoner.'

Her eyes widened.

Inside the house another wallskin settled into a chosen image. Forest. Zoe was surrounding herself with all the beauty she'd never had as a child.

Jeff caught her gaze through the window. She touched her wrist-bag and chewed on her lip. Her skinsuit flickered black and grey and blood-red.

'So, she saved you?' Elya said, beaming.

'No,' he replied, gentle, laying a hand on her shoulder.

Movement flickered in a window to a room Zoe had not yet entered.

'No,' he repeated. 'She stole my heart.'

Elya frowned. 'You mean…you love her?'

More movement in more windows.

Zoe's eyes widened and she backed up against a field of daisies.

'I mean,' he said, the hydraulics in his fingers creaking subtly as he tightened his grip on Elya's shoulder, 'that to stop me from leaving, she stole my heart.'

He tapped his chest, solid titanium ribs beneath scarred skin. 'The control circuit to it, anyway. She found me unconscious outside the prison and took me to safety. But she stole the switch that can kill me.'

He touched the patch over his empty eyesocket. 'That, and other things. She carries the control switch in her wrist bag. Ready to turn my heart off if I disobey.'

Elya flinched beneath his fingers, glancing back and forth between Jeff and her mother. 'You're lying!' She pulled, straining toward the house. Jeff released her. She could not, after all, breach the unbreachable or break the unbreakable.

She pounded on the door, screaming her mother's name.

But Zoe could not hear, and her attention was elsewhere; fixed on the wraith-thin figures seeming to approach from all directions. Their hollow-cheeked gazes and haunted faces held terrors from Jeff's past—and her future, if she didn't co-operate.

For the demolition man was correct. The psych hospital had held the cast-offs of the wealthy. The children whose gene-mods didn't take and whose parents wanted the resulting imperfections out of sight. The playthings of Hegemon scientists. The poor couldn't afford regrows, only cybernetics—and someone had to be the test case for prototypes.

Jeff stared at his hands. Perfect on the outside, but inside his skeleton was metal, half his organs replaced. Both his eyes. His heart. And he was one of the lucky ones.

The rest of his friends now stalked Zoe inside her safe

house. Not sent to the flipvoid, but trapped inside the windows; lost between worlds by the scientists attempting to play with space and time.

His cyborg eyes had always seen them; all the years he'd lived there. His friends had endlessly stalked the halls. Never sleeping. Never letting those that could see them sleep.

Seeking freedom.

Demanding it.

Making him promise.

They'd pounded ceaselessly on the glass, just as Elya did, now.

Jeff stretched his mouth in a grimace. He closed his eyes, briefly, shutting out the images. Ten years since he'd escaped and not a night passed where he didn't see them, still.

But soon... soon he'd be free and so would they. Then he could rest. It would have been a decade earlier, but for Zoe.

Elya pounded on the door again, crying. She could not see the phantoms, only the abject terror on her mother's face.

Zoe could see them. With the eye she'd taken from Jeff— to replace that which her father stole from her. With that she, too, saw between worlds. But to her they were horrific apparitions, not lost friends desperate for release.

Jeff grinned mirthlessly. And they knew whose fault it was that they had been kept prisoner this last decade. He'd told them, today.

Zoe ran to a window, smacking it with palms open in surrender. She pleaded silently; begged, retreated again from his friends. They might not be able to touch her, but he knew they could drive her mad.

How well he knew.

She paled. Her skinsuit was black, now, her body trembling. Knives flashed in ghostly hands. Blades pointed at her eyes. He'd briefed, knowing what she feared.

She screamed, her mouth open, silent. He held up his wrist and pointed to the bag there.

Next door in the neighbour's yard, lights flashed on. Voices lifted, demanding explanations. The deep-throated bark of hounds joined Elya's wailing cries.

Jeff frowned and pointed again to the wrist-bag. He was running out of time. He had gambled everything on this one chance. If the neighbours appeared now…

All she had to do was give back what was his. She'd helped him escape once and he'd thought her a saviour. But she'd bound him to a new form of torture—of slavery. In seeking her freedom from fear, she'd sacrificed his. And dozens of others'.

For that he could not forgive her. Nor would they.

The gate next door squealed open. Jeff set his jaw. She had to give in. If she didn't he would be taken away. Back to somewhere like the psych ward he'd escaped. He couldn't do it. Couldn't go through it all again.

He stared coldly at her imploring terror, keeping his own mounting fear at bay.

Finally, with fumbling fingers she opened her wrist-bag and held up the gleaming silver disc. Such a small thing, was autonomy. With that she could stop his heart.

For a moment his steady gaze locked with her defiant one. Her thumb hovered over the print detector. One touch was all it would take. He merely smiled and pointed at Elya, waiting outside the unbreakable door, watching through the unsmashable windows.

But not far behind him, the crunch of feet on gravel. If she saw the neighbour, his chance at freedom was gone. He held his breath. His heart, for once, stuttered and stumbled.

Then her shoulders slumped. She let the unit fall. With a booted heel she crushed it, forever setting him free.

'You! What's going on?' The sharp voice of the pastel woman cut through the gloom.

Jeff didn't respond.

'Mummy can't get out!' Elya stopped pounding the door, her face streaked with tears.

The woman gathered Elya into her arms and glared at Jeff. 'Well? Get her out you...you creature. Ugh.'

Jeff collected a laser cutter from his toolbox, carefully not meeting her eye. 'It's nothing serious, ma'am. My mistress has just locked herself into the house by accident. Locks aren't programmed, yet.' He held up the tool and set it. 'This will get her out. No need to worry.'

She held Elya tightly, interposing her body between Jeff and the child. 'You don't deserve such a sweet girl as your mistress. I want you off the property. Things like you are too dangerous around this child. You don't belong here.'

'No, ma'am,' he replied. Systematically, Jeff drilled a small hole through each of the windows.

Faint laughter of the damned echoed as his friends, his fellow madmen and lost souls were, at last, released as well.

When the final window was pierced, he destroyed the door lock and the panel clicked open. Mother and daughter reunited in trembling tears.

The pastel woman put her arms around Zoe and Elya, comforting their fears, offering them sanctuary next door.

Now they would all be safe.

And, perhaps, he could find where he did belong.

END

1715 hours: Intrusion

Zev Smith

Zev leaned around the booth and eyed the three women sitting behind.

'Doesn't make that Zoe woman cruel. People make mistakes,' he said, bitterly. 'Just proves you can't fecking trust scientists, if you ask me. Especially ones working for the Hegemon.'

'Eavesdropping again, Zev?' Lieutenant Bligh folded her arms. 'Didn't you say you had maintenance to do? Something about the rich water containment unit needing constant upkeep?'

'I have it under control.' He chuckled. 'And you weren't exactly whispering. Besides, with Ab away playing hero—as he does—he likes me to keep an eye on Vell and make sure this place fecking-well stays quiet.'

Bligh glanced around. 'You could probably leave that to me. It is my job, after all. Not a lot else happening.'

Zev checked his wrist chrono. 'I've got half an hour before the next maintenance cycle's needed on the rich water. Everything else can wait. Want to hear about a real bitch of a woman? In the Grey Guards, too. Well, an elite unit called Spirit Hunters.'

A quick frown gathered on her brow. 'I've never heard of a Spirit Hunters Unit.'

He shrugged. 'We're talking three hundred years ago, for sure. When the Grey Guards' job was to protect the grey fuel miners. The planets the Hegemon was mining for grey fuel were stripped. Destroyed. To the point where even the ghosts of the dead fought back.'

'What?' The bounty hunter woman—Cordelia Bane—fixed a sharp gaze on him. 'Ghosts aren't real. People being stuck in the flipvoid is one thing, but the dead are dead.' Old pain flickered, tightening her hard jaw.

'Oh, I don't know. Ghosts could be real, Cordy.' The third woman—Clare someone—turned to Zev and laughed, the sound full of mischief. 'But ghosts rebelling against the Hegemon? Pull the other one. I think you've been stuck on this backwater station too long. You're starting to believe the stuff you hear from the wrong sort of people.'

'Think what you like.' He shifted into their booth and signalled Vell for another round of drinks. He wasn't averse to spending time with three interesting young women. They exchanged questioning glances but moved to make space for him.

He sipped at his scotch. 'Those were some serious rebellions. Killed millions of Hegemon citizens and Grey Guards. That's why the Hegemon switched to rich water. The death toll grew too fecking high for even them. What happened on Amarion-5 was the last straw.'

Terralight

Pamela Jeffs

300 years ago

Five Driller teams dead so far. Mining for grey fuel on Amarion-5 has ground to a halt. Why do the Hegemon authorities always wait so long to call me in?

I tap the communicator button at my wrist. The red signal light shows an active connection.

'Amarion-5 Off World Base,' I say. 'Cyanna Ryan confirming landing. Ship damaged. Require transport assistance for return. Please acknowledge.' I wait. Static hisses from the speakers in reply.

I try again. 'Please acknowledge.' More static. I sigh. Some kind of magnetic interference. I'll need to find higher ground to improve the connection.

I look out across the sea of shifting, orange sands. The planet doesn't look like much but you can never tell which ones will choose to fight back. Usually it's the younger ones that prove a problem for the Hegemon—they still hold a greater awareness of themselves.

But Amarion-5 is old, she is still awake, and she is defiant.

She has created a spectre army to see to her defence. The reason I have been called in. I can't say I blame her. This planet's peoples were murdered; slaughtered so her rivers of grey fuel could be mined to power Hegemon starships.

If I were such a planet, hell, I'd fight back too. I feel sorry for Amarion-5, but I'll end the planet's rebellion to further Hegemon interests. It's what they pay me to do, after all.

Sometimes I wonder if that makes me a priestess or a murderer. The gods know I've been called both in my time.

I look back toward the wreckage of my shuttle. The small ship lies half buried in the desert sand. I was lucky to make it down intact. A low-orbit collision with satellite debris has left the shuttle hull scarred and battered.

I turn away. The vessel did its job by making the landing but now it's useless. Just another skeleton that will be left to rot in the heat of the desert sun.

I squint at the horizon. The same breeze that ruffles my hair blows across the ocean of sand. And not only the sand. The fluid plains are dotted with stone ruins and stunted purple thorn bushes, shedding their pollen as grey dust into the thin air. It is a grim, bleak landscape telling a story of wreckage.

The cloudless sky that arcs overhead is an ominous wash of dark mustard, the colour of a half-healed bruise.

For a moment I wonder what this place looked like before the Hegemon mining crews invaded, before it was changed from a *Level 1: Habitable* planet to a *Level 9: Dead-Zone*. But I do not let my imagination reign. Years of experience have taught me that to consider what *was*, against the canvas of what *is,* is the surest way to heartbreak.

I unclip the hand-held onnocular from my belt. Through it, the planet's view is magnified. More thorns, lonely broken buildings and sand. I click down the scanner lens. Green laser lines crisscross the viewscreen. A list of numbers cycles down the right side. Atmospheric composition, ground temperature, air toxicity and humidity. The results concur with my ship's scans. Air breathable, no water. Fine by me. I'll only be here a short while.

I drop my gaze to the last number on the list—the spectre-plasm readings. They spike in concentration to the north. I increase the onnocular's magnification. A blunt-edged stone ridge sharpens into view.

The height I need for my comms to work will be there. And beyond it will be why I've come.

I clip the onnocular back onto my belt and re-adjust the terrablade resting in the holster at my side. The distant ridge is a smear on the horizon. It's a fair way out but, armed and with my water canister full, I can make it.

As I walk, the planet's distress becomes obvious. Its acid emotions leech from the ground, rising—poisonous—through the soles of my boots. The bone deep ache infects my knees, elbows and teeth. I clench my fists. All planets over-soaked in blood emanate like this. It doesn't bode well for what I'll find over the ridge.

And what that is, I have seen a hundred times before on a hundred different worlds. Armies of the dead, riled with self-righteous purpose and having already lost their lives, fighting with nothing else to lose.

A spirit will lead them, one who in life was respected. Sometimes a warrior, other times an elder. That is the phantom to watch, the one who leads the pack. The receptacle of the planet's purpose in working to ensure victory at all cost.

But even so empowered, those shades are not indestructible.

In all my years, I have never yet suffered a defeat.

I grasp the hilt of my terrablade. The weapon is the secret to my successes, a weapon that can both disperse spirits and subdue the core of an unquiet planet. Its solid weight bounces against my side as I walk, reminding me of my purpose. *Secure the planet at all cost.*

But with purpose comes danger, and wielding the weapon's tech is hazardous. Modified hydrogen atoms impregnated into the metal, when activated to become terralight, can draw off a wielder's own spirit—if that wielder is not careful.

Experience has made me cautious. I am careful to avoid its use merely to settle the smaller, less important tragedies I pass—the shade of the twin-horned, horse-like creature wandering the dunes, driven by the memory of a terrible thirst; or the Hegemon soldier who sits against a broken wall with his legs missing, his shade calling pitifully for his mother.

Without the danger, the priestess in me would ease their lingering, but the murderer is more practical. I see no use in risking my life to solve problems that are not my own.

#

The orange and yellow coloured ridge is relatively easy to climb. Horizontal leaves of stone, stacked like books and worn smooth by the wind-driven sand, act as steps. I look down as I walk, imagining what the final battle here would have sounded like—the cries, the moans of the dying. Had no one heard the broken sobbing of a heart-sore world, unable to absorb any more blood, crying for it all to stop?

The wind rises as I crest the ridge. I squint against the sand that runs with it, hand up to protect my face. I step down from the small plateau and follow the faint track into the shallow valley below.

From here, I see this world was not always a desert. The remains of a river crawls toward the east. A silver-white forest of dead trees lines the cracked clay pan. Long, wicked spines sprout from pale branches, standing stiff against the elements. Their tips are hung with macabre wind chimes made from the armoured skeletons of Hegemon dead.

The bones dance and I sense eyes upon me. I scan my surrounds. The dirty, yellow light from the sky casts shadows against the white trees. Another gust of wind, the bones clatter again. Then the eyes reveal themselves. They belong to a woman who steps out of the forest across the river, an active terrablade held upright in her fierce grip.

I pull my own sword free of its scabbard. The hydrogen atoms in the weapon begin to glow red as they process the heightened levels of spectre-plasm in the air. The woman, dressed in the same severe dark grey uniform as myself, pauses at the centre of the dead river basin. Another elite Grey Guard Spirit Hunter.

'Do you live or do you linger?' she asks.

'I live,' I reply. 'You?'

The woman lifts her chin. Her eyes, a pale green, cut through me. Her glare is cold and calculating. I respect the scrutiny. Caution is the prerogative of any good hunter.

I seem to pass her test.

'I live,' she says, lowering her blade. Its glowing tip hovers just shy of the ground. 'Why are you here? The Hegemon contract for this world is mine.'

'You are mistaken,' I say. 'Amarion-5 was granted to me.'

The woman's eyes thin. 'When?'

'Yesterday. I deployed this morning.'

The woman's eyebrows rise. 'You must be Cyanna Ryan then?'

'Correct.'

'Well, they'll be happy upstairs to hear you've arrived. I'm the Amarion-7 base station Hunter. When they didn't receive your landing confirmation this morning, they sent for me to find you and finish the job if need be.'

Amarion-7—the smaller sister planet to Amarion-5. It's close, but not that close. She must have been deployed from her own base as soon as I missed the landing confirmation. I'm surprised they sent someone so quickly, but then again the Hegemon is desperate for mining to begin again.

My fingers touch my communicator. 'Some issues with interference. I couldn't get through.'

The woman shrugs. 'Not to worry. Glad to have found you. It's probably a good thing to have two blades here anyway.' She points to the forest. 'With the amount of spectre-plasm here, we might be looking at a caging event.'

Caging. I frown. It's an unnatural use of the terralight power—a cruel, unholy way to end spirits already aggrieved by violent deaths. Never a first-action solution.

'Surely it won't come to that,' I say.

She walks up out of the riverbed and stops in front of me. 'I guess we can hope.'

'We more than hope. We work to avoid it.'

The woman's eyes narrow even as her lips crease into a cold smile. Unease crawls along my spine. Something about this woman doesn't sit right. To ease the discomfort, I holster my terrablade and offer my hand. She ignores it.

'Liv Carson's the name,' she says. She points with her chin toward the dead forest. 'And what we're looking for is in there.'

My hand drops. I look back at the skeletons dangling from the trees. 'The décor certainly gives one pause.'

The woman chuckles and my heart sinks. A sense of humour in a spirit hunter isa telltale sign that they're new to this kind of work, and a clue that they do not yet have a healthy respect for warnings given by the dead.

'Oh, I don't know,' says Liv, smiling. 'It's nice in a dark, stay-the-hell-off-our-planet, kind of way.' She lifts her glowing blade and points it toward the trees. 'Shall we go and see if they have the kettle on for us? Upstairs sent me here in a rush this morning and I missed my first coffee.'

I find her levity uncomfortable. It could be the sign of a reckless nature. But I hold my thoughts close.

'Lead the way,' I say.

#

It's cold inside the dead forest. Spectre-plasm leaches from the ground in bright tendrils that spin upward in uncanny spirals. The sand, ribbed and mounded up against the dead trees, is darker here also. Every now and then we pass remains—bones sticking like toothpicks out of the dirt; a dusty Hegemon helmet.

Liv pauses by one of the trees. She uses the tip of her terrablade to dig clear a half buried body from the foot of it. I frown at her use of the weapon in such a way. The tool of our trade demands respect.

Her actions finally reveal the mummified body of a native. Lithe of form, horned, rough skinned and clawed, it looks to be more savage animal than humanoid. But the desiccated gash across its throat shows that it was killed the same as any other living thing can be.

'Look at that,' says Liv. 'Ugly things.'

I shrug. 'Not ugly. Just different. I hear they were a brave race. They fought well. It took twelve Hegemon battalions to see them finished. Not many of our soldiers returned.'

Liv looks impressed. 'I'd never fight for my planet like that. But then again, it's a shithole world on the edge of the Erdani system. All rocks and reptile farms. No-one would be interested in it anyway.'

Not unless they found grey fuel on it, I think as I look at the native and feel a moment's sorrow at the waste of life.

Liv seems to lack any such compassion. Done with the corpse, she glances over her shoulder. 'Anyway, as fun as it is talking about home, I'm more interested in killing something. Let's keep going.'

The trees open out ahead. The piles of dried bodies mound higher. Hegemon and native alike. They carpet the ground, and it takes all my effort to avoid stepping on them.

Liv has no such qualms. She takes a direct line to the clearing, crunching her way over the bones. I frown again. Her lack of respect for the dead is disappointing.

The ache in my joints and teeth intensifies as I enter the clearing. Here the sand is no longer orange but dark brown—heavy with old blood. I clench my teeth against the planet's pain. This is where the final stand was made, where the most lives were lost.

From the corner of my eye, I see Liv stumble. She must be

feeling the effects of the planet's emotions also.

She sucks in a deep breath. 'By stardust,' she curses. 'Be damned but this planet is angry.'

'Not angry,' I say. 'Anguished.'

Liv looks dubious. 'How can you tell the difference?'

'Think of worlds as mothers,' I say. 'This one has had her children murdered. She is grieving for them.'

Liv scoffs and pushes herself upright. 'It's just a planet.'

I disagree. Perhaps that is the difference between being a priestess and a murderer.

I unsheathe my terrablade and press the activation key on the hilt. My fingers tingle as the metal awakens; light racing down the length of the blade as it blazes to life and phases into the translucent, part gaseous compound that dispels spectre-plasm. The active terralight, coloured red, illuminates the clearing.

Liv's blade follows suit. I look into the wall of forest that lines the clearing.

Where are they? Where are the dead?

It doesn't take them long to arrive. The ghosts emerge from the trees like pillars of smoke. Hundreds of them. Their tall, transparent, willow-like forms are clad in bloodstained robes. Their green skin is like roughened bark. Horns, elegantly twisted into crowns, adorn their heads. All are armed with wicked looking spears.

Then I see the elder spirit that leads them. His horns are piled higher and are more elaborately woven than the rest. As he enters the circle of light thrown by the terrablades, I see that his spear is no memory, but made of true steel. I glance back at the others and frown. Every spirit's weapon is the same—very real.

The elder's voice rasps, sounding like sand grating against stone. 'Your step offends. Leave here.'

Liv answers, 'Stay down, shades. This land is no longer yours. Yield.'

I glare at her. Any experienced spirit hunter knows to speak to the dead respectfully.

The elder's teeth grind. 'We will not,' he says, 'without a fight.'

Liv grins. 'More than happy to oblige!'

Before I can diffuse the situation, Liv has rammed her blade, tip first, deep into the ground.

'*No!*' I cry. 'Gently! Or the planet will revolt!'

Liv glances at me, her eyes reflecting the red fire of her blade. Her lips peel back. 'Who cares about the damned planet? We're here to kill ghosts—so let's kill them!'

I growl in frustration. It's too late now to try a kinder approach. I whisper an apology to Amarion-5 and press the tip of my own blade into the ground. It slides through like cutting into butter. Then, feeding off the old blood in the earth, the terralight in the blade expands.

A shard of lightning hurtles into the planet's core, seeking to smother its life force. The sudden flux of the world's response hits like a hammer—a wild, desperate wave of ancient emotion that travels through the blade and into my body.

Amarion-5 gathers her deeper resources to attack. I firm my grip on the hilt of the blade. I brace my feet against the desecrated soil.

Bleed-off power from the terrablade coils across the ground. Raw and red, it carves into the ranks of advancing spirits. The ghosts fall to its touch, their screams fading as they crumble to ash.

But it isn't enough. Our work is doomed to failure. The planet fights hard; the phantoms too numerous.

Not enough time.

I hear a cry. Liv stumbles as the ground at her feet opens. Her offending blade dislodges, leaving broken edges of earth glowing red in triumph.

The planet has given her ghosts the opening they need.

Liv staggers back as the spirits reach her. She cries out, swamped.

I draw my own blade free, releasing the planet's core. I rush to Liv's aid, my boots floundering in the sand as I go.

One metre. Two metres. I'm standing over Liv. I turn the glowing, translucent length of my blade against the horde.

Their ghostly flesh presses against the knife's edge and the run of their spectre-plasm slicks my wrists. They are just memories, dying, but the priestess in me screams along with their despair.

This is no way to end the brave dead.

Liv rallies. She rises to fight by my side. Splattered spectre-plasm and the acrid smell of burning terralight surround us. We fight.

We fight.

But still we are failing…

'We need to cage them!' screams Liv as she ducks under the wicked point of a spear. The wielder falls on the edge of her blade. Another spirit takes its place. 'We have no choice!'

I curse, trying to think of an alternative solution. But the ghosts surge forward again, almost overwhelming me. I duck another spear thrust and swallow my reservations. Liv is right.

Better to end the already-dead, than join them.

'I'll go left,' I yell back.

I step to the side and drive the tip of my blade back into the ground. Again I feel the planet's recoil. I ignore the gut-deep feeling that what I am doing is wrong.

Then, with the ghosts milling alongside me, I run left, trailing my weapon in the sand.

A slice of light follows the line of the blade. Breathtaking and deadly it rises like a curtain into the desert air. Liv moves in the opposite direction. A fiery terralight glow follows in her footsteps.

We will need to meet precisely at the other end to ensure we encircle the shades.

Cage them.

I run. My leg muscles burn but I maintain focus on the end game. The sand drags at the blade and sucks at my feet. I force myself onward.

The ghosts realize what is happening. Their strident battle cry raises the hairs on my skin. I take in a deep breath and hope that whatever gods are watching will forgive what we are about to do.

The trees seem to clutch at me as I run. Their spikes bite into my shoulders. Vicious. Blood from a hundred small nicks runs down my arms and legs.

I glance over. The glow of Liv's blade keeps pace with me off to the right. The ghosts sprint, trying to overtake us. I speed up and shift direction, circling around to the right.

Moments seem like hours. The ghosts run neck-and-neck with me. I glimpse the elder spirit, his horns glowing red in the light thrown from the blades.

His gaze locks onto mine. Condemnation blazes in eyes that glitter like an animal's—green and wicked. *Your choices define you,* his scrutiny seems to say. *Murderer.*

Guilt washes through me. Unwilling to hold the weight of his unspoken accusation, I look away.

Liv emerges from the trees to my right. Her face is red, her legs pumping an uneven tattoo across the ground. We are within touching distance as we pass each other, just enough space for the light of our blades to connect.

The elder's unearthly, despairing roar makes me stumble. The wall of his soldiers strikes the terralight barrier. Their screams pierce the air as they are reduced to ash.

I turn to look at Liv. Her terrablade lies in the dust as she stands with hands on knees sucking in great breaths of air.

Then I hear another mighty roar. The elder. Over the top of the wall he emerges, the length of his spear used as a vault to clear the barrier. He lands between Liv and me. Before I can help her, the elder raises his spear. Liv only has enough time to stand upright. He plunges his weapon through her chest.

'*No!*' I run, but I'm already too late. The elder roars in victory. A spray of blood coats Liv's lips.

The murderer in me wakes. I shift the grip on my sword, every muscle in my arm tightening. My blade, its length still burning with terralight, drives through the elder's heart.

There is satisfaction in seeing his head fly back in a wordless cry. Satisfaction in watching the terralight eat away at him. In moments his body is a pillar of ash. He crumbles and is gone, motes carried away on the slight breeze.

I kneel by Liv's side. Her eyes are open and her throat works as she struggles to breathe.

'Thrice-damned ghosts,' she whispers. 'I let them get me, didn't I?'

I have nothing useful to say, no words to ease her regret.

'Did we get the rest of them?' she asks.

This I can answer. 'We did. The shades have all been dispersed.'

'The shades have *all* been dispersed?' She laughs. Another bright gush of blood washes across her chin. 'You don't know, do you? I thought maybe you did, that you thought you could trick me. But you really don't…'

I frown. 'What don't I know?'

She laughs again, this time ending on a choking cough. Her eyes squeeze shut and her hands clutch at the haft of the spear protruding from her chest. I place my hand over hers. Her skin is hot against my palm.

She grimaces and pulls away. Her eyes glitter with the

light of last life rallied.

'You didn't land on Amarion-5, Cyanna. Your ship crashed.' She bares her bloodied teeth. 'You're dead!'

I leap to my feet. My heart pounds. I look down. My body seems real. Solid. My terrablade is a heavy weight in my grasp.

'I can't be dead...' I stutter. But I don't remember my actual landing. Only the struggle of the descent through Amarion-5's atmosphere, and after that leaving the ship.

And if I still lived, her skin would not have felt so hot to me.

I step away from her, the spectre-plasm leaking rapidly out of her dying body suddenly ominous. Liv turns her head to look at me, her cheek resting against the dark sand. Her gaze, still cold, bores into mine. In her eyes I see she finds my confusion amusing.

Her voice is wet sounding, 'You have to admit it was clever of me to use you. A ghost to kill ghosts. Pretty funny, hey?'

But I don't have a sense of humour.

I don't find it funny.

Not funny at all.

My blood rages, boiling through my veins like fire. Darkness creeps in at the edges of my vision. I see, again, the innocent native spirits I just helped to disperse. I step back to Liv's side as life fades from her body. Her shade rises from the ruin of her death. She smiles when she sees me.

'Hey,' she says, flexing her fingers. 'This being dead thing isn't so bad.'

But the murderer in me surfaces again. Hot and searing, my anger burns away the morality of the priestess. I raise my weapon. The red light of its power washes over Liv's face.

'You don't deserve to linger,' I say as I plunge my terrablade through her.

Her eyes widen. Her form fractures and falls to ash.

And, when I lower my blade, it is done.

I am alone—the last left to stand as this planet's protector.

And protect her I will.

END

1730 hours: Reality Check

Cordelia Bane

When Zev finished speaking, Ori let out a disbelieving snort.

'You're talking horror stories for children. There's no such thing as magic swords and ghosts. And I know the Hegemon did some awful things back then, but that was a small group of very specific people. You can't tar the whole Alliance with the same brush.'

Cordelia leaned back as Vell placed another drink in front of her, this time a straight redwater. She didn't have enough credits to keep drinking fireon. The fickle light in the bar sparked ruby glints in the depths of the liquid.

She fingered the scar on her chin and eyed Ori. There was something about the young Grey Guard that made her want to open the kid's eyes to the universe. The lieutenant had been brought up in a privileged, Inner System world, but there was a spark there. A spark of possibility that the kid could see the corruption in the Hegemon and the Inner Systems for what it was, if the veil was stripped away.

Cordelia sipped her drink, considering her words. 'It's not always about science, sometimes you've got to consider the influences of higher powers.'

Zev sneered. 'You don't seem the religious sort.'

Cordelia considered her reply and nibbled on a steamed dumpling from a plateful Clare had brought from the refectory next door. Not bad. Salty and redolent of herbs. Best not to ask what the meat inside, was.

She shrugged. 'I'm not religious. But I've heard about shit that would make your hair curl. Three hundred and fifty-year-old stories about bat-winged, metal-skinned monsters to be precise.'

'That's a pretty specific description,' Clare said.

Cordelia smiled. 'She was a pretty specific kind of monster, that the Hegemon wanted to use for a pretty specific kind of reason.'

Monstrous in Nature

Pamela Jeffs

350 years ago

In this life, I'm strapped to an examination table. My body languishes, half alive, half dead—half formed—as part mechanical, part skeleton. My bony hands, at least, are free. I reach down and press a shuddering palm to my leg. A fire rages in my thighbone, so hot as to wring tears. If I could cry.

My touch meets new metal skin. I must have passed out during the last procedure. I don't recall them fixing another panel to my frame.

I inhale a breath into the flexible metal lungs they gave me ten days ago. Again, I ask myself, why have I been awoken from my long death?

Why am I being clothed in a living metal skin?

A human—or Terran as I've learnt they are called in this age—enters. It's the old one, Professor Gareth Mortimer. The man who applies to me his process of re-animating bones. Of re-instating movement and sensation that transfers across into the living metal. He is the violator of my natural death and the source of my pain.

My enemy.

Today, he carries a covered board. On it lies a slight mound concealed beneath cloth that shimmers blue like Earth's oceans of old.

'Morning, my dear,' he says. 'I have a gift for you.' His teeth are too white against his lips when he smiles. He reminds me of a gorgon I once knew. Not a smile to trust.

Gareth pulls a trolley closer and positions the board on it. 'Today I give you an identity. Unless you confirm, once and for all, which of the Three you are?'

I glare at him, hoping my still-skeletal face carries enough impression to convey my outrage. They have already manufactured a large part of my body, my torso, legs and arms. But my head and hands are bare bone. They are the only parts of me that belong to the old world. Those and the power of my voice.

'No?' he frowns, seemingly disappointed. 'Okay, suit yourself. Then you will get what you are given.'

His removes the fabric sheet on the board with surgical precision. A metal face emerges, polished silver, with cupid lips and long, narrowed eyes. But it is not my face. It belongs to my sister, Alecto. So, Gareth guessed my identity incorrectly. But in doing so, he has also revealed his purpose in re-forging me.

Alecto was of Anger.

That means that Gareth wants a fighter. He wants blood spilt. He wants power.

Well, he has awoken the wrong Daughter of the Night for that.

I am not the Soldier Daughter. I am the Avenger.

Or at least I was, long ago.

A small, fine-boned woman enters the room. Alice is her name. Her arrival always precedes the pain. I struggle against my bonds.

'Use the wrist straps,' says Gareth. 'And check her wings are secure.'

Alice leans over me, her eyes avoiding mine. I struggle again, straining the flexible metal sheeting of my wings against the bolts fixing them down. But it's of no use. The restraints are biolocked to his signature or Alice's. I cannot remove them. I have tried. So many times.

Alice is loyal to her job and much stronger than she seems. With my wings checked, she buckles the bracing straps around my wrists. Their leather bites into my exposed bones, pulling me down tight to the bed.

Gareth brandishes a drill, its tip wicked sharp and gleaming in the acid white lights of my prison cell.

'Here we go,' he says.

The drill bites into my iron-hard cheek bone. Bitter pain

blossoms across my skull. But I won't give these mortals the satisfaction of hearing me scream. My teeth grind against each other as the invasive sound of the tool grates.

Gareth screws the drill down deeper, the tip digging and scraping at my frame. Alice produces a cloth, dusting and cleaning away the gritty leftovers, letting them fall to the antiseptic floor.

The stench of bleach fills my nostril cavities. A stiff brush, wet with the stuff, tracks a line across my forehead. Then down my cheek. The touch is that of a rapist against my virgin bone.

Alecto's face is placed over mine with careful precision. The edges of the metal mask scrape across my sensitive bone as it settles over my eyes and sharp-edged teeth. The fit is uncomfortable and the steel burns like ice.

Gareth aligns his drill again. He pushes down on the first bolt. The sheet of metal gives slightly. Then he presses the trigger. The sharp fixing bites through steel and directly into bone.

I suck in a tortured breath. A part of me wishes he would just kill me. It's my last thought as the kindness of darkness claims me again.

#

I awaken to agony. My wrists are no longer bound, but my cheeks ache with a weight like ancient winters. I have no wish to touch my new face. It represents a symbol of forced change, of identity stolen. I do not weep, for it is not the nature of my kind, but in this moment, I do long for the company of my two sisters. Or, better yet, the embrace of Gaea; the warm darkness of my mother's breast.

The laboratory is quiet. I lift my head briefly, ignoring the pain. The humans are still in the room, huddled around the computer consoles built outside the glass barrier of my cell.

Their faces glow sickly pale in the light of the screens. Their voices mutter and murmur, a jumbled mess of quiet words. But their tone seems happy. The experiments on me have been a success. I curl my fingers. Nails press against my palm. A new steel palm.

So they gave me hands today, also. I inspect them, disappointed to see the details are wrong. The nails I have been given are smooth and rounded like a human's. When I was myself, my nails were ebony claws.

But at least the drills might quiet now I am complete.

Doctor Gareth notices I am awake. He locks his gaze onto mine. He smiles his gorgon smile then stretches his arms over his head. The dark brown residue of my powdered bone still mars the front of his white lab-coat.

'Let's call it a night, guys,' he says. 'Great work today. I'll tidy up here. You can all head back to the dorms.'

Gareth thinks he has achieved great work? All he has done is won a dangerous enemy.

I scowl, nursing my hatred as his scientists file out of the room. I notice Alice glancing over her shoulder at me. For the first time ever, her gaze finds mine. There is strength in it— the strength I've always recognised in her, but there is also something else.

Connection.

Then she passes. And I am left to wonder who exactly she is.

Gareth enters my cell. He moves so smoothly, a slick of slime probably follows in his wake. His touch is warm as he tracks one finger down the new, sleek metallic skin of my cheek. I shudder.

'Earth's mythology has always depicted you as a monster. But not anymore. My dear, I have made you beautiful.'

I scowl, feeling my face move and mould to express it—a strange, unfamiliar sensation after my expressions before being tied to rigid bone.

Gareth frowns. 'Come now,' he says. 'That makes you look just plain ugly.'

If he undid the belts holding me down, I would show him just how ugly I could truly be.

He looks down at my body, his eyes appreciating the lines he has created.

'Look,' he says. 'We don't have to be enemies. I knew it was you, Alecto, the moment I saw your bones on Mount Olympus. And I saw the potential of our union. Speak to me, please. You owe it to me. I have given back a life taken from you centuries ago.'

He is alone and wants me to talk. The time is right to do so. I carefully weave my magic into my words, not the magic of righteous death I would usually deal to the guilty, but threads of truth and of justice.

A trial before the judgement.

'I am not Alecto.'

Gareth's eyebrows shoot up at the rich, baritone sound of my voice. 'Then who?'

I ease more power into my words. I have my own questions to be answered. 'Where are my sisters?'

Gareth scratches the side of his nose. He seems unaware of my influence. 'You were found with one other skeleton like yours on the mountain,' he says. 'But it was crushed beyond repair. You were bought here alone.'

Alone? And one of my sisters lay alongside me, unrecoverable? Which one? Where is the other?

'Why am I here?'

Gareth blinks like a wide-eyed deer. He is completely in my thrall. 'The Hegemon knows you are one of the ancient Earth Erinyes—a Greek Fury.'

'Who are the Hegemon?'

'An intragalactic government with and interest in economic trade.'

'What do they want from me?

'They intend to use you and your powers as a weapon.'

'But I am not interested in fighting.'

'What you want doesn't matter.'

'But I am a goddess.'

'Once, maybe. But to them you are a myth. An immortal skeleton covered in sheet metal. Power is the currency of this age. You are owned. You are property. You will be the weapon that defines the future of the galaxy.'

'What future?'

'Apocalypses,' whispers Gareth, his eyelids almost closed. 'Your strength will be used to cull worlds. Worlds where mining grey fuel is profitable—fuel to power starships. You will be sent in as Mistress of the Slaughter, First General of the Hegemon Armies. You will destroy civilisations so other, greater ones can rise.'

'That is murder.'

'No. That's the Hegemon's plan to ensure their continued business interests.'

'They cannot force me to do it.'

Gareth taps his temple. 'You have a purpose-built control chip in there,' he says. 'They will make you do it.'

Shocked, I drop the threads of persuasive power fortifying my voice.

Gareth blinks as his mind clears. His forehead furrows and his eyes narrow. 'Okay, you need to tell me right now. Which Fury are you?'

Still possessed of the image of ravaged worlds, I answer without thinking, 'Tisiphone,' I say. 'The wrong sister to have resurrected for killing innocents.'

'Tisiphone. Avenger of the Murdered.' His mouth screws into a knot. 'How ironic. But I guess it makes no difference. You will do the job you're built for. And if you rebel, they will dismantle you. Either way, I get paid.'

A chill creeps down my spine.

As Gareth turns to leave, I remind myself who I am.

I am a goddess of vengeance and retribution.

I will never become the monster they wish me to be.

But, as the weight of my metal limbs settles around me, I wonder if I really have a choice.

#

The solitude and silence of the laboratory is welcome. It allows me the space to mull over my situation. Possibilities circle my mind, manifest and are rejected. I must find a way to escape.

A noise at the far end of the room catches my attention. I lift my head, straining against my bonds. In the far, shadowed corner of the room, a sliver of light breaks the darkness then shutters off. A door opening then closing. A silhouette passes behind the computers and steps into the light.

It's Alice.

She presses her access card to the panel by my cell door. The glass slides open and she steps in. Again I feel the spark of connection as her gaze falls on mine.

Alice speaks first. Her voice is hard, like steel. 'I know you can talk. And you must understand that your powers will have no effect on me.' Her expression softens. 'How are you feeling?'

'Better if I were not here.'

Alice nods. Her ebony hair, tied back in a ponytail, shines as she moves. Her eyes narrow. 'I am sorry for the trials you have suffered, but I had no choice. I needed you alive.'

I've endured too much to trust this woman. 'Who are

you?'

Alice's mouth turns down. She moves to my side, her fingers tracing the dome headed bolts that fix my wings to the table's top. 'Do you remember the day you died?'

The memories of that time are hazy at best. Something about decimation and ruin. 'No.'

'You destroyed your own sister that day. You pulverised her bones against the rocks of your homeland.'

An image of my sibling, Megaera, blossoms before my eyes. Broken winged, green-blooded, and lying dead on a cliff-top. 'I killed her?'

Alice nods. 'And there was no shame in it, Tisiphone. You did what needed to be done. She betrayed her purpose, despairing at the shortcomings of humanity. She called upon you to join her—to end the Terran race and along with it, every heartache you existed to avenge. You killed her, but she injured you so critically you died, also. Before anyone found or could save you.' She sighs. 'Do you not recall?'

Alice's knowledge of both my name and my past unsettles me. How can a human know such things? 'Who are you?' I ask again.

'Look harder. Do you truly not know?'

I don't. Her features are unfamiliar to me. But that means nothing. Centuries of death have left my memory fragmented. 'No.'

Alice bites her bottom lip. She pulls a tool from the trolley. 'How about we let you up to get a better look?'

The bio-wrench she holds against the living metal of my

wings feels cold. *Scrape. Scrape.* Alice undoes the first bolt, then the next. Soon my wings are free. I surge upright, feeling my old bones and new metal tendons stretch and move in my new body. I raise my wings high, their tips scraping gouges into the ceiling. Alice helps me off the table. I can't believe I'm free. It's too good to be true.

'What do you expect from me?' I ask.

Alice gently turns me to face her. Her green eyes bore into the metal orbs that make mine. Something. Something deep in her gaze awakens a memory. Of ebony wings, of gods and clear skies. Of rage.

Recognition blossoms like the sun.

My sister. The third of three. The Fury of Constant Anger.

'Alecto! Is it truly you?'

My sister's cold façade breaks, her predator smile is one I am most glad to see. Then it fades.

'I am sorry, sister,' she says, 'to have put you through all of this. But it was necessary.'

Her mood darkens mine. 'Of what do you speak?'

'I have been alone in the world. Keeping the course has been difficult, but I have managed until now. But the universe as you knew it has changed; galaxies have opened and a multitude of alien species have been discovered. But this growth has been detrimental.

'The despair and evil we once fought together are now compounded. And in our sister's stead, others work toward achieving what she wished for.'

'The destruction of civilisations?'

Alecto nods. 'And our home, Earth, is on that list. Other planets will follow.'

'And your plan to solve this includes me?'

'Yes. But I couldn't waken you. Not until I found Gareth in the Hegemon's Galaxy Collaborative University. An arrogant man with a dark soul. But a man with an interest in the mythology of our perished sister. I learnt the Hegemon had enlisted him for illicit work.

'So I joined his team and helped develop the Living Metal technology. Then I fed him stories that led him to your bones. I even suggested you might be me, the dark goddess of his dreams. He was all too willing to follow the clues and find you.'

The far door to the laboratory opens, a knife-edged glare carving through the intimate darkness. A silhouette cuts the glare—tall, lanky.

Gareth.

'What are you doing, Alice?' he snarls, stepping into the circle of light beyond my clear prison walls. 'She is dangerous. She needs to be restrained.' He reaches the first computer console and stabs at a button. The door lock panel bleeps to red.

Alecto's face ripples in frustration. A brief flash of needle-sharp teeth and luminous red eyes. Then her human mask settles back into place.

'Unlock the door, Gareth,' she says, quietly, calmly. But her voice is not the one to hold the power of influence.

'You are out of your fecking mind if you think I am going

to do that.'

I step up to the glass. 'You have nothing to fear from me, Gareth. Open the door. Please.'

The professor's eyes droop. 'Stop it,' he murmurs.

I push into his mind, inexorable. 'Release the lock.'

Gareth's hand twitches. He fights me, but his mental strength is mist-thin against the might of my power. He falters. His face hangs slack and pale in the ghostly luminescence.

'Release the lock,' he whispers, his mind lost in more ways than one.

Gareth's finger drops. The lock indicator turns green. The bolt slithers back into the frame with a quiet *shush*.

Alecto stalks past me. A predator with her eye on prey. Her fingers lengthen as she moves, her pale fingernails blurring into razor-sharp ebony claws.

I almost feel sorry for Gareth as he stands, unable to defend himself.

My sister's claws strike, carried on the strength of her righteous purpose. Gareth's windpipe pops wetly as it is torn clear of his throat.

The professor stands swaying. Being merciful, I hold him under my thrall. His eyes remained fixed, uncaring of the mortal blow dealt him.

I hold him until his legs give out and his body slumps to the blood-soaked linoleum. Still, I hold until his heart beats its last beat.

Then I let him go—a bundle of slack bones and withered skin.

Alecto's eyes are two bright coals. 'He did not deserve that mercy, sister,'

'A gift to him for returning me to you.'

She seems unconvinced. Her gaze slews to the lax corpse. 'The others will return, soon. We need to leave.'

I glance at the far door, still open and spewing light into the laboratory. Already footsteps echo down the corridor beyond. 'Lead the way then.'

Alecto shakes her head. 'We must destroy the computers. All research into Living Metal is filed there. It is too dangerous to leave behind. We cannot afford others to be raised from the dead.'

I shudder. Ancient gods and goddesses, re-woken, would wreak havoc in this time.

'Then we burn it,' I say. 'We burn it all.'

Alecto smiles, her grin painted wild with glee. She clicks her fingers and a flame erupts, cupped in the cradle of her palm.

'It's good to have you back, sister.'

#

Midnight. We alight on a mountain plateau due east of the shadowed valley where the burning Hegemon facility huddles. From here the flames consuming the buildings and the remains of Gareth's team gleam as a red-gold pyre against the indigo backdrop. A crumbling of metal and stone into ash that swirls, glittering, high into the night sky. There is something satisfying in witnessing the demise of the place that re-birthed me. A wrong made right.

'It is done,' I say, watching the flames.

'It is,' replies Alecto. 'And their backups and records on the Hegemon Core computer destroyed as well. None survive who can tell of your return.'

'What now?' I ask.

My sister's eyes remain trained on the distant brightness. Her hand grasps mine, long claws extended to press against my palm. Her wings, two black scythes, arc over her back, their soft leather panels rippling like oil in the cool night breeze. 'Now we save worlds.'

'How?'

Alecto turns, the lines of her face furrowed with an ancient weariness. 'We combine our powers. Then we negotiate with the Hegemon authorities and convince them that planetary extermination in the search for their grey fuel is not the answer.'

She throws her shoulders back. 'And if they resist, we stand by our purpose. We avenge the innocent. Already so many crimes need to be answered for.'

Her magic stays soft as it encircles me. Where my power is the influence over words, hers is the language of images. 'Look and stand witness. See why this fight is imperative.'

Her images pour into my mind. Grey-edged, bleak and sharp.

Alien battlefields littered with corpses of strange beings.

Living forests torn free from their roots.

Oceans swelling with the bloated bodies of dead creatures.

And powerful leaders on thrones built of coin and blood.

I reel in shock, this modern philosophy of existence beyond my ability to recognise.

'And these creatures call *us* monstrous,' I whisper. 'Of course I will help you.'

'And, when we are done, perhaps both of us can rest in peace,' says Alecto, her demeanour grim.

'That time will come,' I say.

But as her images still circle my mind, I wonder if our ancient skills will ever be enough to turn the torrent and the tide.

END

1745 hours: A History Lesson

Ori Bligh

'Goddesses!' Ori grimaced. 'That's got to be the product of flip psychosis. Someone stayed too long in the flipvoid. Went crazy. No way can that be real.'

Zev dragged his finger through a ring of water left on the table by his drink. 'The galaxy is a big place. Weird shit happens. Can't deny the Hegemon stopped using grey fuel about three hundred years ago. That's only fifty years after that goddess.'

'Nah.' Ori sipped at her drink and ate a dumpling. This definitely had to be the last drink or she'd be hung over in the morning when it came time to officially be registered as on duty. 'They switched to rich water fuel because of the planetary rebellions against grey fuel mining.'

Cordy sent her a cynical look and Clare chuckled.

'What?' Ori spread her hands. 'I'll bet most of that stuff about monsters and goddesses came from the great flip psychosis two hundred years ago.'

She tapped at her temple. 'People thought they saw all kinds of strange crap. One of my ancestors was an astrophysicist and trader. And her mother was a medic who worked with Hegemon medics trying to find a cure for flip psychosis.

'I still have a holo recording the astrophysicist made when the Hegemon seconded her to help them find a drive to replace flipping. She was a scientist and I still don't believe what she says. Had to be psychosis.'

'The Hegemon seconded a trader?' Cordy raised her brows. 'Seems strange. They don't get on all that well. Traders aren't known for obeying the Hegemon Economic Alliance rules. What'd she do for them?'

Ori grinned. 'Not quite what they expected.'

The Stars Like Sand

Aiki Flinthart

200 years ago

When a hunch is wrong, you're an idiot; right and you're a hero. I scowled at my calculations. The math said I should be an idiot. But the presence of Arma, the green planet sailing serenely through this system—where it absolutely shouldn't be—suggested otherwise. I had no time for heroes, but finding Arma did bring us one step closer to a solution. Maybe.

And we needed a solution. If wormhole tech could replace flipdrives we could save thousands of trade families and Hegemon personnel.

Someone whispered my name. I glanced over my shoulder, but the astro lab was empty. Just me, the outdated astro computer and the scuffed grey plascrete surfaces of an exploration ship with years of service under her belt and minimal maintenance.

I rubbed at my eyes. Too many hours and too little sleep.

'Sarva.' Barrett's resonant voice crackled over the ship's com. 'Incoming call on secure line from Luna Base.'

I ran a hand over my buzz-cut hair and straightened, my back crackling. Contact from Luna could only mean one person and the expense of such a call made it worrying. 'I'll take it here.'

'Then Gav wants your help with a fluctuation in the flipdrive regulator. He said you'd be familiar with the older model we're using.'

I rolled my eyes but said nothing. The implication that my trader-family was too poor to upgrade their drive wasn't worth correcting. We'd upgraded a year ago. But Gav was a planet-born earther to the bone.

'Oh,' Barrett added, 'and the captain wants that report asap. In person. Take the shuttle as soon as you're done with your call.'

'Right,' I acknowledged, only half-listening. A tap on the screen switched the display from the astro charts to the long-distance comms screen.

My mother's familiar face flickered into view, the low-res image skipping and warping with interference. She must be using the cheapest call option. My heart contracted. She looked so much thinner than when I'd left, a month before. Her hair was almost grey and the circles beneath her eyes were dark bruises against pale, lined skin.

'Ma?' I wasted no words. Spacers rarely did. Air was a luxury and cross-galaxy calls insanely so.

Her lips stretched into an almost-smile. 'They're sending us on another trade run. Tomorrow. We can't afford to stay on Luna any longer.'

I gripped the edge of the plascrete desk. 'Damn them! There's too much risk of flipdrive psychosis. You had funds for another six months. What happened?'

Her shoulders slumped as though all her fifty years had descended on her at once. 'Price hikes. With everything in such short supply, the few trader families still allowed to flip can charge whatever they like for the goods they bring from the colony planets. You know your father. He's willing to take the risk.'

She sighed. 'But there are fewer traders each week that can or will. The flipdrive psychosis is spreading. Faster than the med sector thought, even.'

'Any news on why?'

A frown deepened the creases between her brows. 'I've been over and over our flip records—and those of every other trader in the sector. Of course the Hegemon Core won't give me access to the Grey Guard ship records, so I don't know what's happening with their crews.

'But none of the traders stay long enough in the flipvoid to cause the sensory deprivation insanity—the psychosis. We're all careful that way. Multiple short flipvoid hops. It must be some sort of disease we're picking up in the void.'

I twisted my mouth. 'I'm the wrong person to ask, Ma. I'm an astrophysicist who dabbles in flipdrive physics. You're the medic. But it's no wonder the Hegemon is panicking. With all the new colonies, the trade families were stretched even before this pandemic.'

I snorted. 'And the Hegemon was putting more pressure on us to fulfil impossible trade demands. Like driving the traders to exhaustion would actually help.'

She stilled, her gaze thoughtful. Then she rubbed a thin hand over her face. 'I'm sure they'll work it out. I've been helping the medics here, trying to find a reason or a cure. I'm sure I'm close to something, too.'

'Surely they'll let you stay if they know you might have a solution?'

Shaking her head, she spread her hands. 'Money talks. It's either another trade run or we go down to Earth. And gravity's a drag.'

I managed a wan smile at the oldest spacer pun in the galaxy. 'If we bring back this wormhole tech, will we have the funds to refit?'

She grimaced. 'We'll have to. The *Roadrunner* has carried our family for close on two hundred years. Will do again, once you get back. The wormhole tech you're chasing sounds so promising. Make sure you get it from those people.' She frowned, fingering the medic's badge on her lapel. 'But don't hurt anyone.'

'I don't have a lot of say in who gets hurt, Ma,' I said. 'The Grey Guard seconded me for this mission the minute I posted my findings on the Hegemon Core computer database. They're running the show. If they want to force these people to give up their tech, I don't think I can stop them.'

I pressed my lips thin and studied her sunken eyes. 'Not sure I want to, anyway. I'll do whatever it takes to keep you and Dad safe and in space.'

My mother stiffened and touched her badge of office again, her frown deepening.

I changed the subject. 'Where are they sending you? On trade, I mean?'

'Delta sector somewhere.' She shrugged.

'That's a full ten flips!' I blurted. 'It will trigger the psychosis for sure.'

My mother lifted her chin, her eyes steely. 'We're spacers, Sarva. Earthers think we're weak because we've adapted to low grav. But we're tough. You know that.'

'Toughest there is,' I replied automatically, finishing our family mantra.

'Space is in our blood and bones. Flipping's part of us, and we of it. When you get back, we'll be waiting, I promise. Go.' But tears glinted in her eyes and her hand trembled as she reached for the end-call control.

The screen blanked into grey snow. I swore and threw my stylus aside. It rebounded off the wall with a *ting* and spun lazily back, slow in the ship's quarter-grav. I caught and snapped the stylus into its bracket out of habit then stared out the window at the swathe of sharp stars stabbing through the endless black.

My fingers curled into fists. Dammit! I pushed off the desk and covered the floor space of the tiny lab in four long paces.

'Sarv?' Barrett's disembodied voice interrupted. 'Cap's waiting for your signal. His exact words were: *Get her arse into the shuttle and down to the surface, now.*'

'Acknowledged.' I snatched up my dress jacket then hesitated with one arm half in the sleeve. 'Wait. Why?'

'Wouldn't say,' he replied. 'He said to send you and only you.'

'But I'm not fit to go planetside.' I frowned at the blank screen. 'I can give that report over comms. What's he need an astrophysicist for? Isn't he negotiating with the Empress or something?'

'Just go, Sarva,' Barrett's tone held wry weariness. 'We all know what you are. If he's asked for you, it must be important.'

I cut the connection before I said something I'd regret, and shoved my arm into the other sleeve. My throat thickened. I liked Barrett. But after two months working with him and the other six crew on the *Tornado,* I'd still not earned enough respect for them to overlook my spacer history.

Even though my calculations led us to this lost colony and the chance to investigate the wormhole-generating tech these people were rumoured to have, it wasn't enough to overcome an earther's disdain for the spacer-born.

Swearing every step of the way, I hurried to the shuttle.

#

'Reporting, Captain Zoya.' I stood before his desk and tried to ignore the aches in my knees and back; the trembling of my thighs under Arma's four-fifths gravity. I could feel my spine compressing.

Sucking the humid, dirt-scented air into my lungs hurt and I coughed before continuing. 'Regarding Arma's location, sir, I still can't explain why it's here. But I guess that's why it's been lost for a few hundred years.'

Zoya nodded at a chair and I sank gratefully into it. He sat rigidly in another and frowned at me. The Arma'ans had set him up as a guest in a house near to where our first shuttle had landed, five days before. Just a simple dome of stone, as all their houses were, but full of natural materials unheard of on Earth for hundreds of years.

I ran my hands over the sensuously-smooth timber chair and snuck looks out the warped glass at the actual trees, scattered thickly between dome-houses of red stone and more timber. The Arma'an people were low-tech: no steel highrises, no planetary defences, no aircraft. Nothing but small towns, agriculture and animal-powered vehicles.

And the sky.

I squinted. So very blue, shading into green. Not a star in sight, except the orange sun. It made me feel claustrophobic and agoraphobic at the same time. Vids were nothing compared to seeing the real thing.

'The report was just an excuse to get you down here,' Zoya growled. 'I need your help, Sarva.' He rubbed his fingers repeatedly over his thumbs, his frown deepening.

'Sir?' I swiped a hand over my head and tried to ignore a growing pressure; a not-quite-headache in the back of my skull.

'You're a civilian.' He tugged on his severe grey uniform jacket and cleared his throat. 'But you're also part of my crew. And you know what's at stake here.' He leaned forward, into a beam of sunlight, the grey at his temples bright against his short, dark hair. 'We need these people to give us their wormhole tech.'

He frowned out the window. 'Though I'm beginning to doubt it exists. I haven't seen anything to even *hint* at an ability to travel through space in any form. Damned backward plebs, the lot of them.'

'Yes, sir.' I studied the restless motion of his hands and drew my own conclusions. He'd been here five days and hadn't yet been called before the Empress to negotiate. He was desperate. The far-reaching Hegemon was desperate.

Without an alternative to flipdrives the Hegemon's fleets of traders and their military escorts were useless chunks of metal, plascrete, and carbon nanotubes. Economies, communications, worlds, lives depended on the network of merchant spacers—and the Grey Guards' protection. My family. The Captain's career. So much rode on the success of this trip that my head spun.

I sucked a heavy breath and braced myself. If he was anxious enough to call me down, this wasn't going to be good news.

'They want you,' he said baldly, glaring.

I blinked. 'What? I don't understand. Who want me?'

He flapped a dismissive hand. 'Not you, by name. But you're the only one that fits their criteria.'

I raised my brows and waited. The pressure in my head mounted, becoming a drone of noise, almost like a deep, slow voice slurring incomprehensible words.

'The Empress won't speak to anyone who hasn't been purified in some damned-fool pseudo-religious ritual.'

'And?' There had to be more or he'd have gone through the ritual himself.

'And they'll only talk to a female of child-bearing age.' He grimaced. 'Apparently they view them as the most valuable members of a society. Damned backward colonials. You're the only non-essential crewmember that fits the bill.'

My fingers tightened on the wooden armrest until the edges bit into my skin. I chewed on the words I wanted to spit at him. Non-essential? I was the one who'd got us here; found the planet that would save the fecking Hegemon and make his retirement possible. Now I was reduced to the importance of reproductive organs?

He held up a hand. 'Don't ask me why. I don't know. But this is our only chance, Sarva.' He scrubbed lean fingers over his head. His gaze slid down my over-slender frame. 'I can't force you. And, believe me, if I could send someone—'

'Not a spacer you mean?' I said, curling a lip.

He shrugged one shoulder. '—not as…breakable, I would.' He glanced out the window. 'Shit. The temple delegate is here. Decision time. Will you?'

I struggled to my feet. The air was molasses and the ground a quagmire, sucking at my legs. Every bone ached already and the low droning deep in my brain just wouldn't stop. But, apparently, I was tough. Who was I to disagree with my mother?

'Sir.'

'Good. I'll make sure you get a significant share of royalties from sales of the new wormhole tech.'

'Define "significant", sir. On record, if you will,' I said levelly. 'And they go to my family if I…don't make it.'

He raised a weary brow. 'Trader to the bone, huh? Let's say enough that your family's ship will have their drive installed free and will get first shot at five prime trade routes.'

I swallowed and tried to keep my face calm. Five trade routes. That meant my parents would be able to keep enough profit to buy a second and third ship and never go planetside again.

'Deal,' I managed.

'Oh.' Zoya reached into his desk drawer and pulled out an injection pen and a translator collar. More sophisticated than the normal comms gauntlet most people used. 'Here.'

The collar I clipped around my throat with shaking fingers. It sat uncomfortably over my voicebox, warm and faintly vibrating. I pressed the pen to the mastoid bone, behind my right ear, and pushed the button. Wincing at the sharp pain, I worked my jaw and fingered the lump under the skin where the aural translator now sat.

He nodded. 'Shipboard computer has translated thousands of language recordings over the last five days. The local language is derived from a couple of Indian dialects from Earth. The language has shifted in the last few hundred years, but the computer compensated. Hopefully. Try it.'

'I...I don't know what to say,' I stammered. The box at my throat emitted a liquid, sing-song string of sounds in a feminine voice far more sultry than my own. I flushed.

'Here. You'll need this.' He thrust a medipack at me. 'Analgesics and sleeping pills, along with water sterilizers, immune boosters, antihistamines, and multispectrum antibios.'

I accepted it.

'And this.' He handed me a palm-sized scanner. 'A bit old-school but easier to hide than the new glove-comm. Use it to scan any tech you find. Send the data straight to the ship's processor.'

'Anything else, sir?'

Zoya shook his head. 'Only that you'll be taken to the Temple of the Sushum.' He pointed out the window at the tallest stone dome, protruding above the canopy. 'The ritual is supposed to take between a day and a month, depending on how you handle it.'

'A month!' I gulped and clutched the medipack to my chest. 'I can't survive that long here, even at only four-fifths grav.' Admitting my physical limitations to an earther went against the grain, but he needed to know.

Zoya's jaw hardened. His dark eyes glittered. 'We don't

have that long, anyway. It's not common knowledge, but the rate the psychosis pandemic is spreading means the Hegemon only has enough flipship pilots for about four more months' worth of trade. It takes longer than that to train decent navigators and pilots to replace the sick ones. After that, the Hegemon collapses into chaos.'

He paused to let that sink in then added, 'I've sent a message to Headquarters. They're expecting to hear back within two days.'

'What if I haven't seen the Empress by then?' My heart stuttered.

'Two gunships are due here in three days.'

I gaped, speechless and glanced out the window at the peaceful town. There were over three million people on this planet. My mother's words echoed in my head. Was I prepared to let the Hegemon kill millions of innocent people in order to save the precious trade network—and my family? I ground my teeth, tasting resentment. Two days. I had two lousy days.

The Captain held out a hand. 'Good luck. I expect twice-daily reports. If we don't hear from you, we'll take this fecking planet by force when the gunners arrive.' Distaste passed over his face. 'But I'd rather not go down in history for genocide.'

'Then you shouldn't have joined the Grey Guards,' I said grimly.

Enjoying his startled expression, I shuffled out the door.

#

Spacers live with mortality embedded in their daily thoughts. Emptiness and death outside a ship, minimalism and life inside; separated only by a thin wall. Our lives were simple and complicated all at once.

Here, on the planet, there was no clean awareness of death. There was only overwhelming complexity. Life in all its forms sought to engulf me as I exited the Captain's dwelling. Every breath of unfiltered air. Every step on the filthy, cobblestone street. So much life and open air. I resolutely ignored the vast sky above.

I was grateful to be transported to the Temple of Sushum in a closed carriage, drawn by what could only be horses, if my memory of old Earth animals was right. The swaying and jolting over stone-paved roads made my spine and pelvis hurt. The heat, and the clamour of people speaking, singing, and shouting outside in the streets, made my head ache.

I lifted a red silk curtain and watched the chaos of colour and sound. The smell of over-ripe fruit and horse-dung. The reedy wail of a musical instrument. We were passing through a marketplace of brightly-striped tents, their tables piled high with strange fruits and shimmering fabrics. It became too overwhelming and I had to close my eyes.

I slipped an analgesic tablet under my tongue and tucked the medikit back into a thigh pocket. But, by the time I was ushered into the Temple of Sushum's towering stone dome, I could barely think straight or even breathe.

Thin trails of blue smoke rose from incense sticks embedded into pots of sand outside the temple's bronze doors.

The sick-sweet scent almost made me gag. I swallowed saliva and struggled up the stone steps.

The temple doors closed behind me with an ominous bang and I stopped, trying to get my bearings. With the closing of the door, all sound from the town's cacophony stopped. But pain hammered at my skull from the inside and I swallowed again. Vomiting on the temple delegate would be an undiplomatic start to things.

My eyes adjusted to the gloom and the temple's interior took shape. Overhead, the red stone roof vaulted in a perfect, self-supporting dome. In the centre of the white-stone floor lay a huge depiction of a silvery serpent, coiled tightly in on itself, surrounded by a thick black-stone circle. From the middle rose a black plinth. A white cloth covered whatever sat on it, leaving only lumps and bumps that my imagination couldn't interpret.

Around the walls were a series of paintings, all connected by a sinuous, blue-grey line; perhaps a river. Images of people dancing, of green-blue planets, of houses and unfamiliar trees, of various different starry night skies. Apart from those and the plinth, the room was empty and bare.

I turned in a slow circle, listening for footsteps or voices. Nothing. Hopefully they would send someone soon and I could lie down. In the huge silence, the not-quite-audible rumbling in my head threatened to overpower what little sense I could muster.

'Namass.'

I jumped and barely registered the translation to 'Hello' in my ear.

Turning, I looked down at a slim, dark-eyed, older woman, who pressed her hands together and bowed. Awkwardly, I returned the gesture, my bones protesting. Spacers were always tall and thin but I towered a full head and a half over this woman.

Normally, amongst earthers, my height gave me a sense of power, false though that might be. Here, I just felt uncomfortable and gangly, unco-ordinated beside her grace and economy of movement.

The contrast was heightened by our clothing. She wore something complicated and flowing in a stunning shade of dark purple, edged with gold embroidery. I wore practical spacer-grey overalls with my formal grey dress jacket. She had presence and elegance I envied. She bowed again and a long, grey-streaked braid slipped over her shoulder.

'Kusuma,' she said, pointing to herself. My earpiece translated that as 'flower'. It seemed more likely to be a personal name, so I repeated the word as she'd said it and she nodded, smiling.

'Sarva Blythe,' I laid a hand on my chest. A string of liquid sounds emerged from my throat-mike.

Her eyes widened and she sucked a quick breath. She stepped closer, peering into my face. 'You are the one who found our world, yes?'

I nodded.

'It is good.' She smiled, her heavy eyelids drooping. 'I am pleased the Captain sent you, not another. We knew only that the Seeker was female and of childbearing age.'

'The Seeker?' The capital letter was, somehow, audible.

Kusuma nodded. 'That is the term for one who finds us through the sushum.' The translator supplied a meaningless definition. A tube of some sort running down the spine. 'You're only the second in three hundred years.'

I smiled politely. 'I found you through the starcharts and a computer.'

Her chuckle was liquid and, earther or not, I couldn't help relaxing under the sun of her openness. But every muscle ached and every lungful of scented air was like breathing in water. I just wanted to lie down.

Kusuma strolled towards the decorated walls and ran her fingers over a painting of two people standing in this very room, their arms uplifted and a great light surrounding what might be the plinth.

She glanced back at me and tilted her head. 'How, exactly, did you find us?'

'I…' I shrugged, still studying the picture. 'I was going through some old star charts and light wavelength analyses, looking for hints of wormhole technology. I saw a reference to Arma and saw the signature for an active, stable wormhole in its data. When I couldn't find it in the current Alpha five-seven charts, I tried Beta seven-three on a hunch.'

'A hunch.' She sent me a dry look. 'There are hundreds of possible sectors and millions of stars, yet you believe you just happened to look in the right place, first off?' She strode back and peered into my face. 'You're a scientist. A mathematician.

What are the odds of that?'

'What are you saying?' I moved a pace back. The thick floral notes of her perfume made my stomach churn again.

She laid a hand on the covered plinth. '*We* called you here, Sarva. Through the sushum that binds us all—spacers, especially are sensitive to the sushum.'

'Called me? That's ridiculous.' I rubbed at the ache in the back of my head, certainty melting beneath her calm. 'How, then? And why?'

'We need a second pilot.' Her fingertips danced lightly over the odd shapes hidden beneath the white cloth.

'That makes no sense. You don't have any spaceships. Unless they're well-hidden.' What lay beneath that white covering? Could that be the tech I was after? But how? The sort of machinery that would plausibly open a stable wormhole couldn't possibly fit on a plinth I could get my arms around.

'Not in the sense that you understand them, no.'

'Look.' I folded my arms. 'I'm here to speak with the Empress about wormhole technology. Millions of people depend on the trader families and the Hegemon. We need new drives for our ships or those people will die of starvation. We have two days before the Hegemon sends gunships, so I don't have a lot of time for riddles.'

Kusuma sent me a cool, amused look, reminding me forcibly of my mother. My cheeks warmed and I cleared my throat. I wasn't trained as a diplomat, my skull throbbed like a disruptor was being fired into my brain, and I couldn't shake the feeling that someone kept saying my name, over and over, just out of hearing. I opened my mouth to apologise.

Kusuma cocked her head as though listening. 'I must leave you for a moment. I'll be back to explain.' She waved a graceful hand. 'Please make yourself at home.' Without waiting, she glided from the room, leaving me standing awkwardly in the vast chamber.

There were no chairs.

'Shit.' The word echoed in a whisper back at me. That hadn't gone well. Plan B, perhaps? I pulled the hand scanner out of my pocket, glanced around, and lifted the white cloth covering the plinth.

Beneath lay a beautifully-carved wooden sculpture of what might be a dragon, but without wings—just a sinuous, scaled body, eyes, and some serious teeth and claws. A quick scan showed nothing of use.

Embedded inside the sculpture was some rudimentary electronics. Possibly a communication device of some sort. But communications with who? Other temples across the world was the most likely answer. Probably just used to control information so only the temple staff could spread news to the population.

I sneered. A standard earther technique for population manipulation. Keep them uninformed and uneducated. Dependent on religion. Disappointing, but not unexpected in what was essentially a primitive, feudal society.

I was wasting my time. The temple was the most complex architecture in this town. Whatever had caused the wormhole signature on the scans wasn't coming from any technology these people had. I should get back to the ship and hunt for something else.

'Ah!'

I jumped at the sound of Kusuma's gentle exclamation behind me.

'Don't *do* that!' I said.

'I see you found the transmitter.' She stepped forward to pat the wooden dragon lovingly. 'It hasn't been used for a hundred years or so. But it's almost time.'

'Time for what?' My curiosity got the better of sense.

Her smile widened. 'For you to help us move house.'

With a glance around at the stone temple, and another at my thin, elongated arms, I laughed. 'I think you have the wrong person.'

'Come. Sit.' She gestured toward a pair of sleek silver-metal stools that rose soundlessly from the floor.

Gaping, I lowered myself gingerly into one, half-expecting it to slide back into the stone. Was there more technological sophistication to this place than I'd thought? More than the scanner had picked up?

'Are you prepared to open your mind, now?' Kusuma tilted her head like a small, brown bird.

I shelved antagonism and swallowed pride. If there was even a slim chance I could help my mother and the other trader families, I had to.

'You said you needed a pilot? Why?'

She settled herself in the chair, smoothing her skirts. 'We knew the Hegemon would find us, eventually. They claim they want an alternative to the flipdrive. But what we have they cannot take. This world is part of the blood system of the galaxy. Part of the sushum—the wormhole network. There are so few left and it is our job to protect this one.'

I sucked a sharp breath. 'Network. So there *is* a method of generating stable wormholes? How? You have to tell me.' I leaned forward.

She studied me for a long moment. 'This is important to you, isn't it? Why?'

'It's important to everyone,' I said, shortly. 'Flip psychosis is killing the trader families. We need an alternative to the flipdrive.'

'Do you? Really?' Her mouth twisted into a regretful smile.

I hesitated, frowning. Acid burned in my stomach. I swallowed down a bitter, impulsive reply and said, 'The Hegemon gunships are already enroute. If you don't agree to give them your wormhole generation tech, the Grey Guard will kill you all. They're that desperate.'

'We know they're coming. And we know why, even if you don't,' Kusuma said, placidly. She flicked her long braid back over her shoulder. 'That's why we called you.'

'Still not making sense.' What did she mean "*even if you don't?*" I'd just explained it. And how could she possibly know the Hegemon were coming? No way Captain Zoya would have told her.

'This...' she touched the dragon's head, '...is actually a type of control system. But it requires two pilots with special gifts, and I am the only one on the planet at the moment. The skill is quite rare.'

I squinted up at the domed ceiling. 'This place can't be a ship. It's stone and not even vaguely airtight. And what about the rest of your people? You can't leave them to the Grey Guards' mercy.'

She gave an indulgent smile. 'Not the dome, the whole planet. We will move our home to a new system. Somewhere safe. For now.'

'What? That's not possible. You can't move an entire planet.' I folded my arms to keep in a surge of bitter disappointment that threatened to burst forth.

Kusuma sighed. 'You're so certain. Sure of us. Sure of the Grey Guard. Sure of yourself. Is there no space left in your thoughts for what's extraordinary in this universe?' She gestured to the intricate paintings on the walls.

'It's a matter of science and physics, not wonder. Our scans show you have hardly any industry. You don't have a source of energy large enough to open a wormhole for a whole planet.'

Her laugh resonated, low and liquid, through the chamber. 'My dear girl, the planet *is* the energy source. There is no technology. They are called wormholes for a good reason.'

She rose and spread her arms wide. 'This planet is an egg. An egg laid by a creature that sees the stars and galaxies as we would see grains of sand. And the wyrm larva curled inside this shell is capable of travelling the wormholes laid down by its parent, but not capable of generating new ones. Only the adults can do that. And they are few, if any.'

My mouth had fallen open at some point and I couldn't find the skill to close it.

Her intense gaze searched mine. 'We must protect this one until its birth. We think that will occur in around four hundred years. It is our task. In that time we will begin building ships to take us offworld when the hatching destroys this one.'

She swung around, fixing me with fanatical intensity. 'So, you see, the wormhole generation "technology" does not exist. And these creatures cannot be tamed or forced to do a mere human's bidding. I doubt they even register our presence. There is nothing for the Grey Guards here. You must help us hide this egg. It takes two who are sensitive to the sushum and you are the first we have found in a decade of searching.'

I rose, staggering beneath gravity and grief. She was insane. The victim of some stupid religious fanaticism. I'd seen it before in worlds where science had been abandoned. There was no salvation here for my family and the thousands of other trader families stricken by psychosis. No hope.

Nausea churned my stomach and I covered my mouth. I had to get back to the ship. To find another solution before my mother and father became the next victims of the psychosis.

But how? There was no time.

Tears blurred the pictures on the walls until the people seemed to dance and the silver river writhed in sickening ecstasy.

'Did you know that it's only the traders who are affected by the psychosis?' Kusuma's throaty voice snapped me back from the brink of hysteria.

I scrubbed at my face and sucked a deep breath, trying to process her words. 'How could you possibly know something like that? I haven't heard any news to that effect.'

The priestess smiled faintly. 'We have sources all over the galaxy. The wormholes allow us to keep in touch with a select few who keep us informed.'

'Spies.'

'If you like. We have a lot to protect. And good reason to fear the Grey Guard.' There was a pause and she pinned me with an unwavering look. 'After all, they're coming here. In their gunships. Which have older flipdrives. Like the ship you arrived in.'

I froze, my aching limbs trembling as the import of her words washed over me. My knees weakened and I stumbled back to sink into the seat, clutching at the plinth with numb fingers.

'Older drives,' I mumbled. 'My father upgraded ours. Got a good deal on the new drive.'

'All the traders did,' Kusuma said, gently. 'The Hegemon isn't sending gunships to obtain our wormhole tech as a substitute for flipdrives.'

'They're coming to obliterate the competition,' I whispered. 'Like they're doing with the trader families. The traders are too strong as a group. The Hegemon has never been able to completely control the colonies because they can't completely control us. So they're eliminating us.'

I buried my face in my hands. 'Some sort of hidden flaw

in the new flipdrives is causing the psychosis—even with short flips and fewer flips.'

'Psychosis is real,' Kusuma said, 'but yes, the new drives are designed to keep traders in the flipvoid just a little bit too long. The readouts are deliberately faulty so the traders underestimate how long they are in the void. And next the Guard are coming after us. Just to make sure the traders have no alternatives.'

She gripped my hands gently and pulled them away from my face. 'You have to help us. We must hide the egg from them. Without it, they can't find the wormholes and the wyrm larva will be safe.'

'No!' I rose again, my mind scattered, heart pounding. The air was a heavy blanket, smothering my chest. 'I have to warn my parents. They're about to do ten flips. They'll go mad!'

Kusuma appeared before me, her knotted fingers clasping mine in a bone-grinding grip.

'Stop, Sarva,' she commanded.

I obeyed, unwillingly, mesmerised by her black-hole eyes.

'Help me and I will help you, I promise,' she said, low and hard.

'How?' Old distrust of earthers tainted my reply with scorn.

Her smile reappeared and the ever-present, distant murmuring in the back of my thoughts burst into choral glory. A nova of light and love exploded in my head.

Now I understood.

'The wyrm accepts you,' she said. 'Now that your mind is

open, you can Seek through the sushum, across the void. Help me and I will teach you to speak with your parents. Together, we will save not only my people and the wyrm, but yours, too.'

She drew me back towards the plinth. 'Come, child. It's time.'

Willingly, I thrust aside doubt and distrust, and lay my hands over Kusuma's. The Hegemon would fail and they would not get a second chance. The traders were tougher than the Hegemon thought.

I smiled grimly and joined my thoughts to Kusuma's. Together we stretched into the universe, seeking the next star along the sushum's silver path. Together we reached for salvation.

For a new path for her people and for mine.

END

1815 hours: Rethinking things

Zev Smith

'Giant fecking space worms?' Zev rose and tossed back the last dregs of his scotch. 'That sounds more flip-psychotic than anything else I've heard today.'

Bligh pursed her lips. 'You don't believe me?' She chuckled ruefully. 'I have to admit I'm not convinced, either. Good story, though.'

Cordy and Clare exchanged amused looks.

Zev shrugged. 'If it's real you've just confirmed everything we were saying about the Hegemon, anyway, girl. Think about it. You really reckon they'll let you go home after you serve your time here? You're dreaming.'

The young lieutenant opened her mouth, frowned, and closed it again.

Clare patted the younger woman's arm. 'Don't worry.

Zev's just another hardened cynic who's seen terrible things and no longer believes in anything good. I'm sure you'll be alright.' She glared at Zev.

He blinked, taken aback. Maybe he had been a bit hard on the kid. He considered what stories he knew that weren't Hegemon-related.

'You're right. I've seen a lot,' he said. 'Heard about a lot of odd things in the void. And I heard a doozy from my grandfather, years ago.'

Clare sent him an approving smile. Cordy just raised a brow and rolled her eyes.

'What?' Bligh folded her arms. 'It's hard to imagine what's worse than a planet-egg.'

'Believe me,' Zev stretched his mouth into a grimace, 'there's worse. My something-times great grandfather was a Terran shark fisher two hundred years ago. Sometimes went voidfishing. He saw all the crazy shit in the void. Loved it. Until he went fishing with an Aquanorian voidfisher. Bad move.'

'Why?'

Tenebrous

Pamela Jeffs

200 years ago

I favour the flipvoid over real space. That non-place of existence between planets. It reminds me of the oceans of my home world, Aquanum. Only darker. A plane of endless black: a plane where monsters roam.

And it's also where my elusive nightmare lingers. A nightmare as real as breathing. One I've searched long years to find and to kill.

Still the hunt goes on.

'Fishin' grounds ahead, Zesa,' I call over my shoulder. 'Better haul that arse of yours and get the customers sorted.'

The ship's viewscreen reflects the cabin and the movements of my first mate behind me. Zesa rises from her seat at the far end of the cockpit. Her short hair glints copper in the bright cabin lights. Her neck, translucent white, gleams like marble against the polished black collar of her armoured voidsuit. She taps a button on the navicomp control transferring radar output to my console.

'Of course, Tiswin,' she says. 'But only because you asked so nicely.'

I shrug. 'Nice is for nursefish, not captains.'

'You're not a real Hegemon captain. You still know that, right?'

I tap the faded insignia on my jacket—a jacket I found abandoned in a bar on a station in the Glondian system. 'That ain't what the badge says, sister.'

Zesa rolls her eyes. 'That's not your badge.'

'Hegemon ain't got no authority here in the flipvoid. That means I'm the bossman and the badge confirms it.'

Zesa's lips pinch together. Her yellow eyes narrow, but there's laughter in her gaze. She dips her chin to glance out the ship's viewscreen. The display panel shows the void. A sea of shadows; darkness shifting and roiling.

She frowns. 'Currents look strong out there. You alright to keep us steady on your own?'

I grin a debonair smile and wiggle my facial tentacles. 'Me? Come on. I eat void currents for breakfast.'

Zesa chuckles, the sound rich like warm chocolate. 'I've seen what you eat for breakfast. Space eel à la carte isn't nearly as dangerous.'

'You've never tried eating the space eel alive.'

'And I thank the Creator for that.' She flips a sarcastic

salute. 'I'm off. Call me if you need anything.'

The cockpit door leading to the cargo bay unseals and opens. Zesa exits, her voice echoing off the metal corridor as she calls the passengers up.

'You can unclip your travel harnesses. Voidsuits are in the lockers. Those of you without aural implants will find your translator and comms earbud in the top pockets. Let me know if you need help fitting them.'

Her voice fades as the door closes and re-seals. The cabin grows colder and quieter without her. Just the tiny, regular beeps of the radar scanner keep me company. It's too quiet. I hate the quiet. It brings memories.

First the slow familiar slither of pain crawling across my chest—a chest half prosthetic, since the day one of my three hearts was torn out. The sensation is in my mind, not real. But even now, after ten long years, the phantom pains afflict me.

And then the waking nightmares. Such nightmares. The visions borne of darkness and teeth and eyes like red coals. In their thrall I taste my blood. My far-left heart is again ripped away and the haunting call of my nemesis holds me teetering on the edge of sanity.

No-one else knows of the visions. If they did, I would be diagnosed with flip psychosis and locked away. But it's not that. I'm perfectly sane. I just need to find and kill the creature that crippled me.

Find it.

Kill it.

Then the memory of the blood I taste won't be mine

anymore.

And the nightmares will no longer eat me.

I take a shuddering breath, thinking of Zesa to try and thaw the ice crawling down my spine. She's my first mate, but also my anchor.

A Yoobrillian biologist here cataloguing void creatures, she found me floating in space all those years ago. She gathered up my shattered body and patched it to save my life. And, when I told my story, she believed me. Maybe it was something to do with the logician in her Yoobrillian nature. But she's been by my side ever since, supporting my quest.

My friend. My conscience.

My tie to reality.

I glance at the radar scanner. Blue pulses of light circle out from the centre, showing nothing more sinister than a small makovoid swarm huddled a klick to port. No creatures the size of small moons lurk here. I growl, hating myself for fearing what I come here every trip to kill. And that which I fail to find.

The Tenebrous.

The memory of it rises before me. Blue and silver skin and rows of wicked teeth stacked like knives. The single kill spot on the roof of its mouth. I press back into my chair, my palms tingling. My breaths come short and sharp.

Then my aural implant buzzes in my ear.

Zesa's voice crackles over the comms. 'We are suited up in here, Tis.'

I blink, and the hallucination fades but my hearts still beat an uneasy tattoo. I take a deep breath and collect myself.

'Good one,' I reply. 'Hang a bit. I'll anchor up.'

'Right-o.'

The lever next to the control wheel slides down in one slick movement. The viewscreen displays the anchor parachutes as they flare out, one from each side of the ship. Two great sheets of treated rhodium, beaten to a shining foil, bell out and gather the flipdrive's excess particles to hold us in place. The surface of each chute, illuminated by its own anchor light, undulates in the void current, beautiful like molten mercury.

'Cargo bay opening,' I confirm.

'Aye. Good to go,' says Zesa.

The escaping atmosphere hisses behind the closed cockpit door. A light blinks red on the console. *Atmosphere purge complete.* The radar screen beeps, changing to register dots aft of the ship. Zesa and our three customers. Four fishers all up.

I close the cargo doors, re-pressurize the bay and then shift the viewscreen display. Zesa, dressed in her black suit is only visible by the blue illumination of her helmet. The others, a Dirty from Earth, an Iscean and a Kronck are all in white voidsuits.

They bob like moths against the dark. Each customer is armed with an electro-rod—a slender, red spear that can be used stun a makovoid at fifty paces.

'Can you give us a heading on the school?' crackles Zesa over the comms.

I glance back at the radar. 'Thirty meters to port. Careful

of the currents.'

'Listen everybody,' says Zesa addressing the customers. 'We need to move quietly or we'll miss. Rear suit thrustors are used for forward propulsion. Short bursts and let the momentum carry you before you use it again. Hand thrustors are only for course corrections. Everyone understand?'

Agreement in three different languages scratches through my ear implant. No translation. I tap it. If I'm lucky, it's usually only the translator function that's finicky, other times the whole unit fails. The damn thing needs to be replaced.

It clicks and the implant comes back online. The Kronck is speaking. One type of alien species, you do not want to piss off.

'You consssssider this sssssneaking up to be hunting?' lisps its insectoid voice. 'There is no honour in thisss. It issss not how Kronck's hunt. The kill must be made face to face. I want to ssssee the makovoid's eyes when it diessss.'

I smile. Customers like this one is why Zesa is in charge of public relations. My tendency toward a "sit down and shut up" methodology isn't always the best way to deal with some aliens.

'This is the only way to capture this type of creature,' says Zesa carefully. 'They're quick, smart and extremely flighty. But, if you will follow my direction closely, none of us will go home empty handed.'

The male Dirty, too stupid for his own good, sniggers. The Kronck growls in return.

But the Iscean steps in. 'Our host is correct. Makovoids

are capricious. Let us put aside our egos and get to fishing shall we, gentlemen?' she says. 'I'm sure we are all looking forward to a fine feast tonight.'

The Kronck grunts, the sound untranslatable, but nothing more is said.

The group, stretched out in a line, follows Zesa past the ship. I track their progress on the radar. Twenty-five meters. Fifteen meters. They are right on the school. I look back to the viewscreen.

Electricity, shaped like lightning, bristles against the darkness. The four fishers are silhouetted against the brightness. Black cardboard cut-outs.

My comms blinks alert, a cacophony of voices screeching against my eardrum. Something about the Kronck shooting too soon.

Something about Zesa being hit.

I duck as the school of makovoid shoots past the ship. Tentacles streaming out behind them, their bullet nosed, sapphire bodies glint for a moment in the ship's anchor lights. Then they're gone.

But the noise is still raging in my ear. Something has gone terribly wrong out there.

'Zesa? What's goin' on, darlin'?'

No answer.

But the Iscean's voice bursts suddenly into my ear, sharp as a knife. 'Pilot, your female has been hit. Her suit is damaged…'

A pause. 'Oxygen convertors are destroyed. We won't get

her back to you in time. Can you bring the ship to us?'

I slam the console. 'Fecking hell,' I snarl. I can't release the anchors because if I do the ship will fall back into normal space, leaving the lot of them stranded in the void.

Only one choice here. 'Can't do. But hold on to her. I'll come out to you.'

I do three things at once. One tentacle presses the auto-pilot. One repressurises the cargo bay and another transfers the radar read to my ocular implant. The blue lines bloom before my right eye in concentric circles, the four dots representing those outside are pinpoints of light against my retina.

Zesa.

I can't lose her.

I race into the cargo bay. Two white voidsuits remain in the lockers. Neither fully charged. I scramble into one. I curl my tentacles into the collar and slip the helmet on. The other voidsuit I tie around my arm.

I pull the manual release lever for the cargo bay doors. The atmosphere explodes from the airlock, pushing me clear of the ship. I engage the suit thrustors and angle my way toward the cluster of helmet lights.

I travel fast, but not fast enough. Every second wasted is a moment less for Zesa.

I growl as the low power alarm blares across my helmet's screen. Dammit. The void currents are too strong, just keeping on course has depleted the first of the power cells. But there should still be enough charge to get me to Zesa and back.

The cluster of lights grows brighter. The view grows

clearer. The limp form of my first mate floats gently in the centre of the huddle. I swallow my desperation.

I'm travelling too fast. My momentum carries me into the circle of customers and scatters them like leaves. As I pass, I catch Zesa around the waist. Her inertia anchors me. Another burst from my backpack does the rest to help me stop.

Hanging in the velvet darkness, I turn her toward me. The right arm casing of her voidsuit crumples under my touch. The oxygen compartment has been breached. The canisters are all gone.

Zesa's face comes into view, bloodied, behind the crack in her visor. Her lips are dark blue, her eyelids flutter and jerk.

Panic swells in my chest. My prosthetic heart shivers, beating out of alignment with the other two. My ID implant activates, registering the high level of stress on my biorhythms.

I blink and the readout switches to Zesa's status.

Transferred patient status: Onset of critical hypoxia. Pulmonary hypertension.

'By the fecking Creator,' I snarl. 'Someone come and help me.'

I turn and find the Iscean female already floating next to me.

'Here, hold her.' I push Zesa into the reptilian woman's arms. She holds her while I undo the spare void suit from my arm and crack open the unit's sleeve covering. Inside, the oxygen generator's canister, the size of my palm, stares back at me. I tear it free, the thin wires connecting it to the suit twist and snap.

'This is gonna be a real patch job, darlin',' I mutter to Zesa's inert form.

The broken top layer of Zesa's sleeve peels back like an eggshell. The stripped wires, where the original canisters were, gleam bright. Quickly, I twist the wire ends together, cursing the awkwardness of my gloves, and then shove the unit back into the compartment.

Zesa sucks in a breath as oxygen floods her suit. Her eyes snap open; their bright yellow hue is a sharp contrast to her violet coloured, half-human, half-Yoobrillian blood.

The Iscean lets go of Zesa. The comms light on the woman's earbud blinks on. 'The helmet is still cracked. We need to get her back before it ruptures.'

'Aye,' I say. 'Collect up the others. We're done fishin' for today.'

#

The Kronck hangs back, strangely silent on the return trip to the ship. It's like he knows that every part of me wants to tear the exoskeleton off his back for what he did. But Zesa has forbidden it.

'Let it go,' she says yet again to me on the private comms channel. 'It was an honest mistake. The Kronck accidently released the safety on the rod. I went in to fix it and it discharged.'

'Or he pulled the trigger. You know, wanting better prey

than a makovoid.'

'Kroncks are rude bastards, but honourable. It was a mistake, I'm sure of it.'

I let the matter drop but the anger still bubbles inside of me. I'm sick of this gig, sick of dealing with ungrateful, useless customers. Especially this whingeing lot. I have a sudden urge to get back on board and drop all of them off at the nearest asteroid. Let them rot there.

But Zesa won't allow it. She'd say we need the credits they owe us.

And she's right. No credits means a trip to the Underground Banker and a visit to that loan shark is never a good idea.

I glance at the radar display again on my helmet visor. The makovoid swarms have all fled. This section of flipvoid is now empty except for the ship and us.

But the ship's mark—it's bigger than it should be.

Almost small moon-sized.

I look back at the ship. Its bulbous lines are clearly visible in the glow of the anchor lights—a beetle pinned against velvet. For a moment everything is still except for faint ripples in the darkness around the ship caused by the active flipdrive.

But then the ripples start to grow. Wider and wider they crease the darkness into ominous waves—small to large. Large to tidal.

Then something else is illuminated—a mountain of flesh, silver, and undulating blue traced through with a line of jagged, brilliant white. A huge head materialises; a maw bristling with a wall of wicked teeth.

The mouth opens wider.

And then the ship, anchor parachutes and all, is inhaled into the monstrous mouth.

'What the feck is that?' yells the Dirty.

My palms turn to sweat. My stomach rolls. But not because our only way back to real space has been taken, but because I finally have a chance for revenge.

I smile, my tentacles tingling. 'That's the fecking tenebrous.'

Without the lights of the ship to hide it, the pale, quavering red light emanating from the edges of the tenebrous' fins is revealed, watercolour scarlet against the infinite black.

Then the glow fades and darkness falls to shroud the monster. It's still there, but hunting; veiled. I imagine the thud of its heartbeat around me.

I let go of Zesa. 'Give me an electro-rod.'

'Tiswin, *no!*' says Zesa. 'Don't be crazy. You can't go after it by yourself.'

A rod is pressed into my hand. It's the Kronck, handing me Zesa's abandoned spear. His eyes glitter in the light from his helmet.

'He doesssss not go alone,' he says to Zesa. 'My kind have hunted the tenebroussss for centuriessss. Few ever return. But when they do, they come with tales of an inssssatiable creature that never ssssstops until everything is consumed—machine and flesh alike. But to kill it gives ussss a chance to sssssurvive. The creature's carcassss will regisssster on a sensor. Another sssship travelling through flip will ssssstop to invesssstigate. They can take us back to real ssssspace.'

Zesa's gaze is like a brand as she watches me take the rod. She knows me too well; knows that while the Kronck is right, that is not why I want to fight. I have waited ten years for revenge. Now is my time.

'I will fight alongssssside you,' says the Kronck, nodding. 'Live or die, thissss is an honourable hunt.'

'Count me in,' says the Dirty. 'That thing's nothin' more than a great big space shark, and I'm considered the best shark fisherman on Earth. I got your back.'

I'm not sure that Earth's shark species are even comparable to what we face, but the human will be good bait if nothing else.

#

The Iscean stays with Zesa. The Dirty and the Kronck fan out around me.

We wait.

We wait.

The light of the tenebrous swells to life on our left. The tip of my electro-rod blares active-white. The other two follow. I press the suit's thrustors and sail toward my quarry.

Zesa's voice crackles in my ear. 'Come back alive, Tis.'

'No fear, darlin',' I reply. 'I'll get ya home.'

'It's *you* not coming home I'm worried about.'

I've no chance to answer. The tenebrous roars, a silent

wall of pressure carried through the void. I increase the force of my suit's thrustors, and sail through the disturbed current unaffected. And so does the Kronck.

But the Dirty wobbles. He tumbles, shunted off course, before readjusting and falling back into place behind us. The power cell alarm beeps again in my helmet. My second power cell is depleted.

Only one to go. It'll have to be enough.

The tenebrous rises as a wall of flesh before us. Its mouth, the size of a battle cruiser, hangs open sucking in the void current.

I am drawn forward. Closer and closer to that bone-lined opening. Closer to the animal's single kill-spot.

I press the trigger on the electro-rod. It burgeons to life. A spider web of electricity crackles out, encasing half of the beast's face. The rest is covered as the Kronck's and the Dirty's weapons activate.

The tenebrous rears and slews sideways as it tries to free its head from the expanding web of power.

The creature lunges forward. It breaks free and draws in a mighty breath. I roll to the side, aided by the quick press of my hand thrustor.

But the Dirty is caught in the flow. He screams as he is pulled into the cavernous mouth. Panicked he activates his electro-rod again.

But he is too late. His weapon is sucked along with him down the tenebrous' throat.

The Kronck appears by my side. 'Aim for the eyessss!' he

screams into his comms bud. 'Blind it!'

I aim my weapon. Electricity blurs to life again. I fire. The Kronck's beam joins mine to fall on the tenebrous' left eye.

The orb of flesh, the softest part of the creature, disintegrates. A clouding mist of yellow blood stains the backdrop of flipspace. The tenebrous shrieks and I smile, teeth bared.

'Take that, you bastard,' I mutter.

The creature rolls away. The pale expanse of its belly is momentarily revealed, pink against the glow of its internal light. Then the light fades.

Silence falls.

The Kronck floats in close. 'My suit issss almost out of power,' he says.

'Mine too. We need to end this soon. Inside its mouth is the way to kill it.'

I look at him. The metallic-looking matrix of his insectoid eyes glitters. He grins at me.

'We can do thisss,' he says.

I like the Kronck. He's an alien after my own hearts.

The tenebrous' light awakens again overhead. Yellow ichor trails from its damaged eye.

'Follow me!' yells the Kronck as he shoots forward. His momentum carries him to the open wound. He rears back and jams the activated electro-rod into the creature's damaged eye.

The tenebrous bucks. The Kronck, still grasping the electro-rod, is flung against the side of the animal. Then the creature drops its great fluke, a fin ridged with sharpened bone and glittering points of red light. It catches the Kronck.

His suit fractures.

My translator crackles to life. The Kronck is laughing.

'An honourable death,' he says.

Then his body, the exoskeleton now revealed, cracks apart like an eggshell. The shattered remains float away, scattered by the void's current.

I grip the smooth edge of my electro-rod. Rage and sorrow war within me, but my resolve is iron-hard.

Zesa's voice sounds small in my ear. 'Please come back,' she says. 'Let it go, Tis. It's not worth your life. Don't leave me here without you.'

'I'll always be with you, darlin',' I say. 'Now be brave. I gotta see you girls get home.'

I sail forward with my suit's power alarm ringing in my ears. I am focused, my hearts beating a slow, steady rhythm. I am ready. I just need to get the timing right.

The tenebrous' mouth opens, a red, light-lined cavern. My suit's thrustors shudder and then, with a final burst, hiss to a stop. The alarm cuts off mid-beep. The suits automated voice activates.

Power shutdown. Three minutes of oxygen remaining.

It'll be enough.

It has to be enough.

The creature inhales again, pulling me deeper into its maw. I sail past the first of ten rows of teeth and down toward the darkness of its throat. I activate my electro-rod and look up. I watch and wait. Wait for the moment. Wait for the spot I saw ten years ago, just past the last ridge of teeth at the top of its mouth. Back then I accidently punched it—that small patch of tender flesh. It was enough for the creature to spit me out.

But today, I am properly armed.

The dark spot of flesh crosses my vision. The size of a melon.

I aim the electro-rod, press the trigger and pour electricity into the beast.

Death is instantaneous. The tenebrous plunges into a nose-dive and a gush of yellow blood waterfalls over me. I lose my grip on the rod. I spiral, blinded, in space. I hit hard flesh. I scrape over razor teeth.

Then silence.

Power shutdown. Oxygen. Thirty seconds remaining.

Spiral. Spiral. Spiral.

I can't see anything past the blood on my visor.

Twenty seconds remaining.

My breath thunders in my ears.

At least the tenebrous is dead.

I can rest easy in that knowledge.

My momentum slows. Hands pull at me. Gloved fingers scrape across my suit visor, smearing away the tenebrous' blood.

Zesa's face appears, her lovely eyes wide. Her lips are stretched to thin lines. She is screaming at me. But the words don't reach me. My fickle comms has failed me.

But I don't need to hear her. I already know what she is saying. And I wish she could save me too. But there is nothing we can do. I'm already breathing fumes.

Ten seconds remaining.

My gaze moves past Zesa's face, drawn by a distant glow. I bark out a choking laugh, delighted by what I see. In the distance hover the illuminated parachute anchors of a Hegemon cargo hauler.

Salvation.

For the girls at least.

Zesa and the Iscean will make it home.

It's harder to breathe. My throat works to suck in air that just isn't there. Only seconds left now. Shuttles ease away from the hauler, coming for us, but their progress is slow against the void-current. I'll be dead by the time they get to us. So close, but so far.

I look back at Zesa. Beautiful, loyal Zesa. I blink and press a tentacle against the inside of my visor. Her fingers line up with my touch.

'Goodbye, darlin',' I whisper.

Oxygen depleted.

Zesa's face crumples with grief. But she holds my gaze as I fight my final choking breaths.

She holds my gaze until I fail, until the darkness creeps in.

The last thing I see are her tears falling.

END

1830 hours: Changing

Ori Bligh

'Seriously? A fish that big in the void?' Ori eyed her chrono. These stories were getting wilder and it was almost time to do the next round of security checks on the docks—although, technically, she didn't need to until tomorrow. And she could use a good night's sleep. Her team seemed to have things under control and the station was as dull as dogshit so far.

Zev shrugged and scratched at his chin. 'Not sure anything that big could live in normal space.'

'I dunno,' Ori said, thinking of her History of Colonisation classes at the Grey Guards Academy. 'Humans took a while to find it, but life was always there, waiting. In the void and out.'

She studied her three companions. None were her usual choice of friends but their stories were eye-opening, to say the least. Was it wrong that she was—for the first time in her life—quite enjoying skiving off and *not* being the duty-bound little good girl from the perfect family living the perfect life? She'd been sent here as punishment. What if it wasn't going to be as bad as she thought? What if the people weren't as awful out here as her parents had led her to believe?

May as well get what enjoyment she could from it.

She signalled Vell for another round of drinks.

Cordy snorted a laugh. 'One of my mother's favourite stories was about an ancestor of ours who was a water miner four hundred years ago. She took life with her into the asteroid belt when Terrans discovered flip tech and first started colonising outside the Sol system.'

'Water mining.' Ori raised a brow. 'Shitty job back then.'

'Still is,' Cordy said. 'But Kat was a smart lady. All of the early colonies depended on her. And her tech.'

'How?' Ori asked.

The bounty hunter smiled at Clare. 'You'll like this story. It involves your name, O'Malley.'

Wet Through and Through

Aiki Flinthart

400 years ago

From this height and distance Gobi didn't look like a Hadean shithole of inequity. It looked…boring. The settlement of low, sandstone buildings straggled fitfully away from the spaceport's scorched-earth liftoff area. Surrounded by shades of red and brown.

Lifeless as every other of Earth's colony planets. If it weren't for the discovery of grey fuel deposits needed for flipdrive tech, it wouldn't have been colonised. Barely habitable at best.

As the water miner's ship soared into the stratosphere, height flattened jagged mountains and empty riverbeds into mere shadows and lines. An artist's impression of a world. Off to the north, a massive dust storm brushed a red-grey smear over the landscape; the painter attempting to wipe clean his unsatisfactory work.

Shon Gibson curled a lip. At least he wouldn't have to breathe the lung-scouring grit when the storm ploughed through the city, later today.

The ship turned and Gobi vanished, taking Shon's old life with it; replaced by a darkening green sky and Callipso III's burnt-orange glare.

Shon unfastened his harness and shoved out of the rear passenger seat. Even with the ship's grav-mod on he still felt the pressure of liftoff as an unfamiliar ache in his bones. He peered out the front-facing window, into the dark future, speckled by distant diamonds and hope.

The hope that he'd made the right choice.

'When are you going to tell me where we're going?' he asked.

Kat didn't reply. Shon eyed the back of her head then returned to watching the globe that used to be his home.

'Gobi control, Gobi control, this is *The Grace O'Malley.*' Kat's mild voice cut through the silence. 'I confirm we've just left atmo. See you in six months with a fresh load of aitch-two-oh.' The Gobi control tower acknowledged and wished her safe flipping.

The faint roar of the planet-drive faded, followed by a stomach-churning moment when the engines switched over to sublight and the grav-mod recalibrated for zero grav. Shon swallowed. Hearing about this from friends who'd travelled from Pan was one thing; experiencing it, another. The descriptions left a lot to be desired. His stomach seemed determined to expel itself through his nostrils.

'If you'd stayed in the seat,' Kat said, 'you'd find it less sickening. The seats have a built-in medic that administers anti-nausea intras.'

'Thanks, but I've had my share of medics.' He pulled the cyc-suit glove off his left hand and waggled his mechanical fingers at her. The subtle whine of its biotronics was probably only audible to him. He twisted at the smallest finger out of habit and let it go out of irritation with himself.

She glanced at the hand with apparent disinterest and went back to her delicate manipulation of the controls. Her fingers, although knotted with age, handled the computer with ease and skill. Why she flew the ship manually, instead of with a neural implant, was a mystery, though.

'Why a prosthetic? Why not a re-grow?' she asked. 'Gobi Med Centre might not be the most advanced in the colonies, but they can achieve that much.' Her tone held neither judgement nor scorn, just curiosity.

Her dark brown eyes, creased by years of life and space travel, met his in a shadowed reflection off the front viewscreen—a ghost looking in through the window at him. She tucked a curl of hair behind one ear.

Her hair fascinated Shon. He'd never seen so much on anyone. It fell to her waist in a grey-streaked, faded-red braid. Not even the Guvner's wife could afford to wash that much. He shoved his cyc-suit hood back and swept his right hand over his own bald scalp.

With a shrug, he slid into the co-pilot seat and stared into the glittering darkness ahead. 'Couldn't afford a regrow. If you're not a key worker then you need to be wet through and through to get one. I was just labour in the grey fuel mine.'

He inspected his hand, hating the cheap, too-smooth artificial skin. The flash of the mining pick; the spray of blood; the horrified fascination of the onlookers. 'After this no-one would take me on, even as labour.

'But I'm not bad with dice and cards, so I got by. Hit a dry patch, though.' He grimaced and flexed the artificial hand again. Luckily River hadn't thought to check it when he'd accused Shon of cheating, stripped him of everything but his suit, and thrown him out into the midday sun.

'Wet?' The lines between Kat's brows crevassed, then softened. 'Oh, I see. That's the latest vernacular for wealth, isn't it? My apologies. It's been a while since I've spoken with anyone from the streets of Gobi. Normally I just unload the water-trailer and flip. Lot of ground to cover.'

Shon slid his gaze sideways, taking in her profile. How could anyone, even someone in her line of work, be so out of touch? She looked to be about sixty-five orbs, maybe older if she'd had gene therapy. Her skin, though papery and wrinkled, still held more water-softness than anyone he knew.

Her skin and hair were the reason he'd shelved his pride and begged to be her apprentice. That and the fact he'd been half-delirious with dehydration. Otherwise he'd never have dared. But he'd seen her and known she had more water than anyone on Gobi. More than the Guvner and all his cronies.

And so she should. After all, she was a winer.

By some miracle, she'd taken him on instead of handing him to the Guvner's thugs. And now he'd never be dry again.

Kat jerked her chin at his hand. 'What makes you think you can do this job?'

He debated how to answer her. This was his last chance. He had nowhere else to go.

If he said the wrong thing, would she send him back on her next run? Or, maybe he could convince her to drop him at one of the other colonies. Anywhere was better than Gobi.

He'd been silent too long. She repeated her question and added, 'What about your family?'

Gripping the fake hand with the real one, he looked away, out into the blackness. 'My parents dried out fifteen years ago. My grandfather moved with them to Gobi from Pan fifty-three years ago and he dried out too.' He cleared his throat, unable still to cry for them. Tears were wasted water. Anger tasted sweeter, anyway.

Kat's thin grey brows snapped together again. 'You mean they all died? And by "dried out" you mean they died poor; of dehydration?' When he shrugged his feigned indifference, she pressed her lined lips together and glared out the window.

Shon stiffened. Should he ask if she was angry with him? No.

'Why'd you take me on?' he asked. She must have had hundreds of applicants for the position and he hadn't even been on the official applicant list.

She flicked him a quick look from beneath sandy lashes,

her lined lips twisting into a half-smile. 'You reminded me of someone I used to know. Name was Adron. He was a stubborn, wily bastard, too.'

'What happened to him?' Shon couldn't help asking, though he wasn't sure he appreciated the comparison. Or the description.

She shrugged. 'He didn't like the isolation. Didn't stay long. It doesn't suit everyone to be out here on their own for months on end. So I took him home again, to Pan.'

Shon opened his mouth.

An alarm flared on the screen to her left. She tapped and swept through a few displays before snorting a laugh, her irritation apparently vanishing.

'Someone after you?' she nodded at the display. A little red blip, surrounded by flashing, changing numbers, emerged from behind Gobi's one small moon.

Shon swallowed. River had the resources. But surely he wouldn't be stupid enough to show his hand so blatantly. Not against a winer and not within range of the colony guardships.

He gave a nonchalant shrug and as rakish a grin as he could manage. 'Can't imagine why.'

Kat sent him an ironic look. 'I was kidding. It's me they're after. They never let up.' Her smile held both pride and a hint of weariness. 'One part of being a winer, as you call us, is outrunning and outsmarting the lumps of excrement who think they can follow me and find out how I mine water so well.'

Shon peered over her arm at the readout. He had, of course, a basic understanding of piloting and space-nav, but barely enough to run the Pan-transport, if he absolutely had to. It was required of all Gobians, in case of emergency.

Kat's system was way more complex, even though her ship was an older model. She'd obviously modified it in her trips to the various other Colonies she supplied with water. Pan and Gobi were relatively new settlements. The older ones were further advanced technologically and some of her ship-tronics were beyond his understanding.

The best he could tell from the readout was that they were being followed.

'It's gaining pretty fast.' He nodded at the red dot. 'Can we outrun it? I thought most of the winers operating in this sector had newer ships than this.'

Kat smiled wider. 'Oh ye of little faith. I have no intention of trying to outrun at sublight.'

'What then?' Understanding dawned. 'Hang on. You can't be serious. You're going to flip? Here? And go where? I thought you operated out of the A-6 Asteroid Belt right here in this solar system. You can't flip that short a distance.'

Kat chuckled. '*He* can't. *I* can.' She patted the display desk in front of her. '*Grace O'Malley* and I have an understanding: she flips us to the Belt and I don't crash her into an asteroid when we drop back into normal space. You might want to buckle in, though. This short a flip-trip is always a bit rough on re-entry.'

Shon fumbled with the buckles, snapping them together even as she punched the ship's flip control. His final coherent thought was that he'd made a mistake and would be lost in the flipvoid.

The sensory whiteout-deprivation lasted only a few seconds, or it could have been years. Shon found it impossible to tell. He could see, feel, hear and taste nothing, not his body, not the chair under his fingers, not even his own heartbeat in his ears.

Nothing.

Just as panic nibbled at the edges of his thoughts, the ship dropped back into normal space. The sudden existence of velocity snapped his body hard against the seatbelts.

Kat's fingers flew over the controls. She flung the little ship into a tight spiral, skimming a jagged asteroid that loomed in the viewscreen.

Shon's head cracked against the edge of the seat. The grav-mod motors whined as they compensated for the vessel's aerobatic manoeuvres. The cold of an anti-nausea intra washed into his thigh and Shon welcomed it as his stomach heaved.

Several tense minutes passed as Kat negotiated the free-wheeling asteroids. The nausea subsided and Shon was able to watch more closely. She seemed to be heading for one rock in particular, one of the largest and slowest-rotating in the viewscreen.

He squeezed his eyelids to a slit, trying to stop the illusion that made the huge boulder look as though it pulsated. Clearly the anti-nausea meds weren't working properly.

As the asteroid approached, a high-pitched pinging echoed in the small cabin. It drove right through Shon's skull and bounced around inside his head, setting his teeth on edge.

Kat eyed him. 'You can hear that?' When he nodded she twisted a wry smile. 'I used to be able to as well. Getting old sucks. Several times, over. It's *Goose* checking *Grace* is who she says she is. We'll dock in a minute or so and it will stop.'

She heaved a heavy breath. 'It'll be nice to be home. I'm away for six months out of every orb and, I have to admit, I'm a little tired these days by the time I get back.'

She spun to avoid a fast-moving rock. Shon concentrated on the conversation to avoid releasing the scream tickling the back of his throat.

'So…' He took a sharp breath as she pointed the nose straight at a deep cave in the large asteroid. 'I know you've been doing this awhile.'

She smiled in irony but said nothing.

He gulped as a house-sized rock slipped past the window. 'Why do you still do it if you're tired? You must have enough water saved to settle anywhere if you wanted.'

She touched a button and an orange light flashed on the console. A matching one stabbed out from the darkness of the cave ahead. Kat took her hands off the panel and leaned back with a sigh.

'There's more to this than just me and water, kid. I'm the best water-miner there is. If I stop, six colonies and fifty-five million people would dry out within a year.' Her lips thinned.

Grace O'Malley lined herself up with the cave and slowly drifted into its depths. The dark maw engulfed them and Shon gaped, only then grasping the scale of the cavern and the asteroid itself. The cavity was clearly built, not natural; the ochre rock walls smooth and laced with long veins of some bluish mineral that emitted a pulsing light.

The ship clunked into its docking station. Kat punched a couple of buttons and faced Shon. 'I can't just walk away from that sort of responsibility in a hurry. That's why you're here.'

He suppressed the automatic curl of his lip at the thought. He would. Given a choice, he'd abandon Gobi without a second thought. Well, the Guvner and his like, anyway. From what newcomers said, Pan was no better. Both colonies run by corrupt, water-thieving officials who kept the workers dry and themselves soaked. They didn't deserve the water in their blood.

The external and internal lights both flicked from orange to green at the same moment and something clanged against the ship's skin. Shon jumped.

'Don't fret.' Kat patted his hand. It was his left. He didn't feel it. 'It's the auto airlock.' She unbuckled her harness and eased out of the seat, her joints audibly crackling when she stretched. Moving stiffly, she unlocked the airlock doors and opened the outer one to reveal a featureless carved-rock tunnel.

'Come into the main living area and I'll show you around.' She preceded him, her stride turning almost jaunty. 'You will have to duck, though. The doors are a little short for you.' She bounced on her toes a couple of times. 'And you may want to watch your step for a few days. I keep the gravity set a little lighter than Gobi's.' She flexed her gnarled fingers. 'Helps my arthritis until it settles down.'

The first few steps did feel strange—but good. The pathway was of some smooth, spongy material that gave beneath his boots. He felt lighter. His body, always weak from lack of water, relaxed.

The dim-lit tunnel was carved from the same ochre, blue-veined rock. Warmth radiated from the walls. And a subsonic, rhythmic thrumming vibrated through his feet. There must be some sort of reactor buried in the asteroid to heat that much rock. Seemed like a waste of energy.

Kat gestured him onward. A few minutes of walking brought them to another airlock door. She was right. The doors were only at shoulder height for Shon, and he wasn't particularly tall.

Kat punched a code into the wall panel, which was also set inconveniently low. The door hissed open. She paused at the second door, waiting until the first had closed before opening it. When it finally swung open, she stepped into the room beyond, a satisfied, anticipatory smile on her mouth as she swept a hand out in a grand gesture.

'Welcome to the *Goose*, Shon. What do you think? It's set for nighttime at the moment, but I just thought you might like to see it before I show you to your room.'

Shon ducked through and straightened. He dragged a deep, shocked breath, so thick with moisture that it felt like sucking something solid into his lungs. He couldn't help but cough. It smelled strange, too, like damp earth and another, unfamiliar scent that appealed to something in his heart, for which he had no name.

It took a moment, but his eyes adjusted to the gloom. Before him opened a vast space, the ceiling too high to be seen and the walls invisible in the dim light. In the centre of the room stood a huge, dark mass of something indistinguishable. Something tall and dark.

Touching a panel on the curving wall, Kat raised the level of illumination.

'What...' Shon blinked in the warm golden light. He stumbled across a soft green floor, almost frightened to put his feet on the stuff underfoot lest he crush it.

He reached out and touched. The surface of the thing dangling before him was strangely smooth, almost waxen, and glossy. Droplets of water stuck to his finger and he touched the tip reverently to his tongue, tasting clean, unprocessed, pure water. He breathed deep again, drawing in the damp—the *life*—that pulsed in this room.

'Are these...actual *plants*?' He'd seen vids in the standard kid's brain-train. Even walked through a virtual forest, but this was just so much more...real.

An earthy smell of wet soil; the drip of water; the variety and intensity of colours. That plants were more than just green and brown was a revelation on its own. They were every hue of those it was possible to imagine, plus greys, yellows, even pinks.

'They certainly are,' Kat said, pride in her voice. 'I planted them when I came. Using seed brought from Earth. One of my ancestors was a botanist on the early colony ships.' She snorted. 'Back when they thought water was as plentiful in the rest of the galaxy as it was on Earth. They help recycle the air here.'

Real plants. Shon could do little more than gaze at the spectacle in disbelief.

The tallest reached up to the distant ceiling and spread dozens of…branches, each one sprouting hundreds of…Shon searched his memory…leaves. Below were more plants, with leaves of different shapes and shades, right down to the narrow, brilliant…grass underfoot.

Dazzled and overwhelmed, he stepped back from the…trees…, off the grass, onto the safe, dry, impersonal surface near the wall.

It felt so wrong for so much water to be wasted in such a way. But so right, at the same time. Envy twisted at his stomach, knotting it around the festering anger already deeply embedded there.

'It can be a little daunting, I guess,' Kat said. 'You'll get used to it. Come this way.' She gave him an understanding smile and motioned him around the edge of the room, toward another of the low doors.

Hardly able to take his eyes off the vibrant patch of life, Shon followed her, cracking his head when he forgot to duck through the door.

They emerged into a smaller room; one clearly designed as living quarters, with very ordinary lounge chairs, a dining table, and a vid screen on one wall. Several doors led off it, one to a small food prep area. Two other doors stood open, offering glimpses of what appeared to be sleeping quarters.

Two of the curved walls were lined with dozens of shelves. But nothing was bolted to the ochre wall and it all looked a little…rickety.

The shelves were crammed with rectangular items of various sizes, all a little bigger than a hand, and with what seemed to be words printed on their edges. The room smelled slightly dusty.

Shon frowned, his mind starting to tick again after the shock of seeing so much greenery. Even though the furniture was perfectly normal, and the cooking area similarly so, everything seemed slightly wrong in the space. Nothing quite sat properly; the vid screen tilted to fit under the ceiling; the shelves were made of what looked like scrap metal bolted together; the benchtops in the food prep area were uncomfortably low and a bowl on it disproportionately large.

Moving into the cooking area, Kat tapped a panel on a food dispenser sitting on the bench, and produced two glasses of some sort of liquid. Shon sniffed suspiciously, then sipped, savouring the sweet-sour unfamiliar tang, reluctant to finish because it represented what would normally be a whole day's water allowance on Gobi.

'It's an old Earth recipe for something called "lemonade",' Kat said, seating herself on one of the couches and drinking deeply. When he didn't reply and continued to stand in the doorway, she leaned back.

'Relax, kid. There's more. Drink. Sit. You must have questions. We can answer some now and the rest in the morning. I don't know about you, but I'm exhausted.' She yawned as though to demonstrate.

He sank onto a chair, sitting on the edge and placing the half-finished cup on the table before him. Gathering thoughts scattered by too many shocks, he touched his fingertip to the liquid condensing on the outside of the cup. Such waste.

'Those trees...' he half-glanced over his shoulder at the now-darkened forest '...this place...what....how?' He hadn't the words to express what he wanted to ask. They disappeared beneath the weight of strangeness.

Kat stretched her neck and swept a stray strand of hair back behind an ear. She gazed past him toward the forest room.

'I found *Goose*. Years ago.' She drank again, holding the translucent cup up to the light. 'I'd been water-mining this belt for a few years, scraping a living using what tech I could beg, borrow or steal—none of it very efficient. Relying on finding asteroids that were mostly ice already, because tech wasn't up to molecular debonding of rocks to create water. Don't know that anyone can do it very well, even now.'

She raised the cup as though toasting. 'Then I brought *Grace* in here to hide from another miner...and found this.'

'But what *is* this?'

Kat gave a soft chuckle. 'To be honest, I'm not entirely sure and I don't completely understand how *Goose* works, even now. She seems to be a mining facility. Either created or modified by an alien race. I've just adapted her to suit me. Took me a few years to get things just right and to translate the language enough so I could understand how to help her properly, though. Luckily she's self-maintaining and was still working fine when I came along.'

'So, it's some sort of giant…machine?'

'In a way. She eats asteroids, breaks the molecular bonds and rearranges them. That produces just a little more energy than she uses so she's self-powering. The carbons and some hydrogens and oxygens I redirect to the food dispenser, which creates proteins and carbohydrates.

'But most of the hydrogens and oxygens are a waste by-product in the form of water—which I take to the colonists. Whatever silicates and minerals are left, after *Goose* takes what she needs, become bonus base materials I can on-sell as well.'

'You talk about…it as though it's alive.'

Kat sent him an amused smile.

He shook his head. 'Alien!' Shon could barely voice the word. Humans had spread from Earth a hundred years before, seeding colonies across their own solar system. But only when they discovered grey fuel had they managed to spread to four more solar systems. Nothing—not even bacteria, plants, or animals—had been found. 'I didn't think anyone had found *any* evidence of alien life.'

Kat patted the wall. 'Nope. *Goose* is the first. Which is why I keep her secret.'

'But,' he said, swallowing acid, 'you've found the solution. You've found a way to produce water for practically nothing. A way to save millions on the colony planets.'

Her smile turned weary. 'I wish it were that simple, kid. But there's no way to replicate *Goose* and she can only produce so much per year. And can you imagine what would happen to her if the boffins got their hands on her?'

Shon ground his teeth. She was lying. Sitting not only on the first evidence of alien tech, but the exact tech the Colonies so desperately needed. Yet she kept it to herself, living in luxury, selling for an exorbitant price what came to her for free, keeping the Colonies in poverty and drought.

Deep resentment bubbled and he threw back the drink with reckless haste to hide it. He pushed aside the bleak memory of his parents' withered corpses, of his grandfather's sunken cheeks and voiceless pleas for water, of the desperate and dispossessed reduced to licking metal in the mornings and gathering their breath into bags for the moisture it held; of the sneering scorn on the face of the paymaster when he doled out ever-decreasing water-wages and gave extra, unpaid shifts to anyone that complained. He mastered his reaction with difficulty, schooling his face into curiosity.

'So…' he tried to keep his voice level '…how long do you think it will take me to learn everything?'

Kat, who had been watching him shrewdly, shrugged. 'Depends on how smart you are and how much you want this job.'

'More than anything,' Shon shot back. That was all truth. He did want this. It was more than he'd hoped for when he'd dared clutch at Kat's hand as she emerged from the Guvner's house. Then, he'd just had a vague, delirious idea that she was the source of water and a hope that she might give him some. He'd been lucky she'd ordered the Guvner's men to release him after they'd grabbed him. She'd given him water enough that he could answer her questions then, bizarrely, announced she would take him as her new apprentice. He didn't even remember what she'd asked, or what he'd said. Thirst had consumed every thought at that point.

'Good. We'll get started in the morning.' She busied herself tidying up and making a basic meal, discouraging more questions.

When she placed it in front of Shon he blinked. The plate contained actual plant leaves, and what looked like other bits of plants, cut up small: red, curved pieces, glistening with water and studded with little pale dots inside the flesh; curved, dark green wedges, wrinkled on the inside and smooth out; long, narrow pods of some sort containing green lumps inside. Shon poked at them, dubious.

Kat laughed and picked one up, crunching it with her yellowed teeth. 'Tomato, capsicum, and beans. The leaves are lettuce. All edible and good for you, I promise. Much better than the nutrition bricks you grew up on. I grow them here, in the garden. This is how our Earth ancestors ate. It's what your body needs to be healthy again. Eat. Drink.' She waved a glass at him.

He did, forcing the stuff down though the tastes were strange and the textures unpleasant. She smiled and nodded encouragingly.

After dinner, she showed him to the spare room and Shon lay on the too-soft bed, staring at the too-low ceiling, listening to the deep thrumming through the walls. Right outside the door was more water and more plant-life than he'd ever imagined existed except in dreams and stories. And, if he played his cards right, it would ensure his survival and safety for the rest of his life.

#

He must have slept, for he woke feeling rested and alert. Better than he had for many years. Some sort of alarm chimed, musical and irritating, by his ear. He squinted at a display that showed time.

Assuming he was supposed to start the day, Shon rose and made use of the waste facilities. Even here there was actual water, just there with the turn of a spigot. He stood for several guilty seconds at the sink, letting the cool, sensual, slipperiness of water wash over his hands.

He glanced in the mirror and frowned, turning his face from side to side. Already his eyes were less sunken, his skin smoother. Imagine what living with this much water every day would be like.

Shaking himself irritably, he flicked off the tap and marched out into the common room. It was too easy to be seduced by this lifestyle. He needed to be careful.

A middle-aged woman entered the room, lush, auburn hair rippling to her waist. She stretched and yawned, then grinned at him.

'Don't know about you, but I feel better already. Sleep okay?'

He gaped at her. 'Who…?'

She laughed. 'Sorry. Forgot to warn you.' She waved a hand vaguely at the ceiling and walls. 'One of the side effects of living here. By-product of the breakdown process is a regenerative radiation for organics. Reverses DNA epimutations, as far as I can tell. I think that's how *Goose* was still functioning for so long.'

Shon kept staring.

She laid a hand on her chest. 'I'm Kat. Promise. Age catches up with me when I leave on the delivery run. Part of the reason I need an apprentice. Too hard on me, these days, and I can't let the colonies down. I have to stay for at least six months to get the full effects and be able to last through the next delivery run.' She grimaced. 'Aging fast is a bitch, though. The arthritis is the worst.'

'How…' He blinked and inspected the back of his real hand. Smoother and softer. Was it just because of the water? 'How old are you?'

She screwed up her nose. 'Not sure. At least a hundred and thirty, I'd say. I lost track at around a hundred.' With a sigh, she turned away and began fussing with the food dispenser. 'That's about when my husband and son left.'

Shon's arm itched and he peeled back the cyc suit to scratch absently at the skin. Kat glanced over her shoulder and pointed.

'You may find the regen field grows that back. I haven't lost any limbs, so I don't know for sure, but it's possible.'

Shon sat down at the table with a thump, staring at his

mechanical hand. Was it possible? He flexed the fingers and absently fiddled with the smallest one.

Kat plonked down a bowl of something steaming and sweet-smelling. 'Eat. My own mix. Don't ask what's in it, but it does have sugar so it might be sweeter than you're used to.'

Shon scooped a spoonful of the greyish mess and lipped at it dubiously. In spite of the appearance, there were so many tastes in it he couldn't speak. He savoured the sweet, spicy flavours, closing his eyes.

'Good?' she asked. When he nodded, she added, 'Took me ages to program it for just the right arrangement of molecules. There's been a lot of trial and error. A lot of errors.' She stared vaguely over his shoulder, darkness shadowing her youthful features, then shook herself and smiled.

'But the result is amazing. After breakfast I'll show you the control room. Show you how to feed *Goose* her daily intake of rocks. She can do it herself, but she gets a better meal if an operator picks out asteroids high in the rare earths. She seems to like those.'

#

Kat led him up a narrow flight of stairs. The risers were too close together and too shallow. Shon had to walk on the balls of his feet. They emerged into a long, narrow hallway-like room. On one side, a bank of windows overlooked the plants and Shon paused for a moment to drink in their astonishing beauty and variety.

Kat nudged him and pointed at the other set of windows. Smaller and thicker, they looked out onto the asteroid's surface, and beyond into the field of tumbling, turning, drifting rocks that made up the A-5 Belt.

Shon gazed at the slow-motion dance for several long, silent minutes, mesmerised. 'Why don't they hit us?'

'Force field. Repellent field.' Kat shrugged and touched a screen, frowning at the display. 'Not sure which. *Goose* just seems to be able to fend them off. Look.'

She pointed at a series of incomprehensible diagrams on the screen. 'This shows that the main water bladders are about half full and the reserves are full. It'll take about another four months to fill them all the way. By then you'll know enough about how she works and you can do the delivery run to Pan as a trial.'

Shon started, glancing at the tumbling asteroids.

She laughed. 'Don't worry. I'll pilot you past the belt then come back in one of *Grace O'Malley's* escape pods. When you finish you can message me and I'll come out and bring you home.'

'Home,' Shon said. His arm itched.

'Hmmm,' Kat frowned at the screen and tapped a few buttons. 'Odd.'

'What?' He peered over her shoulder but could make no sense of the images.

'Looks like one of the other winers is coming a little closer than I'd like them to.' She pressed another button and an image of the asteroids outside appeared. She zoomed in on one quadrant and tapped in a query. 'Still too far away to identify.'

'Is it a problem?' Shon flexed his artificial hand, twisting the little finger.

She shrugged. 'Pretty unlikely they'll pick this particular rock to investigate. The repellent field makes sensors think we're pretty boring. No water, no high concentrates of minerals. I've put *Goose* into stasis, which means we're energy-silent.' She tapped the screen a few more times. 'They'll move on before it becomes a problem.'

'What becomes a problem?'

'After about five days of no food, *Goose* starts to weaken and shut down systems. It gets pretty cold and stuffy in here.' She sent him a quick grin. 'No oxygen or heat. But we can always retreat to *Grace O'Malley* and draw them off then circle back.'

Shon glanced at the forest room. 'And the plants?'

Kat grimaced. 'Yes. They'd die. Not much I can do about that, unfortunately. I have seed banks, but it would take a good forty years to bring it back to this point. Better than dying or giving *Goose* up to those pirating bastards.'

'Who?'

Kat sighed and pointed out the window. 'C'mon. You've met winers, haven't you? Most are a bunch of amoral shitholes that would sell their grandmother and hold the planets to ransom. They hate me.'

Shon turned a bewildered look on her. 'But why? You're one of them.'

She jabbed a finger at him. 'Now *that* was an insult. They

hate me because I don't charge what they consider market price for water. I trade my cargo for base supplies. Only what I can't make or grow myself. I refuse to profit off a basic life necessity. How could I when I get water for free? These bastards would do anything to take this place. Once they had her…' She shook her head.

Shon swallowed and stared at the screen image. 'So Gobi, Pan and the other colonies. What would happen to them if you stopped delivering?'

'They'd dry out,' she said bluntly. 'The other winers can't possibly supply enough for the current population levels. Not without what *Goose* produces. And they'd kill her trying to work out how she does it.'

She scrubbed at her face, suddenly looking older again. 'Dammit. Still heading this way.' She rose and paced to the window overlooking the forest. 'Not now. I've sacrificed too much to have it all destroyed now.'

The asteroid trembled and juddered. Shon staggered, thrown offbalance. He grabbed at a counter for support. Klaxons and alarms blared. Yellow lights flared across the screens.

'What's happening?'

Kat jabbed at a few screens and the alarms stopped. 'I had to shut off the repellent field to dampen the detectible energy output. It makes us vulnerable to asteroid strikes. That was a small one. No serious damage. But if that damned ship doesn't turn away soon *Goose* will be badly damaged.'

'Doesn't this thing have any weapons?'

Kat shook her head.

Shon made a noise of frustration. 'Then can't we distract them? Use the *Grace O'Malley* to lead them away, like you said.'

Kat's shoulders sagged. 'I guess we'll have to. No.' Her head snapped up and she pierced Shon with a sharp stare. '*I'll* have to. You have to stay here and re-activate *Goose* and the repellent field as soon as you see them follow me.'

'What? No! I can't. I have no idea...' Shon looked helplessly at the screens.

She dragged him over and pointed. 'You can. I'll show you. Here.' For the next five minutes, she took him through the startup sequence, step by step, making him repeat it until he had it action-perfect.

Then she checked the screen one last time and scowled. 'Still coming. Right. Walk me down to the *Grace* so I can show you how to operate the manual override on the airlocks.'

'What, why?'

She sent him a bleak look. 'In case they don't follow me. It'll be up to you to keep them out until I get back with reinforcements.' They entered the forest room and she kept walking. 'I'll flip to Gobi and get the Guvner there to mobilise troops.'

Shon stopped, breathing in the scent of life and water. 'You'd give this over to the Guvner of Gobi rather than these winers? How is he any better?'

Kat grimaced. 'He's not. But with hundreds of troops, he wouldn't be able to keep her a secret. He'd have to send scientists to feed her. At least people would still get their water.'

'No,' Shon said. 'They wouldn't. The Guvner is the last person I'd trust with this. You've seen his house? He has *grass* around it. His wife has hair almost as long as yours. He has a *shower* in his waste facility room. He would be the one holding people to ransom. But he'd hold *all* the colonies, not just Gobi.'

Kat spun on her heel, red hair flying. She marched up to him, fisted the front of his cyc suit and pulled his face to hers.

'Then give me an alternative, kid.' Her eyes fixed on his, searching, digging into his soul. 'Don't you get it? *Goose* isn't just alien tech, she's an *alien.*

'This is an organic life form you're standing in. A fecking great animal that eats rocks and excretes water. If the winers get hold of her, they'll kill her. Now you're saying the Guvner will do the same? So give me another choice. Help me save her. Help me save Gobi and Pan.'

Shon gasped and stared wildly around. The pulsating he'd thought was an illusion; the thrumming walls; the heat. It all made sense. He swore and stared out into the void. *Goose* shuddered again. Another hit. More klaxons blared.

'Feck!' He fumbled with his artificial hand. The limb came away from his flesh with a slight sucking sound, leaving the scarred stump exposed. He thrust it at her.

'Take it. Put it in the escape pod. Send it through the belt then set it to auto-flip into the sun or something.'

Kat took it, holding the hand gently, almost lovingly. She

turned it over and inspected the interior mechanism.

'Homing beacon?'

Shon nodded, his cheeks burning. 'I was desperate. Gambling my last water rations. Cheating. River caught me. He would have killed me on the spot but I told him I had a plan that could make both of us rich.'

'You thought you'd scam me,' she said flatly. 'Tell me things you figured I couldn't resist when we met. Earn my trust then steal the secret of my success and hand it to this gambler for what, a few lousy litres of water? A job?'

He nodded.

Kat sighed and released him. 'You played the part well, kid. Let's hope it's not too late.' She turned away and stalked towards the docking bay, his hand still in her grip.

In the doorway, she paused and looked back. 'Is your name really Shon Gibson?'

'Yes…great-grandmother.' Shon lifted his chin. 'My grandfather, Adron Gibson, told me to name my daughter "Grace" if I had one. Told me to keep an eye out for you.'

She smiled. 'I'm glad you did. And do it again. I'll be back, soon.'

'I'm counting on it.' Shon saluted and watched her disappear into the docking bay.

END

1900 hours: Beginning of the End

Cordelia Bane

Cordelia glanced around the Zoo, marvelling again at the variety of species represented even in such a backwater place. She shook her head.

'That's one story that never made it into the history books, though. My mother said Kat managed to keep it all hush-hush. For all I know the *Goose* is still chomping on rocks in the Gobi system's A-5 Belt somewhere.'

'Maybe,' Clare mused. 'Be fun to go check. The *Grace O'Malley,* huh. Excellent ship name.' She squinted at her chrono and stretched. 'Which reminds me…Getting late. Better get back to *Il Mio*.' She rose, swayed slightly and yawned. 'Walk me to the docks, Cordy?'

Cordelia checked the time. It wasn't that late. Only about 1900. All the bar's darkened corners were full, as were the main tables and the three functional habipods. The evening was really only just getting started. But she'd always had a harder head for drinks than Clare. So she slid from the booth.

The whole party exited the Zoo, none of them steady on their feet. Cordelia waved to Vell and the caninoid nodded in return.

At the door, Ori paused, her gaze unfocussed. Must be checking her ocular implant feed.

'Something from your Grey Guard team?' Cordelia asked.

The kid nodded. 'I've got a ship to inspect. Coming in with a radiation leak so I want to make sure it's not going to blow the whole place up. Better go. Nice to meet you, Clare. Cordy.'

Zev growled a laugh. 'You do that, girl. I've gotta do the same from the inside. One more check on the rich water containment tanks.' He threw a casual salute and staggered off.

Ori strode away in the opposite direction.

Clare hooked her arm through Cordelia's and grinned.

'She's a nice kid. Bit uptight about something. I'd trust her in a fight if I had to, though.' She eyed Zev's retreating back. 'Him, too, even if he is a bit of a grump.' She studied Cordelia closely. 'What's next for you?'

'I need more work,' Cordelia said, leaving an expectant silence.

'Sorry.' Clare shook her head. 'I've got nothing. The one bounty I had out has been…resolved at the Raspberry. Ordinary courier work in a week or two, maybe? But nothing right now.'

'Never mind. Let's get you back to Mac on that shiny new

ship of yours.' Cordelia pressed her lips tight. She needed big money, now. Otherwise she'd be the one with a bounty on her head. Feck!

#

Cordelia watched as Clare stomped up the gantry and into her ship. She was sorry to see her go. It was always too long between their catchups, especially with them both so busy.

A beep on her comms drew her attention. She blinked, activating her ocular implant. Lines of glowing blue data blossomed across her vision. A new bounty had been listed. Excellent timing. For an Abaforth Krultius suspected to be hiding here on Asteri Station. Cordelia hit *considering* option before anyone else could take the job, then skimmed the details.

Aquanorian. Drug smuggler.

She clenched her jaw.

The Aquanorian was a child killer, too. Done. She tapped the *accept* button.

Cordelia spun on her heel, just as Clare's ship blasted clear of the dock. Catching child killers was her personal brand of happiness.

She would try the Zoo. The Aquanorian barkeeper might be back by now. They were a reclusive species and the few who'd left their home planet tended to know each other. Maybe he could point her in the right direction. He seemed a decent sort—one of the better life-forms on this station. Good chance he would willingly help her to catch a child killer.

Cordelia stepped onto the teleport pad. 'To the Zoo,' she instructed the computer.

Predator in the Black

Pamela Jeffs

Planet Aquanum: 500 years ago

The view is clearest here, from the rookery lookout. Pencils of light paint the teal-dark sky—a meteor shower punching through the atmosphere, each missile glistening white before breaking apart and fading to embers.

Abaforth curls his lip-tentacles gently around his chin, tasting the air, his scientist's mind turning, making connections and forming theories. Is it just debris from a passing comet or something more sinister? He has no equipment strong enough to pursue an answer, no way to discover the truth. He only knows that last time the sky burned like this, all but Abbalon Island drowned beneath an asteroid-struck sea and a lot of his kin perished.

Whose turn will it be to die this time?

Abaforth braces himself against the lookout railing and scans the sky. Other than shooting meteors and scattered cloudbanks, nothing else seems to warrant further concern. But his shoulder blades are itching—a sixth-sense sign that not all is what it seems. He looks down, past the wild waves that swell and boom against the island's craggy beaches and to his left.

To the city.

Cephas huddles sheltered in the broken-edged crater of the island's dead volcano. Home to the largest of the Aquanorian tribes, the guano-stained, grey buildings cluster close to grim stone cliffs. The Gathering Place—the Octari's hall—with its spired turrets towers above the others. Once a grand building it now stands a faded beauty, decorative ocean friezes and facades blunted by the touch of salt and elements.

Abaforth's fingers press against the salt-slick stone of the battlement. Cephas holds a certain, rugged splendour but he prefers it here in the lookout. Here the stone gulls sing and wind fills his lungs to bursting. He can think clearly surrounded by the true heartbeat and cadence of the world.

A wave, larger than the others, smashes the cliff's foot below. Abaforth turns back, inhaling the mist as it rises around him—a mist that catches the meteors' light and smells of iodine and salt.

A burning sky and a raging sea.

His shoulder blade itches again.

A rattle of rock draws Abaforth's attention. He swivels to see Jaskal emerging from the cliff stair, the boy's face flushed with the exertion of his climb. His breath rasps in and out as he moves to stand next to Abaforth. At only ten winters old, the young Aquanorian hatchling prefers the solitude of this place as much as Abaforth does. His deformed tentacles, hanging limp like sea-worms around his chin, make him a target for the other children—children he comes here to avoid.

Jaskal's hands worry at the edge of his fish-leather jerkin. He looks like he's been crying, wide-set eyes puffy and rimed red. Abaforth frowns.

'What did they do this time?' he asks.

Jaskal looks away. His tentacles ripple awkwardly in the breeze. 'The others wouldn't let me go hunting with them.'

'And?'

'They took my spear. Said I was too weak and useless and shouldn't own one.'

Abaforth's hearts twist painfully for the boy. Jaskal is the Octari's son but it means nothing to the young ones. They lack respect and withhold their acceptance. Pitiful. Abaforth squeezes Jaskal's shoulder.

'You are far from weak, my boy. Yours is a greater strength and one they do not understand. What you have is honour and decency and those qualities are the currency that defines good character. Those hatchlings that hound you are the weak and useless ones, for they have neither.'

'I wish they knew that.'

Abaforth's mouth twists into a wry grin. 'They will. One day.'

Jaskal sighs, as if to ease the weight of his sadness. He

looks away, up to the light-streaked sky. 'What are those sky-lights, Abi? I saw them from down below.'

Abaforth drops his hand from the boy's shoulder. 'It's a meteor shower.'

'I like them. They look like a cloud of lumifish.'

Happy to encourage a lighter topic, Abaforth waggles his tentacles. 'Let's pretend they are. But only as long as we don't let a sharkling lurk in the shadows behind them.'

Jaskal chuckles, his mouth stretching into a lopsided grin. He points. 'That red light up there. Just behind the cloudbank. That's the sharkling.'

'No!' says Abaforth feigning shock. But then his gaze lifts higher. A bloated star sails into view. Two of his three hearts skip a beat.

It's a Hunter Asteroid. The same type that destroyed his world last time.

A predator in the black.

Asteri Station: Current day

Absinthe places the polished shot glass on the rack. It's edge, worn by years of hard usage, clinks softly against the metal frame. A brittle sound. He picks up another. Habit has him surveying the room as he works. A sly surveillance that doesn't cause alarm amongst the more unsavoury characters that frequent the Zoo. He doesn't mind them coming here to drink, as long as their credits are good and they don't cause any problems.

At nine hundred years of age, Absinthe has no interest in tolerating trouble.

The teleport pad, located on the rear wall, blares to life with both green light and a piercing screech. The noise doesn't resonate too well against the delicate sensors of his aural implant, and worse the implant tries to translate the sound for him. Garbled static is the result. Absinthe's scarred lip tentacle twitches in reaction. He rubs his ear to clear the static.

Damn telepad. It's just a victim of the ten-year maintenance slide of Asteri Station.

Zev, the maintenance manager, tries to keep things running—whinges about the state of affairs on a daily basis—but funding from the Hegemon is fickle at best. Still, Absinthe needs to talk to Zev about getting that pad fixed.

The teleporter has delivered a stranger to the bar. A woman—Terran by the look of her and dressed in one of those rare, full-length chametek jackets. Must be the one Vell said spent the afternoon in the Zoo chatting with Zev and the new young Grey Guard lieutenant.

She steps off the transport pad and pauses, turning her flint-glare to scour past the habipods and into the darker corners of the bar.

Her gaze rakes past the insectoid Kronck crew that Absinthe knows to be organizing an illegal hunting sortie to the planet Derria; past the Isceans with soft, whispering snake voices; past the Terran gunner pilots playing poker in the front area.

Foreboding crawls up Absinthe's spine. The woman's

gaze is an iron-edged blade—swift, clean and unapologetic.

She turns toward the bar. The lights flickering in the out-of-order habipod to the right of the telepad catch the line of her chin, and the edge of a long, thin scar that caresses it. Absinthe has seen enough. He doesn't need to see the weapon concealed in her jacket to know she is trouble.

To know she's a bounty hunter.

Everyone on Asteri Station has some kind of past they are trying to escape. Those that reveal themselves to Absinthe across the bar when they're in the bottom of their cups are usually repentant for their crimes. If they aren't, well, a quiet word to Sergeant Yang of the Grey Guards usually sees them shipped off pretty fast to the prison ships.

As the resident barkeeper, Absinthe makes it his business to protect the station and its inhabitants. This place and these people are important to him—they represent family and a home.

Absinthe curls his ivory and teal coloured tentacles around themselves. He takes a deep breath. So who needs his protection this time? Whose secrets will he have to hold close?

Planet Aquanum: 500 years ago

The streets are soaked in the falling asteroid's red light. Terrified Aquanorian citizens gather in the Octari's hall. The Octari herself sits on her raised dais, dressed in the silver-blue ceremonial armour of her office—Protector of the People.

Abaforth pushes his way into the crowd. Jaskal clings to

his heels. Abaforth's boots, wet from his climb across the beach, squelch around his feet. Their sodden heels imprint puddles onto the lacquered shell floor.

Citizens, standing in groups, mutter and move aside as they recognize him. Abaforth Krultius is First Scientist. He will no doubt know what is going on.

Abaforth kneels at the bottom stair of the dais. Jaskal continues up and climbs into the Octari's lap. His mother curls her arms around him. The boy leans into her.

The Octari's elaborately braided tentacles hang from her chin like pale milk. Others, woven just as elaborately sit atop her head, fashioned as a crown of office. Her jet-dark eyes fall on Abaforth. Warmth and trust emanates from her gaze—born from a friendship grown around shared respect and a love of Jaskal.

'What news do you have, Abaforth?' Her voice holds steady and calm but Abaforth senses the anxiety in her tone.

'Octari,' he says, pushing strength into his voice for her. 'An asteroid comes. We must flee to the high-mountain tunnels and seal the entrances. Our city will be drowned in the deluge when it hits.'

Jaskal shifts. The Octari, older than all others, would remember the tragedy of the last impact. She lost her mate, Jaskal's father, in that devastation. With ghosts of the past haunting her eyes, she delivers her order.

'Make haste, citizens,' she calls out. 'Gather only what you must. We head for our underground fortress.' Her voice drops to a whisper. 'And may the sea spirits save us all.'

Asteri Station: Current day

The woman stalks to the bar, predator-like, with long steps and easy movements. She drags a stool away from the counter, the legs screeching across the scratched floor. She rests half a cheek on the seat, half off. Her right leg hangs in the air. A pose chosen to keep her hidden guns clear for a quick draw, surmises Absinthe.

'Fireon water,' says the woman, 'with ice.' The drink is one of Absinthe's own chemical creations—a contradiction of flavours, a mixture of fire and frost.

The colours of the woman's chametek jacket sleeve shift to match the scarred bar top as she reaches out to tap her wrist implant on the credit reader. The machine beeps and flashes red before deducting the five-credit drink fee.

A hard drink for a hard woman. Absinthe pushes his shoulders back and readjusts the front of the Terran Hawaiian-style shirt he wears. He turns over a clean glass and touches the drink nozzle to the rim. Chilli-red liquid coils thickly into the bottom.

'I haven't seen you around here before,' says Absinthe, keeping his voice light. 'What's your moniker? What brings you to Asteri Station?'

The woman gulps the drink down in one go. She doesn't even wince as the burning fluid slides down her throat. She places the glass back carefully and inspects the thick residue trickling down the inside of it.

'I'm Cordelia Bane,' she says.

Absinthe holds his expression neutral. The woman's reputation precedes her—a bounty hunter who operates outside Hegemon rules, one whose moral code doesn't always match up with everyone else's idea of right.

Bane grins, the smile wicked. 'C'mon, makovoid shark got your tongue?' She tilts her head, so that her scar lifts to the light—rugged like an ugly secret. 'Most people have heard of me before.'

'And so have I,' says Absinthe, keeping his tone friendly. 'You are quite the bounty hunter, I hear.'

She opens her jacket to reveal the sleek, square lines of a high-tech disruptor. Its silver casings gleam like new dycerium against the grittiness of the Zoo's finishes—a cold weapon, malevolent. The hilt of an old-school dagger also glints wickedly, sheathed deeper in the jacket's shadow.

'Best there is,' she says.

'Better keep those out of sight. Don't want the Grey Guard confiscating them.'

'I'd like to see them try.'

'So would I,' says Absinthe imagining the slender, pretty Ori trying to take this battle-hard woman down. He places another glass of fireon water in front of Bane.

She shrugs. 'Besides, I've already met Ori. Nice kid.'

'But you haven't told me why you're here.'

Another gulp and the glass clinks back to the bar. Bane leans in conspiratorially.

'I'm looking for someone,' she says. She flicks a loose

strand of her short hair off her forehead and looks at Absinthe. 'Maybe you could help me find him.'

Something about her tone sets his tentacles on edge.

'He's an Aquanorian like yourself,' says the woman.

Absinthe swallows. The Aquanorians are a small community on board the station. Only five in total, all close to him and all were criminals at one time or another.

He uses his left chin tentacle to place the dirty glass carefully into the washing rack. 'Who exactly are you looking for?'

Planet Aquanum: 500 years ago

Abaforth reaches the end of the tunnel leading to Cephas city and presses the release panel. The metal hatch concealing the entrance activates, the lights around its rim blinking red as it rolls up and away.

Rubble coated in dried kelp tumbles in through the opening. He kicks at it, cursing as his foot punches through the pile and into a metre-long corpse of a half-rotted sharkling. He shudders at the white eye of the animal staring sightlessly at him from amid the plant fragments. 'Here dwells death,' it seems to say.

And death there is. As he emerges, a dark and shattered landscape meets him, a landscape painted black. The sky, the sea and the stone. Cephas is gone. Only broken foundations left to mark the location of The Gathering Place. No other homes nor buildings left—everything swept aside in the deadly king-waves that followed the asteroid's impact.

Abaforth clenches his teeth. He turns toward the devastated beach, looking up at the fractured Rookery as he goes. No stone gulls wheel on the lofty heights. The wind soars silent without their songs. Abaforth frowns, bitter tears stinging the backs of his eyes. What will become of the Octopi tribes now?

He kneels down to press his palm against the ruined ground—the broken body of his homeland. Sharp rocks prickle his skin. He closes his eyes and breathes in deeply. But even the smell of salt is gone, replaced by a strange scent.

Abaforth lifts his hand. It comes away coated in a black fluid. He sniffs it. Sickly-sweet. He picks up three rocks coated in the stuff and places them into his pocket. He cleans his hands down the front of his tunic and with one last look at the rookery, turns back to the tunnel he came from.

Survival. Rebuilding. One step at a time.

Asteri Station: Current day

The fireon water has lent a pink flush to Bane's pale cheeks. She presses a finger to the bartop and swirls it around a ring of condensation left by the glass. 'The fugitive's name is Abaforth Krultius. He's old—been on the run a long time. Wanted for drug smuggling and murder. He killed a young boy back on his home world.'

Absinthe releases a slow breath. He eases in another. Quiet. Confident. Abaforth Krultius is a name he's not heard in a long time.

He frowns, letting his tentacles wilt around his chin to show disappointment. 'No one here by that name.' He pours yet another glass for Bane. Maybe if he can get her drunk enough...

'I expect he uses an alias.' The drink disappears down her throat. 'Who is the oldest of your kind here?'

'It's rude to ask an Aquanorian their age,' says Absinthe picking up the glass. 'So, can't say for sure, but I suspect at least three are approaching millennium birthdays.'

Bane's eyes narrow, her pert white teeth nibble at her bottom lip. 'You are sure? Three of the same age?'

Absinthe squares his shoulders. 'Yes.'

The answer seems to disappoint the bounty hunter. She lowers her chin, her scar disappearing into shadow. 'You see, Absinthe,' she says, 'I have a little secret I should disclose to you.'

She shakes her head. 'I really despise liars. Especially when they are murderous bastards that deserve to be rotting on a prison ship. In fact, I hate liars *so* much...' she taps her temple '...I went into massive debt to the Underground Banker and had a special little mod chip installed that tells me when someone is lying to me.'

He blinks.

Bane's face hardens.

'Well that's just fecking unfair,' snarls Absinthe.

Planet Aquanum: 500 years ago

A stone, now clean, falls out of the extractor and into the collection pan. The scraper pads Abaforth developed using the sieve from one of the air purifier replacement filters, drips the black fluid that previously coated it into a glass vial below.

Abaforth smiles. As far as he can tell, the liquid coating the island is leftover sediment created when the asteroid vaporised on collision with the planet. This liquid— this liquid he's named "black"—is exactly the miracle the Octari has been pushing him to find.

Something she can use as trade with aliens to help rebuild the world, fast.

Without his old surface labs it's been hard, but he has done it. He has distilled and tested the compound on himself and the results have exceeded his expectations. The drug is safe to use, stable to ingest and presents no negative side effects—a drug that brings only light and happiness to the user.

To make the Octari even happier, Abaforth's developed a formula to create the compound synthetically. So sweet. Black. Addictive.

With it, a future can be secured for the people.

Abaforth dips his finger in the black and raises it to his lips. It sizzles pleasantly on his tongue sending shivers up his neck. Sparks of light, painted in impossible spectrums, blossom across his vision. Black it is named, but when ingested, it gifts brightness.

Abaforth blinks the colours away. His mind clears. He plugs the vial shut and curls his massive hand around it. The

Octari is keen to present this compound to the citizens—this special tisane that not only settles frayed nerves, but one that will open new economic trade opportunities with their planetary neighbours—the Axxines.

The credits from such trade will rebuild new homes for an Aquanorian population in sore need of them. Give hope to those who have lost so much.

#

The Octari's underground hall is a far cry from the grandeur of her previous abode. No shell floors adorn the hollowed out cavern she has claimed as her Gathering Place. Oiled kelp torches gutter in makeshift wall sconces. The smoke from them rises, staining dark the primordial stone and tainting the air bitter.

Abaforth bows, his long chin tentacles curl and twist around his knees. He straightens. The Octari's gallery is empty this time of the night, the citizens now long abed. She has asked for a meeting of secrecy to ascertain the usefulness of Abaforth's compound. She looks weary but pleased to see him.

'Do you have it?' she asks.

Abaforth lifts his hand. The vial glitters ebony in the uncertain torchlight. 'I do, my Octari.'

Asteri Station: Current day

The station's service corridor reverberates with the thud of Absinthe's boots. Both hands and all facial tentacles reach for and grasp the plasma conduits bolted to the walls, propelling him along. Behind him the bounty hunter's footsteps are a whisper-fleet patter on the grated gantry.

She had looked surprised to see him move so quickly. He'd been through the bar's back door and into the service hatch access near Zev's office before she'd even blinked.

Not that it stopped her for long.

The smell of vermin shit and service oil carries up through the vents leading from the lower levels of the station. Absinthe leaps over one vent, then another. He knows these corridors well—the dark veins of Asteri Station—knows where each one leads.

Knows which one will gift him escape.

He's had an escape plan prepped and ready for years. He always does, in every place he settles—ever since he took the name Absinthe over Abaforth.

Being a fugitive forces you to be organised.

A third vent emerges in the floor. Steam pours from this one—the rich water breath rising off Asteri station's internal power cores.

Absinthe tucks his extremities close and drops into the opening. The moisture-thick air in the vent curls around his head, pressing against his flat nostrils. It smells of minerals and metal—cleaner than in the corridor.

Deeper he falls. Down. Down. Through the intestines of the station.

Absinthe looks up. The vent opening is a small circle above him. The silhouette of the bounty hunter's head emerges, ringed by background light.

Then the shadow widens as Cordelia Bane jumps also.

Planet Aquanum: 500 years ago

The Gathering Place glitters in the lights of a hundred burning torches. The Octari, resplendent in her formal armour sits atop her grey, stone throne. Next to her stands Jaskal, imperfect in form, but glowing with pride. Abaforth stands next to the boy, his hearts bursting with joy.

'Abaforth Krultius has worked tirelessly to bring us hope,' calls out the Octari, pointing to the glass carafe settled on a stone plinth before her. 'He has developed a source of happiness for all Aquanorians and a resource that we can trade to the outer rim planets.

'Already Axxine ships are en-route to purchase quantities from us. Their credits will allow us to build a new home—a great floating city that will raise us above any future disasters. Today, the future of Aquanum is secured.'

She places a hand on Jaskal's shoulder. 'A future for our children to prosper in!'

The hall erupts into a cacophony of sound. Aquanorians cheer as the Octari nods to her son. Jaskal glances at Abaforth, who smiles encouragingly. The boy steps forward, lifts the carafe to his lips and drinks deeply.

Jaskal raises the empty carafe into the air. Its cut edges

catch the firelight, fracturing it into rainbows that paint his skin.

But then the boy's smile fades. He stiffens and jerks. His tentacles splay out, rigid. The carafe drops from his fingers, shattering into slivers of light on the ground.

Dark-coloured froth dribbles from the boy's lips; his black eyes flutter from left to right. He reaches for shadows no-one else can see.

Then he slumps face-first to the ground.

The Octari's scream shatters the air.

Asteri Station: Current day

Absinthe lands in a practised crouch, booted feet and fingertips his only connection to the gantry. Overhead fluorescent lights flutter on and off—their uncertain gaze casting muted shadows around the vast spherical room that is the station's rich water aquifer. A rusted balustrade sweeps by him, the barrier between floor and deep, still waters.

He sprints toward the far end of the gantry. Bane falls from the vent behind him, her landing punctuated by a huff of exhaled breath.

Absinthe races faster. Old, but still lithe and quick, he sprints for the overflow release valve and the small, security ship he has hidden beneath it in the quiet waters.

'*Halt*!' Bane's voice cracks like a whip, reverberating off the metal walls. Absinthe ignores her. He sucks in a breath.

The platform is only a few meters away—

A concussive blast of sound and a flash of light forces Absinthe to stop. Broken steel struts and sparking wires tumble to the gantry before him.

'You're only worth half as much, dead,' says Bane. 'But I'll aim to kill if you make me.'

Absinthe spins around. His tentacles shift in colour to match his anxiety—white to teal, and back. 'Would you consider being paid twice the bounty to let me go?'

Bane's disruptor sits rock steady in her grip. Her race through the station has her breathing heavy, each pant making her chametek jacket shift and blur in the flickering light.

'Sorry Abaforth. Usually I'd take the cash, but I have a personal problem with folks who kill kids. I consider your capture a public service.'

He sags. 'I doubt you know the real story.'

'I know enough,' replies the bounty hunter, her voice hard and bitter.

Planet Aquanum: 500 years ago

The slow *drip, drip* of water is the only sound in the velvet-deep darkness of the prison. Abaforth focuses on it. He can't bear to dwell on anything else. Not the vision of Jaskal lying wide-eyed and still before his mother's throne, nor the sound of the Octari's desperate sobs, nor even the way Jaskal's chest cracked beneath Abaforth's fists as he pounded, trying desperately to restart the boy's hearts.

But the boy remained dead—the mix of black and his

deformities a lethal combination.

How could he have known? Abaforth had tested the compound. The lab results were conclusive. Black was beneficial to Aquanorian DNA.

It shouldn't have killed Jaskal.

But it did.

And the Octari blamed Abaforth.

Her screams still torment him. '*Murderer! Murderer!*'

Abaforth shifts. His stomach aches, bruised from the beating the guards gave him. At least two of his tentacles were torn from his face. They will grow back, but right now, it is a pain he savours. He curls his fists to his chest and pulls his knees up tight. Tears creep past his eyelids as Jaskal's smiling face hovers before him—a memory painted against the darkness.

The clang of steel echoes. Torchlight blossoms along the passage. An Aquanorian guard emerges from the shadows, leading a tall, broad-shouldered creature with brown skin, a feathered brow and wide yellow eyes.

An Axxine. It must be the one come to collect the first shipment of black, not that the Octari will sell it to him now. She has made clear her stance on Abaforth's drug—better the people of Aquanum die than infect the galaxies with such a poison.

'This is the murderous traitor,' snarls the guard. 'He's set to die at dawn.'

'I see,' says the Axxine. 'And is he allowed to speak with me?'

'Only if you do not speak of the black,' replies the guard. 'The Octari intends for the formula to die with him.'

Abaforth huddles in closer to himself. Yes. That is for the best. Even with all the testing he did and all the promise the drug held, it turned on him, killed an innocent. Jaskal's face fills his mind again. He turns his chin to the wall.

Burrrr-zzzzt.

A blast of light followed by the sizzle and stench of burning flesh fills the corridor. Abaforth starts. The guard lies dead on the floor, the huge Axxine hovers over him with the barrel of his blaster still glowing. The alien's head swivels, his yellow, razor-gaze falling to Abaforth's.

Abaforth shivers, and shuffles further against the wall. His hearts beat unsteadily as the Axxine approaches. Another shot sears out of the blaster, hitting the access panel of his prison door. The plate holds for a moment, squealing out a muted alarm. Then it turns to slag and drips to the floor, silenced.

The Axxine pushes open the panel and holds out his free hand.

'Agree to make black for us using our laboratories,' says the Axxine, 'and you will be given a home on our planet, Axx. What do you say?'

Abaforth hangs on the edge of decision. Jaskal died because of him. He should stay and face his just punishment.

But perhaps, with time, the Octari will understand it wasn't his fault; that he had no way of knowing. Perhaps he can find a way to redeem himself and help his world rebuild. She can't mean to throw away two hundred years of trust and friendship on a mistake.

Abaforth's sense of self-preservation prevails. He grasps the Axxine's hand.

'I'll come,' he whispers, knowing that in doing so he has banished himself to a life of exile.

He truly is the traitor his Octari branded him to be.

But maybe that will change.

Asteri Station: Current day

Absinthe takes a step toward Bane. The hidden craft is so close. Can he distract the woman enough to secure an escape? The bounty hunter presses her finger tighter to the disruptor's trigger. He stops.

'So you would see me condemned then, without a fair trial,' he says.

She sneers, her teeth a brilliant white against her olive skin. 'You were given that trial on Aquanum long ago.'

'Yes,' says Absinthe, lifting his arms wide. 'A trial presided over by my grieving Octari—a mother looking to find blame for the death of her son.' His tentacles curl up into a sneer of his own.

He drops his hands to his side. 'But she was just as guilty as I. Jaskal died because *both* of us wanted to save our world. I committed no crime—I made a mistake. Under pressure and wanting a quick solution, I didn't test my compound completely. I didn't understand the complexities when used in a subject with deformities like Jaskal's. And yes, he died for it. But I loved both him and my home above all else. I would never have intentionally hurt either.'

Bane's eye holds the line of her disruptor's sight. 'Mistake or not, you still went and taught others how to make the black. That pissed a lot of people off.' She flicks the end of the disruptor toward the exit doors on the far side of the circular gantry. 'So get moving. There's a not-so-cosy berth waiting for you on the *Tartarus* prison ship.'

Absinthe sighs. He closes his eyes. A vision of Jaskal rises, still sharp after all this time, smiling and innocent. Absinthe locks his gaze back to Bane.

'I know you won't believe me, but I never sold the formula. I betrayed the Axxine buyer and jumped ship three days after I left Aquanum. But it made no difference. They discovered the drug for themselves on other asteroids, anyhow.'

She hesitates, one fingertip stroking her temple. Then her mouth purses. 'I don't care. At the end of the day they say you're a killer. You're worth three hundred thousand credits delivered alive. That's the only truth that matters to me.'

Absinthe, frowns. Truth. The bounty hunter claims to hate liars—all right then—he will give her his truth. He lifts his chin.

'The grief of others has always been my burden to shoulder. That implant in your head will attest to the truth of that. Listen to it as I say I am neither cruel, evil nor a murderer and what you are doing is wrong.'

'Get moving.' Her jaw hardens.

'So you care nothing for honour or decency?'

Cordelia's eyes widen, then narrow. 'Honour and decency only ever get you dead, Aquanorian. Credits are the only thing I care about.'

He looks up at the ruined wall and gantries above him, saddened as he listens to the quiet lapping of the water in the aquifer. He turns back to Cordelia.

'Don't you ever feel the need to just do the right thing?'

'I am doing the right thing.'

'For yourself maybe.' Absinthe sighs. 'Well then, at least let me have one last drink in my own goddamn bar.'

'You're not in a position to be asking for concessions.'

'And yet you are in a position to grant them,' says Absinthe. 'Just one drink—I won't run again. I'll even pour you one on the house.' He lifts a tentacle. 'C'mon bounty hunter, grow a heart. Do at least one decent thing in your life.'

Cordelia presses her lips together, her disruptor lowers an inch. 'Make it another fireon water and you have a deal.'

'No. It needs to be something stronger. I know. The Murderer's Drink.'

She cocks an eyebrow. 'You mean the Terran spirit, absinthe? Is that meant to be ironic?'

'No,' says Absinthe.

'Then why choose that one?'

'Because the drink is heartless like you. It turns the innocent into murderers, just like you are doing to me. For— make no mistake—you hand me over to the *Tarturus* and you are cementing every lie ever told about me. I'll be forced to become what they say I am.'

He straightens. 'The Hegemon won't let a scientist with my abilities in chemistry rot unused. They'll force me to work in their labs. For their profit. You know they will. It's how they operate. They're just like the Underground Banker, or the Chancer Brothers Crime Syndicate. People don't matter. Profit above everything.'

A conflicted look comes over Cordelia's face, as if she is listening to a voice in her head. Maybe her lie implant is whispering to her, confirming the truth of his words. But Absinthe can't know anything for sure except that his shoulder blades are itching. Not all is what it seems.

The bounty hunter's gaze remains hard, but her gun drops another inch. 'You can have your drink, barkeeper. But then you go.'

'Okay' agrees Absinthe. 'And I will go. My word given on *my* decency and honour.'

'Right,' says Cordelia. 'Because those things are worth something to you.'

'Exactly,' he whispers.

END

1915 hours: Doubts

Cordelia Bane

Cordelia signed Ab over to the *Tartarus* Hegemon prison ship with an angry swipe of her ID chip. The bounty transfer acknowledgement glowed green, indicating a transfer of funds from the Hegemon Core computer. The dycerium doors closed behind him with a hollow, permanent sound that thudded through her chest. Feck.

She ported to the Zoo and sat alone, swallowing down the lump of guilt in the back of her throat. Something felt wrong about taking him in. But facts were facts. Abaforth—Absinthe, whatever he called himself—killed a child. He deserved to pay the price. And he was old. He'd been on the run for hundreds of years. Practiced in lying. Maybe so good he was able to deceive the chip in her head. Nothing was infallible.

Besides, she needed the money to pay the Underground

Banker off. He'd put a time limit to the clearing of her debts—and promised a kill-order on her if she didn't deliver. She ground her teeth and transferred the bounty to the Underground Banker with another swipe at her wrist ID chip. More than half the debt paid, but an uncomfortable heaviness sat like lead in her stomach. Why did she still feel so shit?

'Feck it!' Cordelia threw back her glass of fireon water. The taste however was ruined by a stench that had seeped into the bar when the doors last opened. She wrinkled her nose. Smelled like something dead; half-rotted flesh.

Another beep sounded on her wrist implant. Another bounty listing.

Cordelia blinked up the details to her ocular implant. This was a lucrative one too—large enough to clear the last of her obligations to the Banker. Her lucky day.

She ran down the list of data. Malick Dorsson. Wanted on the planet Derria. She blinked again. This listing came with a photo. It flicked up. She narrowed her gaze, zooming in. The picture was old but she recognised the face.

Zev.

Malick Dorsson was Zev Smith. Fecking hell.

Cordelia tapped her comms. Time to get Ori to the Zoo. They both needed to have a chat with Asteri Station's maintenance manager—about more than just the stink in the air.

Ori Bligh

'What is that stench?' Ori stepped into the Zoo and waved a hand in front of her face. Just as bad here as outside. The stink seemed to permeate the whole station. Something like rotting animal, but underlain with lavender and citrus; like someone had tried to disguise the smell of a decaying corpse by spraying it with perfume.

Cordy pulled down her kerchief, sniffed, then tugged it back up again in a hurry. 'It's worse. Started earlier.'

She nodded at the substitute barkeeper, Vell, who shrugged in the vague way Ori had come to realise meant he was trying to be diplomatic while implying he really didn't care, either.

Cordy added, 'Vell says there are people throwing up from the stink all over the station.'

'I can't smell it,' he said, continuing to mix a purple cocktail. 'And can't find Zev to ask him if there's something wrong with the air filters.'

'I thought dogs had a heightened sense of smell.' Ori put her hands on her hips and glanced around the bar. Most of the patrons had cloths or masks over their faces, lifting them only long enough to drink or eat. 'So, what? You're all just sitting here, waiting? What if it's a disease or something?'

'Filter.' Cordy tapped her kerchief. 'Not my problem, kiddo. I'm just on my next job. Which I need to talk to you about. Then I'm out of here.'

'Later. Let me sort out this stink, first,' Ori growled and stomped toward Zev's office.

'Wait!' Cordy called. Ori ignored her and Vell stepped up to stop the bounty hunter from following behind the bar.

Ori slid through the back corridor and found Zev's office. It was locked. Wrenching at the handle snapped the lock and she shoved the door inward.

'Shut the door, ya stupid girl! Shut the fecking door!'

Blinking in the semi-gloom, Ori obliged and waited for her eyes to adjust. Zev sat hunched behind his desk, staring at his displays. The nearest monitor cast a sick, reddish light onto his face, washing it in pale blood and deepening the age lines into crevasses.

'You okay?' she asked, hesitantly.

'No,' he snapped. 'Feck off and do your job. Get them off the station.'

Ori took a step backward. His eyes were those of a man on the edge. Desperate. Haunted. Limned by old ghosts and new fears.

'Get what off the station?'

'Derrians and their cargo.'

'I can't just throw people off the station for no reason,' she said. 'What have they done? What's wrong with their cargo? Is it illegal?'

Zev scrubbed a hand over his face. 'Sit. I'll tell you. But you have to fecking promise me you'll get rid of them. Don't let them find me.' He nodded at the maintenance log tablets littering his untidy desk. 'I'm all that's holding this place together. You let them take me and Asteri is fecked.'

'Take you? Why?'

'Because my real name is Malick Dorsson.'

Fruitful Negotiations

Aiki Flinthart

40 years ago

'Oh, hell no!' Carmen slapped a hand over her nose and backed away from the table, eyeing Malick's contributions to the menu with distaste. 'What on Earth are those? They smell disgusting.'

Malick Dorsson grinned and attempted to rub sticky sap off his fingers. No luck. The stuff was as thick as glue and the colour of old blood. It stank almost as much as the spiky, clot-red fruit he'd harvested.

Carmen swallowed, her face pale. Sweat beaded her forehead. She laid a hand on her gravid belly and closed her eyes.

'I think I'm going to be sick.' She collected her biohazard suit mask from its place on the camp kitchen wall and suctioned it to her face with a sigh of relief.

'You get used to it.' Mal scrubbed his hands under the makeshift tap that brought fresh water from the stream, then disinfected with the sonic sanitiser. He'd just had a booster for the multi-spectrum vaccines everyone got on joining Exploration, but he liked to be careful.

'Where did you get them?' Carmen's voice emerged, raspy and tinny, from the mask. 'What are they?'

Mal pointed at the five, head-sized fruit dripping scarlet onto the aluminium workbench. 'Found them in a hidden gully about five kilometres west. One lone tree. Apparently, they're a delicacy for the Derrians. They have a huge farm of them outside the city to the south. Highest security complex in the place. Guards. With those poison needle-guns they use, and the snaky cat things they keep as pets.'

He shrugged. 'I sent a drone over the fence and saw the Derrians picking the fruit. I gather they put them in a special drying facility for a couple of weeks until they crack open of their own accord. Guess that's when they're ripe enough to eat.'

Carmen screwed up her nose and prodded one with a fork. The fruit rocked slightly on its wicked, black-tipped spikes. 'Get them out. Maybe the inside is delicious, but they smell like rotting meat. I have to cook dinner before the rest of the team gets back. The captain has invited the Tallest One to sample our food and check out the Hegemon database of trade goods. If these are still here, no-one will want to eat.'

'That's just it,' Mal said proudly. He pointed at the fruit. 'The Tallest One may not like our supplies, and the captain said he'd only managed to get small samples of that yellow mushy stuff they eat as everyday food. So, I figured we can put these in the oven for a few hours and they'll be dried out enough to open.'

He spread his hands. 'I've seen the Derrians outside their homes early in the evenings, sharing meals and talk, exchanging items. Maybe it's their standard way of engaging in trade. We want the Tallest One to be comfortable, right? How better than with their own delicacy?'

So far, engaging the interest of the Derrians and their leader had proven difficult. They seemed to want nothing the Hegemon could offer in exchange for the bounty of their world. At least the Tallest One was willing to come and visit the ship. It was a start.

Carmen sighed, prodding the fruit again. 'Fine. But we don't know how to serve these. Do they get cooked in some way? Some way that will get rid of the stink, I mean?'

'I haven't seen them cook anything or use fire at all, so just drying it will have to do. Sometimes, just showing you tried to understand another culture is enough.'

Carmen sent him a dry look. 'Says the newbie to the four-year vet. Go get ready. The Tallest One is due at sunset.'

Mal casually saluted Carmen and strolled outside. He stretched sore back muscles and wandered to the edge of the camp. To the west lay vast, dark forests, rising to distant mountains of hazy blue and purple. The shimmering sun hung heavy, a ripe orange poised on the mountain range's ragged teeth, about to slide down the throat of darkness.

To the east stood the delicate spires of the Derrian people's one and only city. Well, more of an organic growth than a city. Plants had been coaxed into strange forms. Domes of close-woven vines covered in broad, purple leaves served as homes and storage facilities for a few thousand people. Hollow, living trunks, fifty or a hundred metres high, acted like apartment buildings, straight and smooth all the way up to a crown of delicate branches and scarlet leaves like a spray of blood against the dust-blue sky.

Mal sucked a deep breath of cool, damp air and smiled. He'd joined Exploration only eight months before and here he was on a first-contact mission with one of the best teams in the Hegemon.

He sought the bright spot in the heavens that was *The Wonderer,* the mothership. But the sky wasn't yet dark enough to see her. Behind him, on the stony floodplain, sat her squat, little baby scoutship, *The Wunderkind.* Plump and robust, the silvery craft held just four crew and enough supplies and weapons for two weeks of surface time if the place had proved inhospitable.

But it hadn't.

The planet was a treasure-trove of unusual botanicals and potential mineral deposits, and nothing inimical to human life. Now it was up to Captain Singh to tiptoe through the delicate negotiations with the Tallest One. Negotiations that would allow the Hegemon to explore the world for rare earths, medicinal and food plants, and other rarities that could be valuable to the peoples of the galaxy.

Mal glanced over the lush purple forests and fell into a pleasant daydream. Scientists would come and perhaps discover the cure for flipdrive psychosis or black addiction. Maybe in the very fruit he'd just brought in. They would name the plant after him. He would be famous throughout the galaxy. Sought after by the Hegemon as a consultant. Maybe he could even live here and be the trade ambassador.

Yes. That would be good. There weren't many worlds with such a vibrant, complex biosphere. It appealed to something primal in him. He could bring Cassie and they could produce the children that would replace them. Maybe even an extra. This would be a good place to raise kids.

'Ensign Dorsson!'

Mal jumped at Captain Singh's shout. He hurried toward *Wunderkind*'s temporary extension that served as the dining hall for the crew.

'Sir?' He saluted, conscious of his sweat-stained grey uniform and the faint miasma of rotting meat that still hung about him.

'Report.' The captain surveyed him with shrewd dark eyes set beneath thick black brows.

With a nod, Mal launched into his rehearsed speech on where he'd explored and what he'd found. Halfway through, the captain waved a hand to silence him.

'Yes, yes. Put it in the official document. Well done.'

Singh wrinkled his thin nose. 'Carmen tells me you've sourced some of those *glerran* fruits of theirs?' Mal's aural implant translated the word to *new* fruit, but the language was still incomplete in the database, so it was hard to know what that meant, exactly. Perhaps it contained some vital nutrients for the Derrian people—which would explain why they valued and guarded it.

Singh rose from the table, lithe and fine-boned—as most long-time Exploration members were. 'I want to commend you on smart thinking. They seem to mix business with mealtimes, so we want to get it right.'

He grimaced and paced restlessly, as was his habit when things weighed heavily on his mind. 'Carmen's run a sample of the *glerran* through the analyser and it should be safe for us to eat as well.'

He sent a thoughtful look at Mal. 'I want you to be at the table tonight.'

'Sir?' Mal suppressed a grin, his heart thudding. 'Yes, sir. I'd be honoured. What do you need me to do?'

'I've noticed their leaders never serve their own food, so you'll serve us both.' Singh held up a hand when Mal grimaced. 'Don't get me wrong, Ensign. I also know you're smart and good with languages. Our language database is still very patchy. Two sets of ears are better than one. Might prevent fatal misunderstandings.'

'Thank you, sir.'

Singh scratched at his buzzcut salt-and-pepper hair. 'We *need* to get some sort of trade agreement. A foothold. This world is too unique. Too good a colony site with all this water and plant life. We have to find some way to settle our people here.'

Mal hesitated. 'But what about the Derrians? It's their world. You're not talking about...' He couldn't say the word. The Hegemon had slaughtered millions in previous years in their search for grey fuel. Before flipdrives switched to rich water for power. But surely that wasn't necessary anymore?

With a wave of his hand, Singh dismissed the suggestion. 'Of course not. We're not barbarians. There are two other continents that look promising. We could section off territory for the Derrians here and leave them be. But it will go a lot smoother if they agree to teach us how their ecosystems work.'

He gazed off into the middle distance briefly, his eyes holding ghosts and memories. 'I've lost people to alien life forms before and it's never pleasant. Two to disease. One eaten by some type of semi-sentient animal.' He shuddered. 'We found his remains cooked over a campfire the next day.'

Swallowing down bile, Mal nodded. 'Understood, sir. I'll do my best to encourage the Tallest One to trade and let us start a colony. Does he have a name?'

'We don't know gender yet,' Singh said reprovingly. 'Or if there even is one. We have no idea how they reproduce. So, gender-neutral pronouns, if you please. Zis name is Kanhuna.'

'Kanhuna,' Mal repeated, tasting the word. 'Very good. If you don't mind, I'll go wash and change.'

Singh sniffed. 'Yes. Please.'

#

An hour later and the Tallest One ambled into the campsite. Only a few rays of blazing, ruddy light, bleeding into the sky from behind the western horizon, marked zis arrival. Mal, standing at attention along with Carmen and Lieutenant M'tonga, resisted the urge to lean back as the alien approached.

Kanhuna was well over three metres, slender and whip-like. Beneath pale, lavender skin, the knotted muscles in elongated, bare arms and legs moved like corded, twisted rope. The bald scalp was mottled with shifting patterns of dark burgundy, red, and purple that matched zis eyes.

Seven digits on each hand and foot, Mal noted absently. Digits that wafted in flowing, graceful movements. More like tentacles than fingers.

Singh made a fluttering gesture toward the sky with his fingers and greeted the Tallest One by name. The captain wore a comm glove and his common tongue words emerged from it, translated into the Derrian language—a series of almost subsonic grumblings and clickings, combined with whispers that sounded like the wind susurrating through grass.

Kanhuna repeated the gesture and replied. The faint earthy smell that always accompanied a Derrian drifted over. Mal's aural implant translated the language as best it could.

'I wish the warmth of sun on your face and the cool of water on your feet.'

'May the winds be gentle,' Singh returned. A soft groan

emerged from the comms unit. He gestured at the table, set for three beneath a canopy of glittering stars.

On the table lay a Hegemon trade database tablet. The full list of everything on offer. 'Please, sit. We have much to show you. And our cook has prepared foods your people prefer, but you're welcome to sample ours.' Singh smiled deprecatingly. 'It's not our best, only what we can carry on long trips.'

Kanhuna inclined zis head and eased ziself onto a cargo box, the largest object available to seat the massive creature. Singh and Mal sat opposite: Mal, upright and on the edge of his chair, Singh leaning back, his eyes narrowed.

Once shown how to access the Hegemon data, Kanhuna spent some time silently perusing the images. Occasionally ze would ask about an item and either Mal or the captain would explain its function. Mal suspected, however, the Tallest One's interest was tepid at best and wasn't surprised when ze put the tablet aside.

'The drawings are beautiful.' Zis tendril-fingers waved toward Singh. 'What did you wish to exchange thoughts about? The sun sleeps and so must I.'

Singh frowned and cleared his throat. 'We would like permission to study your people, your land, this world. It is beautiful and our scientists can learn much. We can trade those things in the pictures for your knowledge and help.'

Nodding slowly, Kanhuna said, 'These thoughts are important and require nourishment to grow to full understanding. May we take in nutrients?'

The captain gestured to Carmen. She and M'tonga

vanished into the kitchen to bring out food.

They served the first dishes—steaming plates of flavoured vat-grown proteins and reconstituted carbohydrates. The best *Wunderkind* had, but a terrible representation of the variety of tastes and textures available in the vast expanse of the Hegemon's territories.

Mal shifted on the hard stool. The Tallest One picked up a protein cube between delicate fingers, placed it into zis mouth and chewed thoughtfully. There was silence for a long time. Carmen hovered behind, just out of the alien's sight, nibbling on her nails.

With a choking cough, Kanhuna turned aside and spat. The sticky, masticated lump of protein splatted onto the stony ground. Mal suppressed a smile. He handed over a glass of water. Without comment, Kanhuna swallowed it down.

Singh sent Mal a sidelong look, pinched his nostrils and jerked his chin toward the kitchen. Mal caught Carmen's eye and nodded. Her shoulders slumped but she touched two fingers to her forehead in acknowledgement. Mal drew his shoulders back. Now was his time.

'I'm sorry our food isn't to your taste, zon,' Singh said politely. His glove emitted a series of growls, rumbles, and whispers. 'But we have something you might like better. A delicacy of yours.'

The Tallest One inclined zis head and rumbled, 'Our needs are different. It was to be expected.'

Carmen emerged from the kitchen with two platters, one holding a bowl of the yellow mush the Derrians ate daily, the other covered—whether to hide the smell of the fruit or to do a big reveal, Mal wasn't sure. She placed them in the centre of the table and stood nervously by.

Mal served several spoonsful of the smooth yellow paste onto each plate. It looked and smelled like some sort of curry. He reached for the covered platter.

Kanhuna switched zis attention to Carmen and reached out toward her rounded belly. She started, but held still when Singh frowned. Those long, gentle digits stroked across Carmen's stomach and she shivered.

'Is this one afflicted by a gall?' ze asked.

A look of confusion passed across Singh's face and he raised a brow. Mal subvocally requested his comms glove to repeat the word into his aural implant. He listened twice. It sounded most like their word for an illness or something like a cancer.

'No, zon,' he said, hazarding a guess. 'She's not sick. She's pregnant. With child,' he clarified when the Derrian turned a blank look on him. 'It's how our species reproduces. Sexual reproduction.'

'Ah!' Kanhuna's expression cleared. Ze nodded and held zis arms wide. 'I, too, shall be soon in the time of ripening. I shall give up my place as the Tallest One and prepare myself. Bear the next generation along with my sisters.'

Singh smiled. 'That's wonderful. Let's celebrate. I'm anxious to taste the delicacy Carmen has prepared for you.' He nodded to Mal.

Mal tilted the lid on the platter, just enough so he could

check the contents. On it lay two of the *glerran* fruits, their husks cracked open, the fleshy-pink inside exposed. The smell was now mouth-watering. Almost like real roast meat, seasoned and salted.

'And I,' replied Kanhuna. 'For soon I shall be bonded and have no further need for food taken through this orifice.' She pointed to her mouth. 'And I shall miss it. And my work. It has been enjoyable to work for the growth of our people. And to meet yours.'

'But,' Mal asked, prising loose a flake of the tender fruit flesh with his knife, 'why do you have to give up your place as leader? Our women can still work and be leaders if they wish.'

Kanhuna spread her fingers. 'When it is our time, we join our sisters in the Place of Giving and produce those that will become our sons and daughters. We remain there, until end of days.' Her tentacle-fingers drooped. 'It is honourable, and important, if not as interesting.'

Mal speared the morsel and lifted it to his lips, just to make sure it was edible before presenting it to their guest. The baked fruit melted in his mouth, releasing subtle flavours of pork and salt, rosemary and something else, unfamiliar but delicious.

'The Place of Giving?' Singh said. 'Where is that?'

'The space where our mothers are protected as they bond with the earth, flower into fullness, and bear our children.' Kanhuna stared off into the darkness with something like longing in her eyes.

Mal set the platter's lid aside. He cut a larger slice of the fruit and laid it on Kanhuna's plate.

'I believe you call our birthing place,' the Derrian said, 'the *glerran* fruit garden.'

END

1930 hours: The Last Hunt

Cordelia Bane

Cordelia, concealed in her chametek jacket, lingered by the broken door of Zev's office. She'd heard it all—heard about the fruits and Ori's gasp of shock at Zev's story. Another child killer, albeit an accidental one. Seemed like this station was a breeding ground for them.

Cordelia sighed. Truthfully though, she didn't think Zev deserved the bounty placed on him. He was just another product of the Hegemon's profit-focussed stupidity when it came to dealing with alien species. But still—she needed the credits from this bounty to save her own neck. And if it wasn't her, other hunters would come for him.

She blinked up the bounty details again. The call-out was listed as a "catch or kill". She frowned. Zev didn't deserve to die. She would take him instead to join Absinthe on the

Tartarus.

The door to the office opened fully.

Cordelia, still invisible, stepped aside as Ori emerged looking pale.

Ori glanced back at Zev. 'Don't worry. I'll sort this. I'll have the Derrians moved on straight away. Then I've got that radiation leak ship to inspect. It's just arrived. I'll come back in the morning and we can work out a plan to keep you hidden from the Derrians if they come again.' She shook her head and smiled ruefully. 'Never thought I'd say something like that. I was top of the Grey Guards Academy.'

Zev growled a laugh. 'More to life than the Grey Guards and being perfect, girl. I know that from experience.'

She sighed. 'So I'm finding out. Night.' She strode away.

Zev's voice followed her down the hall. 'Thanks girl. You're saving more lives than one here.'

Ori waved without looking back and vanished into the Zoo.

Cordelia pressed her boot into Zev's doorway as he tried to close it. The old man's brow furrowed and he pushed harder, crushing her foot. She threw the hood of her jacket back.

He gave a surprised grunt and squinted at her. 'You here for pleasure or business, bounty hunter?'

She pushed her way into his office. 'Sorry, Zev. It's all business this time. You are a wanted man.'

He moved just as fast as Absinthe had when she'd outed him. A wrench materialised in the manager's hand and he swung it towards her chin. She ducked, throwing out a leg to hook him off balance. Zev stumbled, and fell against his desk. His maintenance tracking tablets slipped, clattering to the floor. One screen smashed and threw shards of glass in glittering fragments in all directions.

'Stop!' yelled Zev, sliding to his knees. 'These tablets are all that's keeping this place together.' He held a hand out. 'Please—you don't know what you're doing. This fecking station will fall apart without me. No-one else can keep the patch jobs maintained.'

'Sorry, Zev,' she said. 'But if it's not me, it'll be someone else. Look. I like you, so I'll tell you this. The bounty on you is a catch or kill. If you come with me, at least you'll live.'

Zev's chin fell to his chest. 'So, it's to be the *Tartarus* for me too then?' He looked up, his gaze accusing. 'Well, at least thanks to you, I've got Absinthe already waiting for me over there.'

Cordelia swallowed down rising guilt. 'It'll be a real reunion, I'm sure.'

Don't Make the Same Mistake Twice

Aiki Flinthart

Current day

'No,' Ori Bligh said, laying a hand on her stunner, 'I don't care what your engineer says. My job is to inspect every ship that docks at this station for contraband.' She raised her chin. 'By preventing me from inspecting your engineering section, you're admitting you have something illegal on board.' She gave a sweet smile. 'Shall I call it in now, Captain Cabren? Won't take the Grey Guards' cruiser in this area long to get here.'

The *Orion*'s captain held up two hands, palms out. He gave a lopsided smile that sparkled in his sun-gold eyes. Ori pressed her lips thin, ignoring the flush of excitement that swept through her body at the unmistakable look. He was trying everything he could to get out of the inspection. She knew his type. The serial charmer. Only fools fell for them twice.

She returned his puppy-hopeful look with flat disinterest and the gleam faded. He sighed.

'Look, Lieutenant...' he checked her name badge '...Bligh. I'm not trying to hide anything. We just had some engine trouble. That's why we've stopped here. We normally flip right past but we have to make repairs. My engineer says the drive room is dangerous at the moment.'

His smile flickered, laced this time with what looked very much like weary sincerity. 'I know you have to inspect, but can you wait a day until it's not going to kill you?'

Ori paused, trying to assess whether he was telling the truth.

He held out a portable scanning unit in one lean hand. 'Look. Read the engineer's log for yourself. Dated two flips back. We called it in, in advance, remember?'

She gazed at him for a few more seconds, but his composure didn't falter so she took the log and skimmed it. Radiation leaks and a minor misalignment of the flipdrive.

'Fine.' She handed it back. 'You have four hours to effect repairs enough for me to inspect. In the mean time, I want an assurance the ship won't blow up and wipe the station out.'

He held out a hand. 'Word of honour, ma'am.'

Ori shook it, swallowing as the warmth of his calloused palm sent a spike of sheer desire from her chest to her groin.

She let go and wiped her hand on her coveralls. His gaze followed the movement and his smile softened.

She cleared her throat. 'I…I have to finish my rounds. I'll return at the designated time.' She stalked away toward the next docking station.

It had been a very long day, already. She'd been looking forward to going to bed. Did having an overinflated sense of duty do her any good out here on the fringes of the Hegemon? Would it get her back to the Inner Systems any faster than her designated three year punishment term?

'Lieutenant Bligh?' Cabren's mellow voice called. She glanced over her shoulder.

'I hear the Zoo is a decent bar. I'll be there in an hour.' He grinned. 'Just in case…you know…you need to ask me anything else.'

Ori strode away, feeling the heat of his gaze on her back.

#

Against her best intentions, Ori's feet took her to the Zoo an hour later, at 2045. And against her best intentions, her eyes sought out his tall, broad-shouldered form amongst the crowd of chattering transients and morose permanents.

There he was, in one of the corner booths, with two drinks set on the scarred table. She hesitated. Was he with someone already? He sat, staring down at his own hands, a frown pulling his brows together. He must be. She should go.

Then he looked up and that damned smile lit his face like

a nova. A smile just for her. He gestured her over and her treacherous body moved without consulting her brain. She slid into the booth, knowing her cheeks were pink. She was old enough to know better. What was she doing?

He touched her hand and heat pooled between her thighs again. She suppressed a groan. It had been way too long. Maybe she just needed a good screw to get him out of her system?

'Hey,' he said, with that lopsided smile again, 'glad you made it. Didn't think you'd show.'

'Me neither.' She frowned. 'Still not sure why I came, to be honest. It's late.' Almost lights-out cycle for the station.

He tilted his head and grinned. 'My irresistible charm?' When she returned a dry look, he laughed and pushed the drink toward her. 'This is apparently the house speciality.'

Ori eyed the cloudy green mix dubiously. Until now she'd stuck with the gin her parents' distillery produced. Keeping up the pretence? Hoping for redemption, somehow? As though they would know or care.

She picked up the drink and sipped. Not too sweet. Good. A hint of something citrus. The alcohol burned pleasantly down her throat and warmed her stomach. Three sips and her cheeks heated. She pressed cold fingers to them and snuck a look at Cabren.

He was smiling at her, his gold eyes creased into wry amusement.

'What?' she asked, putting the drink aside. Too much of that and she'd start acting like an idiot.

Cabren shook his dark head and draped one arm along the back of the seat. 'Just then you looked like someone who hadn't had a drink in a long time and had forgotten how good they can be.'

'Up until today, it had been a while,' she admitted. 'This one is pretty good, but I have had a few today, already, so I'll pass.'

He leaned forward, gaze fixed on her face, that killer smile just tilting up the corners of his mouth. 'So what brings you all the way out to this rathole station? You don't strike me as an Outer Systems kind of woman.'

Ori shot him a hard look. 'What's a girl like you doing in a place like this? Really? What makes you think I'm not from here?'

He held up two hands in surrender. 'I have nothing against folks who live in the Inner Systems. But they don't know what they're missing. All that luxury and easy access to food and infrastructure.'

He slapped at his lean stomach beneath the grey shipsuit. 'Nothing makes you appreciate life quite like going hungry for a few days so you can feed your crew and power your ship.'

'You think I don't appreciate life? You know nothing about me.'

Cabren raked her with a narrow look, the grin falling away. 'I could make a few educated guesses.'

She gave a scornful laugh. 'Give it your best shot. I'll try not to be offended.'

He pointed. 'Short hair, uniform a size too big, no

cosmetics, but well-tended fingernails, and you move with the most incredible grace. You're fascinating to watch.'

'So?' She raised a brow.

'I'm thinking daughter of a well-off family. One that could afford dancing lessons, gene therapy, and manicures.' He held up a finger when she opened her mouth. 'But one who rebelled against it all and chose a career her parents didn't approve of. Ditched the glam clothing and cosmetics because she was tired of being valued for her pretty face. Am I close?'

At a sharp pain in her palms, Ori looked down at her clean fingernails and discovered her hands were clenched into fists. She relaxed them and reached for her drink with fingers that trembled slightly.

But even the cool drink didn't quench the renewed burn low in her gut when she thought of the life she'd left; her mother's cold rejection; her father's palpable disappointment.

'No,' she said, low. She sucked a long, slow breath to settle the roiling pain in her stomach. 'Well, sort of. Good family. No dancing. And the choice of career path wasn't quite what I—' Her throat closed. 'Look, can we talk about something else?'

'Sorry. Of course. Didn't mean to intrude.' Cabren touched her hand again, lightly. The hairs on her arms stood up and electricity skittered across her skin and peaked her nipples beneath the thick uniform.

Ori folded her arms and sat back. 'How are the engine repairs going?'

He inclined his head. 'Coming along nicely. We'll be

shipshape very soon.'

'In time for the inspection, Captain Cabren?' She grabbed the drink as an excuse not to look into his open, easy gaze.

'Absolutely.' He hesitated, then leaned closer. The clean smell of his freshly-washed hair set her body on fire again and she swallowed. 'Call me Alec?' he said.

She pulled away, trying to clear her head. 'I'm Ori.' The name tasted wrong, but it was too late. And how would telling him her real name help, anyway? That warm look would evaporate into distaste, as it always did.

'So...er...how did you get into...' she waved a hand vaguely in the direction of the ship dock '...whatever it is you do?'

'Trading?' He grinned easily. 'Parents were farmers on Caldera. Shithole of an Inner System planet. Everyone is...comfortable. There's no adventure.'

'Sounds just terrible,' she said.

'For me, yep.' He threw his arms wide. 'Decided I wanted out and saved every credit until I could get a berth on a merchant ship. Parents weren't happy, but I figured it's my life, not theirs. Worked my way up. Bought my own ship about two years ago. Went hunting for new markets outside Hegemon-controlled space.'

His smile quirked into wry understanding. 'And new things to satiate the insatiable Inner Systems buyers. Now I might finally be at the point of breaking even for the first time. But—' he shrugged. 'No. Business talk is boring. We don't have very long together. Surely we can think of something more interesting to…do?'

He slipped his hand under her unoccupied one and drew it to his mouth. With his eyes focussed solely on her face, his lips brushed her fingers and she couldn't suppress a gasp this time.

'Look,' he said, not breaking eye contact, 'I know this sounds crazy, but have you got a room we can go to? I haven't been able to stop thinking about you since we met.' He clasped her hand in both of his, his thumb brushing across the thin skin of her inner wrist. Then he let go and the shock was equally as great. 'If I'm completely out of line, just say so. No hard feelings.'

Ori gripped the glass of her drink so tightly it shattered and sprayed green cocktail across the table and her uniform. She shook liquid from her fingers and shivered as the cold mess soaked through her clothing. No blood, luckily.

Casting a quick look up through her lashes, she smiled. 'Well, I do have to change clothes.' She glanced around the full bar. 'But we can't leave together.' She gave directions to her room and left, every limb and muscle shaking in anticipation.

She must be utterly insane. But the bubble of desire and excitement wouldn't be banished. She'd never felt this intense an attraction to someone. Not even—No, best not to think about him. Not now.

She hurried to her room, stripped off her coveralls and tossed them into the laundry unit. With her bag as yet unpacked, the room looked bare and cold. She hastily pulled a few things from her luggage and displayed them on the shelves and desk. It gave her something to think about other than the immediate future. Her heart thudded so loud she barely heard the door chime.

Still wearing only her underclothing, she opened it. Alec stepped in and the door swooshed shut. Ori slapped the privacy lock. The admiring smile on his mouth was all it took to melt her doubts. She was mad, but it didn't seem to matter.

Alec opened his arms and she stepped into them without hesitation. His mouth, warm and gentle, captured hers and she abandoned herself to hedonistic pleasure.

#

When Ori woke two hours later, the bed was empty but his comforting scent lingered on the linens. She swept her hand across the space and sighed. Should she be glad he was gone or angry? Hard to say. At that moment, memories of lingering, exquisite sensation made her long for him to return.

She sat up and ran stiff fingers through her short hair. Ridiculous. Mutual desire. That's all it had been. Well-satisfied for both of them. Several times. Her cheeks heated and she pressed her fingers to them, unable to stop grinning like an idiot.

'Get a grip, O,' she said, aloud. Her last irresponsible action had put her in the Zoo. This was a one-time thing. Now she needed to put it aside and focus on her job.

A glance at the time display made her swear. Time to do

the next set of rounds. Including the inspection of Alec's ship. So much for an easy first day.

Her gaze fell on a small, red object. A strange and intricate shape, sitting on her desk.

She rose and picked it up, turning the delicate thing over in her fingertips. Paper? Where had he got a piece of that? Only primitive cultures and low-tech colonies used it these days. And how had he folded it into the perfect shape of a flower? Part of her wanted to unfold it, to analyse and understand. But she resisted and set it on a shelf. Touching it with a fingertip, she smiled and turned away to find fresh clothing.

#

'Where's Captain Cabren?' Ori said. 'The inspection is set for now. I won't be put off a second time.'

The young deck crewman who'd opened the *Orion*'s airlock at her command rubbed his hands together. He met her eyes briefly then looked away.

'The Captain's...er...busy, Lieutenant. Said to tell you we just need another half an hour.' He gave a feeble smile. 'If you don't mind, ma'am?'

Ori set her jaw. So that was his game after all. Use sex to soften her up so she wouldn't complete the inspection.

'I do mind.' She laid a hand on the stunner at her hip. 'You can either lead me to Engineering, or I can walk over your unconscious body. Which would you prefer?'

The boy muttered something rude, sighed and turned away, gesturing for her to follow. Partway down the clean, grey corridor, he paused and thumbed a button on a wall panel.

'Cap, she's coming down. Sorry.'

Too late, Ori realised she should have instructed him not to inform Cabren. Now he would have time to hide whatever it was he didn't want her to see. Feckit.

The crewmember strode ahead, not looking back to see if she followed. Acid boiled up from her stomach. She'd called it right from the start. She was the fool who fell for the serial charmer. Had she learned nothing?

But what was he hiding?

#

'What the hell is *that?*' Ori hesitated at the doorway to the Engineering section, gaping. Where she'd expected to find a regulation flipdrive, there was a floor-to-ceiling, clear tank containing some sort of pale green liquid. Tubes and wires sprouted from it in all directions.

One wall was a bank of screens flashing incomprehensible readouts. Behind the tank lay a complex array of huge, enclosed cabinets of varying sizes, all connected by tubes and wires that led back to the tank.

Then the…*thing* inside the tank swam into view and Ori jumped back. She'd read about a lot of different species at the Grey Guards' Academy and seen a few come through the Zoo and the station, already. But she'd never seen this before.

More tentacles than she could count, extruding and vanishing apparently at random. An amorphous body that kept changing shape, sliding along the tank walls, squeezing into corners. At least eight pairs of eyes. Possibly some sort of mouth in amongst the tentacles.

Alec strode into the room, frowning. He caught sight of her and smiled.

'Ori! Good to see you. We just need half an hour and we'll be ready. Let's go to the bridge.'

That glutinous surge of warm desire filled her again and Ori backed away from his outstretched hands.

'Damn you, Cabren.' The realisation of what he was solidified in her gut.

An empath. He must be. It was the only explanation for why she'd succumbed to his charm so easily.

'You've been manipulating me. Why? So I wouldn't see this?' She pointed at the creature. 'What is it? Are you keeping it prisoner? Selling it off to some collector of rare lifeforms?'

'I can explain,' he said, reaching out again.

She whipped her hands behind her back. He must need touch to establish empathic control over her feelings. 'No. Come near me again and I *will* stun you and lock you in the brig until the rest of my Grey Guards arrive.'

He halted, swiped a hand over his short, dark hair and grimaced. 'I'm sorry. Truly. I needed to buy time.' He waved a hand at her and at himself. 'You, me, us… it wasn't just—'

'Don't say it,' she snapped. 'Don't even pretend. I can't believe I fell for it. You're good, I'll give you that. But if you don't tell me what this thing is and what's going on, I'll call it in right now.'

Cabren glanced at the tank, his weary expression softening into a rueful smile. He laid a palm on the clear surface and sighed. In the tank, one tentacle uncurled and stroked the barrier, gently, like a lover's touch. The creature's skin flashed into shades of grey and dark purple. Cabren nodded.

'She's a Pelcorian.'

Ori folded her arms. 'Never heard of them.' She subvocally queried the Hegemon's Core database and drew a blank. Apparently the Hegemon's supermassive computer had never heard of them, either.

'No.' Cabren scrubbed at his scalp. 'Pelcor is a mostly water-world.' He gestured vaguely. 'Way outside the Hegemon's reach. We found P'tlana—Pat, we call her— beached on an island, dying. Our medic was able to help. But she wouldn't have survived back in the ocean. So, we brought her on board.'

'To sell to some collector, I suppose.' He had all the hallmarks of a smuggler, now she saw him clearly. Undoubtedly the ship was riddled with contraband, secreted into hidey-holes. A thorough search with a sniffer-bot would find any of the drug, black. But what else was he hiding?

She pressed the button on her wrist unit that would summon the three Grey Guards stationed here under her command.

With a shrug, Cabren patted the tank again. 'Initially, maybe. Then Pat here turned out to have an instinct for navigating the flipvoid. And she loves it. You should see what she can do! It's incredible. Cuts our trip time in half.' That nova smile lit his face again and Ori glared until it faded.

'So, what you're saying is that you have an alien life form imprisoned and are using her to improve your drive efficiency,' Ori said coldly.

Cabren opened his mouth, hesitated and grimaced. 'I suppose it would look that way, but—'

'Thank you.' Ori held up a hand. As much as his betrayal gnawed at her, she was obliged to handle this professionally. He needed to shut up, for his own good and the good of his crew. 'This ship is now impounded by the power vested in me by the Hegemon. You have the right to remain silent. Anything you say can and will be used against you in the Inner System courts.'

The stomp of booted feet outside rang through the engine room. Cabren blanched and sent her a pleading look.

'Please? Ori. Don't do this. You don't understand.'

'Shut up, Captain Cabren,' she snarled. 'I do understand. I understand your type all too well.' She stepped closer, prodding his chest with a finger. 'You think you can spend your life taking advantage of others. Charming stupid girls into believing you. Exploiting people. Then throwing them to the wolves when you're bored or ready to move on.'

She lifted her chin. 'Did you ever stop to think what would happen to me if I let you go and you got found out later?'

He stilled, closed his eyes briefly and sighed. When he opened them again the compassion there almost undid her. He searched her face and laid a gentle hand on her wrist. 'Someone really did a number on you, didn't they? I'm sorry. Truly. I get it. Men are bastards. If you have to turn me in, then fine. But please don't impound the ship. Don't let the Hegemon take Pat. They'll use her. Drain her dry.'

Ori hesitated. There was no doubting the sincerity in his voice. The genuine fear. She shook herself. No. He was an empath. Projecting the emotion to influence her. The Hegemon would do the right thing with the alien. They would return it to its world if they could. The regulations were clear on that.

She stepped back.

The Grey Guardsmen appeared in the doorway, weapons drawn. She pointed to Cabren. 'Put him in the brig. The prison ship, *Tartarus,* leaves in half an hour. I want him on it.'

'Yes, ma'am,' Sergeant Yang snapped. 'Docking clamps for the ship?'

She nodded. 'Have your men guard the crew while you put Cabren in the brig. I want a brain scan on him, too. Bring me the result straight away. Then put the crew into cargo bay three. There's not enough space in the brig.'

Yang jerked a thumb at the tank. 'Scan that, too?'

Ori hesitated. 'No. Leave it for the Core scientists.'

Yang gestured at Cabren with the stunner. Cabren's shoulders slumped. He cast one frowning look back at the tank, then a pleading one at Ori. When she stared back coldly, his whole body sagged. But he walked ahead of Yang without argument and gestured placatingly at his young deck crewman and engineer, who watched on wide-eyed.

Ori addressed them. 'Get the rest of your crew into the mess hall. You'll wait there until cargo three is ready.'

The young crewman trembled. 'You're not really going to arrest us all, are you? I mean Pat can't—'

The engineer thumped him in the arm. 'Shut up, kid. She doesn't care.'

'Smart man,' Ori said. 'Now go. If you're lucky you'll get charged as accessories.'

Four crew straggled out, followed by the two remaining Grey Guards. Left alone in the thrumming engineering room, Ori paused and studied the great tank. The alien floated near the top, tentacles limp and dangling, all eight eyes closed, skin unpleasant shades of mottled grey and black. Ori frowned. Was it sick? Should she get their medic?

Then it changed to a shade of green that matched the water and became invisible. Only ripples in the liquid and a faint sloshing, audible above the hum of machinery, indicated the tank was occupied.

Ori backed out of the room, taking her hand off the stunner only when the door closed and sealed the engineering section. She let out a thick breath. Her legs shook and, for some reason, her chest and throat were tight. Tears pricked at her eyes.

What the feck? Cabren was a smuggler, preying on the weak and gullible. He deserved what he got.

Why did she feel like she'd just lost her best friend?

#

Ori sank onto a stool at the Zoo bar and stared at the drinks list.

'Usual, O?' Vell's deep, gruff voice roused her.

'Yes. No.' She pointed. 'The house speciality. Where's Absinthe?' The usual barkeeper was away, again. Probably helping someone in trouble on Asteri Station. That seemed to be the Zookeeper's thing—helping people in trouble.

Vell's black lips peeled back into a snarl. 'That fecking bounty hunter friend of yours. Took him to the *Tartarus.*'

'What?' Ori blinked in shock. 'Legit bounty call? Hegemon-sanctioned?'

He nodded.

She swore. 'Nothing I can do, then. It'll be for the Hegemon Core courts to bring to trial.'

Vell's large ears twitched. 'Can't you…I don't know…put in a word with someone in the Inner Systems?'

Ori snorted. 'Believe me, I'm the last person anyone there would listen to. My own family don't even want to hear from me at the moment.'

He opened his mouth, but didn't ask the question. Ori looked away from the caninoid barkeeper, reminded too strongly that Absinthe was gone. And the memory of Ab, with his Aquanorian facial tentacles, reminded her of the Pelcorian in the tank.

'Want to talk about it?' A green drink appeared by her hand. The same drink Cabren had bought her. She stroked the cold glass with one finger, rubbing the condensation between her fingertips.

Her neat, manicured fingertips. The last remnant of her old life. She sipped the sweet-tart drink and the room shimmered behind tears.

Maybe not the last remnant. She had carried the hope of redemption and return for weeks now. Ever since the Grey Guards' Commander had decided three years on Asteri Station would be her fate for stupidity and naivety.

That hope sat as weight in her chest. The weight of expectation. Of family. Of a safe, hammered-out pathway amongst the safe, hammered-down populace of the Inner Systems.

The weight of fear.

Fear that she wouldn't return to the life she'd wanted. The only life she'd known existed, until today. The only people she'd known existed, until today. The only way of thinking she'd known, until today.

Now it was also a fear that she *would* return and would be trapped there.

Which one was it? Which one did she want?

Ori straightened. She looked at Vell. 'A few months ago, I made a stupid mistake. I fell in love with the wrong guy. He hung me out to dry. Left me to take the blame for a crime he committed.'

Vell showed no surprise, but it wasn't easy to read his emotions at the best of times. His ears stilled their constant movement, though, which meant he was listening.

Ori glanced in the direction of the *Orion*'s docking site.

'And I think I've escaped making the same mistake twice.'

'You think?' He wiped the bar with a hygiene swipe and flicked it into the disposal chute with practiced ease.

'I—'

'Lieutenant Bligh!' Sergeant Yang skidded to a halt, panting. The Glondian's slitted nostrils were flared, zis pale skin flushed delicately green with exertion.

Ori swivelled on her seat.

'It's the prisoner, ma'am,' ze handed her a medic's tablet to read. 'You asked for the brain scan report. He's just been put on board the *Tartarus*. They're due to flip out in five minutes.' Ze pointed to the tablet and gave a sheepish shrug. 'Thought you'd want to see this, just in case.'

She ignored the unsubtle dig, took it and swiped through the report, trying to decipher the medical jargon. She slowed and read it again, her stomach sinking.

'Feck! It's not him.' She stared blankly into the distance. 'He said her name was "P'tlana" but that he called her "Pat". And they communicated when he touched the tank. It's *her*. She's sentient.'

'What?'

Ori shoved the tablet back at zon. 'He's not the empath, Pat is! He was telling the truth. She *wants* to run that damned ship. She loves it. She loves *him*. Get hold of the *Tartarus*. Stop it. I'll send the order, too.'

Yang hesitated, she pushed zon away so she could stand. 'Go, you idiot!' Ze turned and bolted.

Lifting her wrist comm, she touched a button and

subvocally commanded Core to send a halt order to the prison ship. Only static answered her. She tried again. Nothing. The channel to every other ship awaiting docking or departure showed green. But the one to the prison transport was blocked.

How? By whom? Cabren? Was he capable of hijacking a heavily-guarded prison ship? It seemed unlikely. Then who?

The flip-out alert sounded and Ori raced to the observation window just in time to see the *Tartarus* blur and vanish, headed for the Inner Systems. Taking Cabren and Absinthe to their fates.

'Feck!' Ori pressed her forehead against the cool glass and tried to settle her mind. There had to be something she could do. She could easily send through a rescindment of the charges, but it would take weeks for Core to process. She could release Cabren's crew.

Oh! The *Orion*. She could at least protect Pat.

The flip alert went again. Then another, more shrill siren blared. The lock-down alarm? A great, tearing and crunching of metal shrieked through the station. The floor shuddered and Ori clutched at a low-grav handle to steady herself.

The *Orion* appeared in the window, her airlock still open, fragments of metal and piping sailing gracefully through the black vacuum outside.

The ship turned her nose toward the Inner Systems.

And flipped.

Around Ori, sirens blared and bulkheads slammed shut, keeping oxygen in until the ruined airlock could be repaired. She could do nothing but stare at the empty space where both ships had vanished.

What the feck had she done?

Only the Hegemon Core computer could have blocked her messages to the *Tartarus.*

She had queried the computer about Pelcorians. The Hegemon Core must have listened in to her conversation with Alec about what Pat could do.

The Hegemon was always looking for new tech that would improve flipdrives. Anything that would increase their reach and profit.

P'tlana had just followed Alec into the heart of the Inner Systems.

Right where the Hegemon wanted her.

Feck. She hadn't made the same mistake a second time. But, out of fear for her career and losing her cushy Inner Systems lifestyle, she'd made a worse one.

END

2300 hours: Decision Time

Ori Bligh

'Zev, we need to open the bulkheads and kill some of these fecking alarms—' Ori pulled up short in the open doorway to Zev's cramped office.

He wasn't there.

His chair lay overturned. His maintenance tracking tablets were on the floor, one with the screen cracked. Four monitors on his desk flashed with warning lights in eyewatering shades of yellow, orange, and red. Muted sirens blared, filling the room with clashing noise.

'What the feck?' Ori swiped through the menus, trying to get her head around his database. One alarm was airloss for the dock where the *Orion* had torn free of its clamps to chase after the *Tartarus*. She slapped the seal on that and the light went green. That siren stopped.

Her security override code released the bulkheads that were trapping people in various places on the Asteri. At least they could get back to their quarters and ships, now. More sirens stopped as bulkheads slid back into the walls.

But others kept wailing. What for?

She trailed a finger down the screen, deciphering the engineering lingo.

Feck! The rich water containment system. Zev had mentioned the power generation unit was old and held together with spit and tape. By the lurid red colour of the alarm, it was in bad shape. Could it be shut down? How long could the station last without power?

She swiped another screen and swore again. Things were past the point of being able to electronically shut down. And manual shutdown required the presence of two administrators—one of whom was Zev. Without his ID code there was no way to stop the power cascade.

Where the feck was he?

Ori glanced out into the Zoo, but it was empty. Even Vell was gone. She tapped her comms gauntlet and queried Sergeant Yang, who didn't reply. Nor did her other two team members. Where was everyone?

As a last resort, she tried Cordelia Bane. The bounty hunter was someone who would keep a level head in a crisis. 'Cordy, you there?'

'Heading for my ship. What?' Cordy's reply was sharp.

'Do you know where Zev is?'

'Yep. On the *Tartarus*. I didn't want to. But it cleared my debt. Sorry, O.'

Ori frowned. 'You took a bounty on him, too? Fecking great. We're screwed, now. Asteri's screwed.'

'I hear the alarms. What's happened?'

'The rich water containment unit is unstable and I can't fix it or shut it down,' Ori said. 'We need to evacuate the station.'

'You don't need me for that. Hit the evac alert.'

'I will.' She hesitated and scrubbed a hand over her face. Maybe there was a good reason she'd only been able to reach Cordy. Maybe it was time to decide for herself who the right and wrong people in the Hegemon were. She'd spent a long time trying to fit in with the Inner Systems people who were supposed to be good.

All they'd done is screw her over; even her parents.

Maybe it was time to choose her own friends and fight her own battles. For the right people.

She sucked a deep breath. 'Cordy, I want your help for something else. I handed someone over to the *Tartarus* and think I made a mistake. I don't think Captain Cabren did anything wrong. Nor did Zev. You shouldn't have sent him over. We need to get them back.' Tightness clogged her throat. 'I need to get Alec Cabren back.'

There was a long silence and Ori tapped her fingernails on Zev's desk, watching the lights speed up and the colours deepen to scarlet. A countdown popped up. Fifteen minutes until the power containment field blew.

'Cordy?'

'I hear you,' the bounty hunter replied. 'I'm having second

thoughts about handing Absinthe over as well. Fine. Get your arse to Dock 4. We'll go after the *Tartarus*.'

Ori bared her teeth. 'Out.'

She slapped the evacuate alert and bolted with the alarm screeching in her ears. She stopped only long enough at her quarters to collect her still-packed clothes and the paper flower Alec had left for her. The rest wasn't important. Not as important as Alec, Zev, and Absinthe, anyway.

#

Fleeing people filled the corridors. The sound of booted feet slapping on metal almost overrode the earsplitting alarms. Ori pushed her way through the crowds of families carrying pets and hastily-stuffed bags.

At Dock 4 she hit the override code for access and let herself onto Cordy's small flipship. A quick command released the airlock connection and set the ship floating free.

On the bridge, Cordy glanced over her shoulder and nodded. 'Strap yourself in. This will be a rough ride if we're going to try and catch the *Tartarus* before it hits the Inner Systems.' She engaged the sublight engines and manoeuvred the ship away from the station.

'What's your plan?' Ori asked.

Cordy shrugged. 'We'll work it out on the way. *Tartarus* is a robotic prison ship so it should be a matter of hacking the locks and guard controls.'

'You say that like it's easy.'

With a grin, Cordy swiped a control on her screen. 'I've lived a grey life, Ori. Trust me. I know how.' She glanced up and swore. 'But that could be a problem if they follow us.'

Ori checked out the front observation window. 'Hegemon Grey Guard cruiser. Must have come in response to the distress signal sent out by the station when the *Orion* broke free.'

The huge, armed flipship eased alongside Dock 8, its airlock extending to connect with Asteri.

'Do we warn them?' Cordy asked, her finger hovering over the comms button.

Ori checked her wrist chrono and glanced out the window again. Almost every family, trader, and permanent vessel had broken free of the station. Tiny silver specs were disappearing in every direction, vanishing amongst the stars. Safe.

'No.' Ori ground her teeth. 'Let them find out the hard way. Otherwise they'll come after us. We need time on the *Tartarus* uninterrupted.'

Chuckling, Cordy sent her a sly sideways glance. 'Now you're starting to think like a bounty hunter. You know there's no going back, don't you?'

With a thick sigh, Ori nodded. 'I know. I was deluding myself, anyway. There was never any going back. Alec was right: I wasn't meant for an Inner Systems life. The Hegemon isn't what I thought it was. The people I grew up with aren't who I thought they were. And I don't want to be like them. Punch it.'

'None of us were meant for that life, kiddo. Welcome to my world. And Zev's. And Ab's. Let's go get them.'

Cordy programmed the flip course and ramped up the sublight engines to put space between the ship and the Asteri. And the Hegemon cruiser.

Just as the flipdrive engaged, a flash of brilliant orange exploded in the blackness behind the ship.

The Asteri, the Hegemon cruiser, and Ori's career in the Grey Guards.

All gone.

Ori couldn't bring herself to regret it.

Not yet, anyway.

END

If you enjoyed this story collection, please take a moment to leave a positive review on Goodreads and wherever you purchased from. It helps other readers find authors they love as much as you do.

About the Authors

Pamela Jeffs

Pamela Jeffs is a speculative fiction author living in Queensland, Australia with her husband and two daughters. She has numerous short fiction pieces published in recent national and international anthologies. In 2017 and again in 2018, Pamela was nominated for an Australian Aurealis Award in the category of 'Best Science Fiction Short Story'. Her debut collection, titled *'Red Hour and Other Strange Tales,'* was released in March 2018 and her follow up works, titled *'Saloons and Stardust'*, and *'Five Dragons',* in 2019.

Discover other titles by Pamela Jeffs at:
www.pamelajeffs.com

Short Story Collections (Speculative Fiction)
Red Hour and Other Strange Tales
Saloons and Stardust: A Collection
Five Dragons

Connect with her on Facebook
https://www.facebook.com/pamelajeffsauthor/
Twitter: @Pamela_Jeffs
Instagram: @pamela_jeffs

Aiki Flinthart

Aiki lives in Brisbane, Australia. Her short stories have been Aurealis-award shortlisted and also top-8 listed in the USA Writers of the Future competition, as well as published in numerous online magazines and anthologies. She has 13 fiction novels and 1 non-fiction book published to date, with more to come. When not writing and running a full-time business, she likes to do fantasy-approved hobbies such as martial arts, archery, knife-throwing, lute-playing, and belly-dancing.

Discover other titles by Aiki Flinthart at:
www.aikiflinthart.com
Or

Blackbirds Sing (Historical fantasy)

The 80AD series (YA Adventure/Fantasy)
80AD Book 1: *The Jewel of Asgard*
80AD Book 2: *The Hammer of Thor*
80AD Book 3: *The Tekhen of Anuket*
80AD Book 4: *The Sudarshana*
80AD Book 5: *The Yu Dragon*

The Ruadhán *Sidhe* novels (YA Urban fantasy)
Shadows Wake (Bk1)

Shadows Bane (Bk2)
Shadows Fate (Bk 3)
Healing Heather (Bk4—publication 2020)

The Kalima Chronicles (YA Adventure/Fantasy)
IRON—Book One
FIRE—Book Two
STEEL—Book Three
A Future, Forged (Prequel - publication 2020)

Other Novels
Sold! (Contemporary Romance/Adventure)

Short Story Anthologies
Return
Like a Woman
Elemental

Non-Fiction – Author writing resources
Fight Like A *Girl* – Writing Fight Scenes for Female (and male) Characters

Connect with her on Facebook
https://www.facebook.com/aikiflinthartauthor
Twitter: @aikiflinthart
Instagram: Aikiflinthart